PRAISE FOR
LAST CHANTS
Featuring super-sleuth Willa Jansson

"It's a treat to watch the normally levelheaded Willa crawling around in the woods, searching for naked gods."
—Marilyn Stasio, *The New York Times Book Review*

"The real pleasure is Willa, who alternates between humor and annoyance at her predicament—and whose love-hate relationship with men strikes a chord with many female fans."
—*Entertainment Weekly*

"Learning to tell the difference between the evil killers and the good weirdos is half the fun of this . . . enchanted mystery."
—Patricia Holt, *San Francisco Chronicle*

"Readers will find *LAST CHANTS* an unexpected gift that will stay with them a long time after they finish reading it."
—Harriet Klausner, *Ed's Internet Book Review*

"An intriguing plot, well developed with interesting characters in a picturesque location. *LAST CHANTS* rewards a read."
—Judith Kreiner, *Washington Times*

"Fortunately, Willa is back in fine form in her fifth adventure. . . . Matera has produced a first-rate mystery, exhibiting her usual hallmarks of excellent plotting, solid characterizations, and brisk pacing. A sure thing for fans and a great way to introduce new readers to an outstanding mystery series."
—*Booklist*

"Few writers possess Lia Matera's wry humor, especially when it comes to putting down lawyers. . . ."
—*San Jose Mercury News* (CA)

Books by Lia Matera

Designer Crimes*
Face Value*
A Hard Bargain
Prior Convictions†
The Good Fight
Hidden Agenda†
The Smart Money
A Radical Departure†
Where Lawyers Fear to Tread†
Last Chants*†

†A Willa Jansson mystery

*Published by POCKET BOOKS

LAST CHANTS

A WILLA JANSSON
MYSTERY

LIA MATERA

POCKET BOOKS

New York   London   Toronto   Sydney   Tokyo   Singapore

This book is a work of fiction. Names, characters, places and inci-
dents are products of the author's imagination or are used ficti-
tiously. Any resemblance to actual events or locales or persons,
living or dead, is entirely coincidental.

POCKET BOOKS, a division of Simon & Schuster Inc.
1230 Avenue of the Americas, New York, NY 10020

ISBN: 0-671-88096-9

First Pocket Books printing June 1997

10 9 8 7 6 5 4 3 2 1

POCKET and colophon are registered trademarks of
Simon & Schuster Inc.

Cover art by Alan Ayers

Printed in the U.S.A.

To Brendan Rehon,
Mike Matera, and Dan Matera;
boys will be boys,
but not nearly long enough.

ACKNOWLEDGMENTS

Behind any book that deals, even tangentially, with shamanism, mythology, or cybernetics there's an author indebted to scores of writers and scholars. This author must, at the very least, thank Thinking Allowed Productions and Jeffrey Mishlove for their provocative video interviews with today's most original thinkers. I am especially indebted to Joseph Campbell, Michael Harner, Terence McKenna, Fred Alan Wolf, Rupert Sheldrake, Arthur Young, Brugh Joy, and Huston Smith for their mind-opening books, interviews, workshops, and audiotaped lectures. Without their insights, my characters might have lapsed into uncomfortable silences. However, any maladroit misstatements of fact or philosophy are mine alone.

I am also grateful to the anthropology museums in Victoria, Quadra Island, Prince Rupert, and Vancouver (University of British Columbia), British Columbia, and in Neah Bay, Washington, for their help in researching native cultures. For matters closer to home, I'm grateful to Russ Imrie and his Costanoan Indian web site.

ACKNOWLEDGMENTS

Anyone interested in learning more about shamanism, or wanting an extensive bibliography about it, should contact the nonprofit Foundation for Shamanic Studies, PO Box 1939, Mill Valley, CA 94942.

Anyone interested in a less complete and more eccentric bibliography will find one in my web site at http://www.scruz.net/~lmatera/LiaMatera.html.

LAST
CHANTS

CHAPTER ONE

I spent three glacial years earning a piece of paper that read, "Willa Jansson, Juris Doctor, With All the Rights and Privileges Thereto Pertaining." Not surprisingly, after that people expected me to be a lawyer. Resisting the temptation to confound expectations (not to mention default on my student loans), I became a labor lawyer, then a corporate lawyer, then a federal judge's clerk. But after years of nit-picking, hairsplitting, and matter-of-fact assertions of the preposterous, I had few illusions about the work—or the rights and privileges thereto pertaining. With three jobs in four years, I was serving notice more often than I was serving Justice. And as the novelty of solvency wore off, I found myself growing tired of lawyerdom. My creditors, unfortunately, were as sold on the idea as ever.

But I hadn't had a chance to tire of my latest new job yet. I was walking there now, crossing Market Street to begin my first day as a multimedia lawyer. I had no idea whether I'd like the work, but I surely liked the sound of it. Multimedia law; so nineteen-nineties: a career for someone who'd dumped her sixties baggage to lay scratch on the information superhighway.

But this morning, in nonvirtual reality, I was on foot.

Market Street, as usual, seethed with impatient cars. I was too fond of my Honda to expose it to stripping, scratching, and parking-fee gouging. I was also a nervous driver, especially at rush hour. So I'd taken the bus from Haight to Market.

Apparently, this was the strategy of choice for multitudes of white-collar workers. The crosswalks were barely wide enough to corral all the lawyers and brokers and bankers, their shoulders hunched and fists stuffed into raincoat pockets. We were a dour army storming the Financial District, crossing the Maginot Line between warehouses and high-rises, between the chatter of Spanish and cranky Anglo silence, between cheap beer and ferny wine bars.

I lingered at the corner, waiting for the light to change. I was anxious about the new job. I didn't have the best track record; I'd never managed to feel like part of a team. Maybe it was my fault. But from my perspective, previous coworkers had seemed conventional and humorless, at best. At worst, they'd seemed heartless and pretentious. My parents had frequently driven me crazy, but they'd accustomed me to better company.

Along Market, only the homeless dawdled. Con men flashed jewelry to people heading into discount stores. Teenagers offered body parts for rent. Begrunged runaways panhandled. San Francisco didn't offer many self-employment options.

And since I was one of the few lawyers without a legal thriller in the works, I needed this job.

So at the green light, I let the yuppie river sweep me across the street. The sudden corridor of high-rises reminded me of rafting through the Grand Canyon. Thousands of hurrying workers resembled a white-water rush. I tried not to think how long it would be until my next vacation.

I'd spent the last week whipping up enthusiasm for work. If my pattern held, I would maintain a positive attitude almost until lunch.

It was a hip job, at least. I'd scandalized my Bohemian parents two years ago by selling out to a big-bucks L.A. firm. It was the most elegant mine I'd ever toiled in, but I'd barely lasted a year before my inner canary died.

I'd been unemployed almost five months now, with no acceptable explanation for leaving big-firm practice. I'd used up the money I'd saved. And I'd come to an uncomfortable conclusion: If I'd taken low-paying work I liked, instead of trying to accumulate cash in a job I loathed, I'd still be employed. I'd be solvent, and my résumé would be unblemished.

No thirty-six-year-old woman should have to admit that her parents were right.

As if that weren't bad enough, I owed my new job to my father.

It started when he fell in love with the idea of an on-line democracy. He began playing with friends' computers. Then he discovered a latent artistic streak. He all but adopted a former psychedelic poster artist who now taught computer graphics courses. He spent days on end with a bad-boy cybernetics guru, San Francisco's notorious "Brother Mike." He began accumulating the cast-off peripherals of acquaintances caught in upgrade frenzies.

My parents' Haight Street apartment underwent a transformation. The BOYCOTT GRAPES posters were tacked over with fractal designs. The old Gestetner machine, veteran of a million political leaflets, was replaced by a color ink-jet printer. Stacks of flyers were thrown out, superseded by e-mail petition drives and downloadable polemics. My mother, seeing the potential to fill thousands of mailboxes, adapted quickly to electronic proselytizing.

At first, I'd thought this was an idiosyncrasy of my parents, one of thousands. But I'd been surprised by the flow of people through their apartment. I'd come to realize that many old friends of the family, activists and flakes alike, had taken to computers as they'd once taken to bead looms. They used them for cartooning, comic-book writing, collaging, video splicing, and writing music. The Woodstock Nation had moved out of the mud and into cyberspace.

A friend with some programs to copyright told my father about a law firm of "technohippies," as he called them. He'd heard they were looking for the right associate.

Confronted with a three-figure bank account, I phoned the firm immediately. I collected letters of reference, and I took crash courses. I watched computer graphics videos until I recognized stylistic tricks. I risked comas reading software copyright journals.

At my interviews, I tried to pass myself off as a nerd, babbling about programs and patents as if the knowledge predated the interview by more than hours. I stressed nonexistent L.A. media connections. I used the term *infobahn*. After two weeks and four meetings with the named partners of Curtis & Huston, I was hired.

Only now, in the crunch, walking to work on a drizzly Monday morning, did I begin to wish I were back in bed.

I hurried up Montgomery to the heart of the Financial District. Most of my San Francisco jobs had been nearer the civic center, in tawdrier digs bordering neighborhoods of housing projects. This 'hood was scrubbed clean and accented with flowers. It smelled of pretzel carts and espresso, Bay wind and auto exhaust. Around me, jostling workers added occasional whiffs of wet wool and hair mousse.

I gave a stationary cop, speaking into his walkie-talkie, a wide berth. So did the rest of the rush hour foot traffic—it was too damp to stop and gawk. Passing him, I glanced in the direction the cop had been looking. Across the street, a crowded half-block away, was—to my astonishment—an old, dear friend of my parents.

For a split second, I pondered crossing to him. I didn't love all my parents' friends, especially my mother's friends, but I did love Arthur Kenna.

In that instant, though, I saw what the cop had seen: that Arthur was holding a gun.

A gun. I stopped, shaking my head. Arthur holding a gun? I'd have been less shocked to see my own mother—pacifist, vegetarian, Gandhi extremist—with a weapon.

But within seconds, I saw something even more shocking: Arthur was pointing the gun at someone. Another pedestrian stood, back to me, with his hands up over his head in classic mugging pose.

Except that Arthur would never, ever mug anyone.

Arthur Kenna was a mythologist, an ethnobotanist, an anthropologist, a sweet old scholar, and practically an uncle to me. He'd told me he'd been beaten as a child for refusing to hunt; he'd felt even then, he said, that to take up a weapon for sport "disparaged the Great Mother." His best-known theory, popularized on a Public Broadcast System nine-hour special, was that most violent acts required cultural indoctrination, a warrior mythology; that they did not, in fact, explode from primally encoded urges. Ironically, the same people who scorned our "victim culture" derided his thesis as naive. They contended it was natural to brutalize, but unnatural to complain.

Arthur's rebuttal was too well documented to be dismissed with macho sneers. And it was sincere; he didn't believe in violence, nor did he believe that it was hardwired into us.

And here he was, holding someone at gunpoint?

I couldn't believe it. I *didn't* believe it. For once, I trusted what I knew over what I saw.

Around Arthur, people stopped, obviously aghast, taking fearful steps away. Arthur seemed completely focused on the gun, as if it were some reptile manifesting in his hand. The man holding up his hands was yammering. I couldn't hear what he was saying, only his tone: panicky, high-pitched.

I wheeled around. The cop; that's what the cop was doing, radioing for help before dashing forward to arrest Arthur.

Arthur Kenna, thirty years ago, participated in the now-famous Harvard LSD experiments. A prominent ethnobotanist, he'd been a logical choice for inclusion. He'd made a study of how plants affected culture. He'd sampled ayahuasca and yagé with Brazilian natives, he'd eaten psychoactive mushrooms with Siberian peasants, he'd partaken of a whole dessert cart of botanical highs—and done far more retching than any other profession required. (This had been a major factor in shifting his focus from ethnobotany to anthropology and mythology, he'd told me.) Unfortunately, Arthur had been out of the country when LSD was later declared illegal. He'd been arrested and convicted of a felony the next time he'd been persuaded to experiment with it.

And just a few years ago, he'd been arrested and convicted of felony trespass—for accompanying my parents to a demonstration against Lockheed. Arthur wasn't interested in politics, but he'd been in the middle of a discussion and had tagged along to finish making his point.

I'd had a long, frantic talk with my mother recently. California had passed a law making a third felony conviction—whether the felonies were violent or not—punishable by a minimum of twenty-five years in prison. My mother, flighty activist and bleeding heart extraordinaire, had more than three felony convictions already. One more and she'd never be free again. She'd die in prison.

Now I was watching our kindly old friend on the brink of getting arrested and charged with another felony. Unless there was some explanation I absolutely couldn't fathom, he'd be convicted.

I'd spent two months in jail myself. I wouldn't wish it on anyone, much less a seventy-year-old mild-mannered scholar.

Whatever the reason for what was happening, I couldn't bear to imagine Arthur locked away for the rest of his life. I couldn't just stand by.

I only had a moment to alert him. Even then, he might not be spry enough to outrun a young police officer. (If only Mother hadn't dragged him off to that demonstration!)

I charged across the street, oblivious to traffic, though the sound of screeching brakes told me traffic wasn't oblivious to me.

By the time I reached Arthur, it was too late to warn him. The cop was right behind me. I could tell by Arthur's flustered cry.

"Officer!" he said.

That one word, untinged by panic or hostility, dissolved my last doubt. Despite appearances, Arthur wasn't dangerous.

Maybe if I'd bought into, as well as having bought, a law degree, I'd have delivered a "surrender, and let me advise you" speech. But my faith in the criminal justice system could be measured in microns.

I knew the district attorney could find a felony in this situation no matter the excuse or extenuation.

Arthur in prison forever. I couldn't chance it. I had to try *something*.

I was obscuring the officer's view. I took advantage of the fact to twirl as if Arthur had grabbed me, to back myself into his gun.

It was not a good feeling.

I told myself Arthur probably hadn't released— maybe didn't even know how to release—the safety on the gun, wherever it had come from and whyever he was holding it. No matter what, he wouldn't shoot me. Not intentionally, anyway.

"Back away, please," I told the cop. "He's got the gun on me." I worried that it sounded false, sounded silly, maybe wasn't even intelligible English.

Behind me, Arthur was beginning to disclaim. Luckily, he was agitated, stuttering.

"He'll kill me," I blundered on. I looked over my shoulder. Arthur appeared perplexed. "Let him get away." I tried to bore my meaning into Arthur's understanding. "He'll shoot me if you try to stop us!"

I felt like I'd picked up the wrong script. Arthur had, too: "I wouldn't hurt, I'd never—"

"If you back up, he won't hurt me," I interjected. I glanced at Arthur's victim. He looked more surprised than anyone.

"But Willa," Arthur protested.

"Will you what? Will you kill me? Stand back," I urged the cop. Arthur just wasn't getting with the program. "Maybe if you let him go, he'll let me go." I didn't have to work at sounding plaintive.

The cop got macho: "Stand back. Everyone stand back. Give him room."

Bystanders had already practically leap-frogged over one another to get away. And people approaching were halted in their tracks by the sight of a gesticulating cop. (I'd always wondered what could stop urban professionals in their tracks.)

I started backing up, sure if I stepped forward, Arthur would remain rooted, making me the least threatened "hostage" since Tanya.

I couldn't think of a way to get him to half-nelson my neck. So I reached behind me, contorting my arm as if he were twisting it. I forgot to wince, but what the hell. I gave him a backward push.

"Let us go," I said to Arthur, while staring at the cop. "He's dangerous."

Combined with my shove, Arthur got, if not the idea, at least some momentum. As he staggered back,

I matched his steps, keeping as close as Ginger to Fred. I grabbed a fistful of his trenchcoat, then pivoted around him, trying to change our direction. I hoped it looked as if he were in charge.

Arthur rotated with me, thanks to my strategic yanking of his coat. But he protested, voice loud and incredulous, "What are you doing?"

The cop said, "Nothing. Calm down. There's no need to harm the hostage. That won't get you anything."

"Stay with me." I thought I was whispering to Arthur. I was probably shrieking, I was so nervous.

The cop certainly heard me. "Don't worry, lady. Just keep your head." He shouted at Arthur: "Backups are hitting this neighborhood hard. You're not going to get far. Make it easy on yourself."

I let my free hand brush Arthur's nongun hand, then grabbed it. I pulled him along behind me, trying to act like he was pushing.

It didn't seem like much of a plan when I started. A few awkward moments into it, it seemed downright ridiculous. I nearly jumped ship right then.

Except for one thing: Another felony and Arthur would never get out of prison again.

With that thought came an even less-welcome one. If the cops caught us—and there was every probability they would, given Arthur's clueless discomposure and my utter lack of strategy—they'd soon learn I was a friend of Arthur's. They would reinterpret this scene to account for that, and they would realize the obvious: that I was working with Arthur. Except they wouldn't believe my involvement was limited to inappropriate good Samaritanism. They would see me as an accessory after the fact—whatever that fact might be. They might even think I'd been in on Arthur's "crime" (I still couldn't imagine a scenario that would put a gun into Arthur's hand). They'd consider me his accomplice.

At best, I'd be late for my first day of work.

Work: I'd scouted the neighborhood after my job interviews. I'd scoped out the nearest coffee and pastry shops, lunch joints, bookstores, dry cleaners, drugstores.

I'd been impressed with all the back-alley bistros, the mini-plazas with basement delis, the narrow parkways, the labyrinthine connections between skyscrapers. Hurrying, especially driving, through the Financial District gave the impression of big impersonal buildings. But at a leisurely pace, it revealed its architectural grottos and enclaves, its fey staircases and preened alleys.

In fact, we were in front of a tiny plaza now. Sandwiched between skyscrapers, it looked like a subway entrance with planter boxes. But it had escalators up to a barbershop and a travel agency and an escalator down to a market and a deli. The market had a back door. I'd opened it by mistake last week, noticing a storage area with an exit.

I pulled Arthur to the escalator, forcing him to follow me down the moving stairs. I could hear commotion and swearing behind us, people bumping one another in their haste to leave, perhaps. With luck, they would impede the cop.

I yanked Arthur into the market. I let go of his trenchcoat but kept a firm grip on his hand. I dragged him through the store and out the back, to the vocal consternation of its Chinese owners. I thought I heard the cop shout for us to stop, but he wasn't close enough for us to heed him. I opened a storeroom door labeled STAIRS.

I assumed the cop was somewhere behind us, but I didn't look. I told Arthur, "We have got to outrun him. Follow me."

"But Willa—"

"Follow me!" I dropped his hand, willing him to keep up.

I ran up the stairs, to a door labeled EXIT, and pushed out into an alley. I crossed quickly, bypassing the back door of a bank (too obvious) and going into a restaurant. I ran through it, past disgruntled men in tuxedo shirts, and out the back. I ran across the street and into a bank building. I managed to do it looking mostly backward, mostly at Arthur, focusing my imploring panic like a tractor beam.

Arthur remained in tow.

He still carried the gun. "Give me that! Good heavens." I stuck it into my combination handbag-briefcase. It was a miracle no one else had joined the chase.

The cop, I hoped, hadn't kept close enough behind to know which building we'd entered.

We ran up three flights, then through another emergency exit. We found ourselves in a carpeted corridor. A nearby door read LADIES.

I pulled off my jacket, saying, "Take off your trenchcoat. Now."

As Arthur obeyed, I pushed open the restroom door.

"Arthur, you've got to find someplace to hide for a couple of minutes, okay?"

"But Willa, I've been trying to explain this is all a—"

I grabbed his trench. "I'll find you in two minutes," I assured him. "Trust me. Hide."

I stepped into the bathroom. I stuffed our jackets into the trash, covering them with paper towels. Then I wet my hands. I dampened the ends of my hair, an elbow-length reflection of a midlife yearning for my hippie youth. I twisted it into a skinny rope, which I tucked into my blouse. The blouse was high-necked. Without a jacket, I would look as if I worked in the building. I hoped I would look like a short-haired secretary.

I found Arthur idly reading the front-door directory of a law firm with many names. He was right across from the elevator; so much for "hiding."

"We don't have a second to lose," I warned him. "There'll be police all around. We'll have to separate. You take the elevator, I'll take the stairs. I'll meet you on the street."

Could I show up for work without a jacket?

"What happened to your hair, Willa?" He seemed startled by the difference in my appearance.

"Never mind that." I punched the elevator button for him. "Walk toward Market. I'll meet you at the corner."

I dashed back down the stairs. A short service corridor led into an alabaster lobby. A few people waited for elevators, checking their watches. Others pushed through the glass doors of the main entrance. Watching them was the cop who'd been following me and Arthur.

He was intently speaking into his walkie-talkie. I tried to walk past nonchalantly, but my heart was racing. There was a certain unhappy reality that never failed to annoy me; but if it failed this time, I was dogmeat.

"Hey!" the policeman barked. "Did you see anyone on the stair—?"

Before he could say more—maybe too soon—I shook my head.

He scowled, again lifting his walkie-talkie to his lips. Luckily he'd stayed true to guy form. He'd seen me as a blonde, not as someone with a particular face.

I left the building and merged with a river of workers.

Hot from running and worrying, clammy from drizzle on my shirt, I suffered a sudden lack of confidence in Arthur. What if he were caught alone—if he blundered into the police when I left him? Would he name me? Would he tell them what I'd done, thinking they'd believe his exoneration? (One thing about lawyering, it taught you how little the cops were willing to believe. And why.)

My confidence in Arthur was further undercut by the fact that he and my mother were friends. I knew how my mother reacted to being arrested. She was certain being right made her persuasive. Two dozen arrests and five convictions later, she still believed she could change the minds of police and judges; that, hearing her speak with logic and passion, they would be persuaded to take a left turn onto the high road. No doubt about it: In Arthur's place, my mother would admit another's complicity as if sharing an honor. And I knew from painful experience that her most well-intentioned friends could pose the biggest threat to my comfort and security.

By the time I joined Arthur, jittering in perplexity on the corner, I knew I'd better keep an eye on him; that I'd better get him safely out of the neighborhood.

I hoped it wouldn't take long.

For once, I was being unduly optimistic.

CHAPTER TWO

It was taking us forever to get out of the neighborhood. There were uniformed cops on every block. We ducked into buildings, we wound through alleys trying to avoid them. Moments after I dumped the gun in a trash can, we saw police stop an older man walking with a younger woman.

"We'd better keep to opposite sides of the street," I fretted. "But don't lose track of me. Stay right across from me."

Soon after, another cop seemed ready to approach Arthur, though he walked alone. Luckily, he glanced over at me. I pointed out the cop, discreetly, I hoped. He stepped into a nearby bank. The cop seemed about to follow, then went after another December–May couple.

By the time I joined Arthur, we were both as nervous as cats. Lingering a moment in a foyer corner, I snapped, "What in the world possessed you, Arthur? Why were you doing that?"

"Doing what?"

Doing what! "Holding a gun on that guy."

"Holding it on him? Oh my, no. My my, no." Arthur's wrinkled face ironed with astonishment. "Is that what you were thinking? I assumed you realized—I couldn't imagine why you did such a thing."

"Me?" People around us turned. I lowered my voice. "Why *I* did such a thing?"

"Yes! Rushing up like that, pulling me away into this goose flight." His face crinkled like wadded paper. "Really, I was so surprised. But you seemed very determined. I thought you must have a reason. And I hardly knew how to stop you."

"Stop me? You'd be in jail right now, Arthur."

"Oh, no." His tone was avuncular. "I'm sure we'd have straightened it out."

"But you were standing there holding—" I made myself shut up. This was not the place.

"I have no idea why he handed it to me. I imagine the policeman would have asked him."

"Who handed what to you?"

"The gentleman with the scarf."

I had noticed no scarves. I wondered if we were having different conversations. Like many scholars, Arthur tended to focus on fine points invisible to others.

"We should go," I pointed out. "Keep heading toward Market."

His face, as furrowed as a hound's, reflected my discouragement. We'd been trying to get to and across Market Street this last long hour. Instead, we'd seen the insides of several buildings and taken a dozen alley detours.

"Why don't we just talk to them, Willa?"

He'd advocated this earlier, but I'd interpreted it as

a desire to surrender. It dawned on me he believed the police would accept his explanation.

"No way," I reiterated. "They saw you take a hostage. They watched you escape. They'll never believe you."

"I'll take the chance." He wore the same look of naive faith I'd seen on my mother's face before her disastrous arrests.

"Well, I won't. The minute they realize we're friends, they'll label me your accomplice."

"How can you be my accomplice? I haven't done anything."

"You have now. You've resisted arrest. So have I."

"But—"

I turned impatiently. "I'm a lawyer. Trust me." Self-canceling sentences, perhaps, but Arthur took them at face value. He followed me out.

We barely got a half-block farther before another cop seemed to ogle him. This time, Arthur slipped into a building with no prompting from me. I supposed I'd made an impression; he realized he was protecting me now, too.

I waited a few minutes, then followed to give Arthur the "all clear." We continued our parallel progress through the Financial District.

Reaching Market, we saw a police car on the corner. I looked down toward the Embarcaderos. There was another car on the next corner. I looked toward the civic center. There was a car there, too.

They were taking the gunman with a hostage seriously, that was evident.

Even south of Market, along thoroughfares of warehouses and wholesalers, the police presence was noticeable. Street people kept a low profile, lingering in doorways, casting furtive glances at the blue uniforms. I saw a cop questioning a group of men in dirt-streaked clothes.

We walked a mazelike route through a dreary neighborhood that did its business without caring who it impressed.

Eventually, it seemed safe to walk together. But even then, I looked over my shoulder so often my neck ached.

"What did you mean before, Arthur?" I endeavored to squelch my crankiness. I should have been nervously ensconced at work for the last two hours. But I'd jumped into this; it was my doing, not Arthur's. "What about the man with the scarf?"

"I've never been so surprised, Willa. Not here, at any rate. Now, when the Juavaro chief sliced off his rival's ear and used it—"

"Surprised at what?" Fascinating though rain forest etiquette might be, right now I was more interested in us. "What did he do? The man with the scarf."

"He handed me the gun." Arthur had stopped walking. He blinked as if I were a dense student.

"Someone *handed* you that gun?"

He nodded. "And then stuck his hands right up into the air." He mimicked the gesture, looking as if I were mugging him.

"You're kidding. That guy"—I struggled to recall his features, his hair color, anything—"the guy with his hands in the air was the one who handed you the gun?"

"That's right. He handed it to me, put the handle part in my hand, you know. And then ... " He raised his hands higher. "Funny." He let his arms drop back to his sides. "I thought it must be some sort of joke, you know, because of the ululations."

"The what?"

"Ululations." He made a series of quiet whooping noises.

"I don't remember him doing that." But I wasn't sure how long it had been going on before I got there.

"Not literally, of course. Not 'woo woo woo,' but American ululations. You know, 'Help, help, don't shoot'; that sort of thing."

"He put the gun in your hand and started making a fuss." I felt drained of energy. In trying to rescue Arthur, I'd let the man with a scarf get away. I wanted to cry. I am not an intervener by nature. It would be too much if it backfired on me the one time I did it so publicly and dangerously.

"Yes." He nodded emphatically, looking professorial in his turtleneck and cardigan. "So unusual."

"Talk about timing." The man made his move in front of a cop. If it was a coincidence, it was a big one. "Was the man facing you when he handed you the gun?"

"No." Arthur shrugged. "He came up behind me. He put it in my hand, and the next thing I knew he was in front of me, ululating."

"He must have seen the policeman. He must have been following you, waiting until he saw one." I was surprised by the authority in my tone. What did I know? I hadn't even noticed the scarf. "What kind of scarf was he wearing?"

"Wearing?" Arthur looked as if I'd suddenly begun speaking Chinese. "The man?"

"Yes."

"Was he wearing a scarf?"

I felt trapped in a comedy routine. "You said he was."

"No, no, not wearing it. He had the gun in it. I felt it on my hand before I felt the gun. I felt it fall away, out of my hand."

"Did you see it?"

"Mm." He seemed to be pondering, his thick hair shaking slightly. "Just before that, I had the feeling of an eagle."

"A what?" A "feeling" of an eagle?

"Yes, yes. I can't see the scarf, but I can feel its silkiness, and I recall having had the feeling of an eagle."

I picked up our pace. I had no idea what an eagle might feel like. Right now, I was more interested in a cup of coffee.

One of my biggest fears about this morning had been that Curtis & Huston, where I should be right now, made its coffee too weak. I hoped I wouldn't be so late it became a moot point. In the meantime, I could use a triple espresso.

"We'll go to my house." I'd already blown more sensible options. "I'll phone work. We'll figure things out."

We executed a convoluted half-circle through the Mission District, finally recrossing Market. We were north of the civic center now, with perhaps another mile to walk to the Panhandle and another half-mile to the Haight, where I lived.

I had chosen, for better or worse, to stick with Arthur. I told myself it was safer this way: I didn't trust him not to confide in the police. I didn't trust him to be paranoid, evasive, and self-protective; after all, he didn't have my legal training.

CHAPTER THREE

I found my answering-machine light blinking furiously. Four of the messages were from Curtis & Huston. The first two were polite, almost apologetic: Gee, had I glanced at the clock? The third expressed concern; they had set up an appointment that I would soon miss. The fourth was curt; please call them.

There were two messages from my mother. She'd phoned Curtis & Huston to speak to me. Her squeaky voice informed me that I wasn't at my new job, and the secretary didn't know where I was, and she didn't sound happy about it. Her second message consisted of a breathless run-on: "Willa June, it's almost lunchtime; you wanted this job so much; where did you go; why didn't you call them; are you all right?"

I should have phoned work sooner, should have come up with some excuse. I just hadn't been able to think of one.

I went into the kitchen to put on water for coffee. I still couldn't think of one. I'd overslept? Passed out? Gotten lost?

Though I had the perfect excuse for tardiness—Sorry, I was taken hostage—I couldn't use it.

I almost dropped the coffeepot when the phone rang again. I went back into my living room in time to stop Arthur from picking up. After the message beep, I heard my father's voice:

"Willa, your mother's very concerned that you didn't make it to work this morning. She's on her way over." A pause. "We certainly hope you're all right."

I considered picking up the receiver. I didn't want him to worry. On the other hand, I didn't see how the truth would console him, and I couldn't lie to my father. Anyone but.

"Are you there, Willa?" The worry in his tone almost persuaded me to lay my troubles at his feet.

I looked around the living room for my clock. There were newspapers strewn all over, clothes from this morning's hurried try-on session. I spotted a corner of my desk clock under some computer graphics journals. I brushed them aside. It was almost one o'clock. The digital clock on my computer—still on since last night—told me to the second how late I was. Our progress had been slower than I'd supposed.

But a woman my age should be able to "vanish" a few hours without her parents freaking out. Hadn't they joined the Peace Corps in 1976 without telling me? Hadn't they left for two years without saying good-bye? My mother could live with her worry.

My doorbell began to ring. It rang insistently for a minute, then the bell downstairs began to ring. My mother was buzzing Ben, my landlord. I listened to his bell, then mine again. Apparently, Ben wasn't home.

"We should let your mother in," Arthur said gently. "Why, I haven't seen her since, oh my, was it before

Alaska and British Columbia? I think before the hunts?"

"You went *hunting?*" This shocked me more than having seen him with a gun. I hadn't quite believed the gun, but this came from his own lips.

"No! Good lord, Willa! The Hunts—a family of Haida craftsmen and artists from the Queen Charlotte Islands. I was introduced by my assistant." His face lit. "Ah, what a fellow he is, what a truly magical fellow. A shaman, a woodsman, a totem carver, and the most remarkable mind! And he surpasses even Rolling Thunder and Black Elk in spirit, in my opinion. He's a blessing. Really, a blessing to me."

"Hm." The doorbell ringing had stopped. That was all I cared about.

I swept some clutter off the couch and invited Arthur to sit. I went back into the kitchen.

I stood over the dripping coffee cone for a few minutes. Maybe Arthur could have explained away the gun incident and maybe he couldn't. Maybe I'd done the right thing in "rescuing" him. Maybe I'd handled this wrong.

I worried about it. I left Arthur alone in my living room, and I nursed a cup of coffee. I let a hundred worries bloom.

Finally, I decided to phone work. I would offer an unspecified personal emergency as an excuse. If they fired me, they fired me. Waiting wouldn't change that.

I found Arthur reading the newspaper, which he'd stacked into a tidy pile beside him. He didn't look up.

I walked over to the phone, which was on a director's chair. My decor, a friend had pointed out, was basic freshman. I'd tried, on occasion, to become interested in my surroundings. But that meant too much cleaning and shopping, and not enough reading and aimless walking.

I started to dial Curtis & Huston. I chickened out. I told myself I should allay my parents' fears first; that I could practice my excuse-making on them.

My father picked up on the first ring. "Willa!" he said in response to my greeting. "Where are you?"

"Home." I watched Arthur jerk back as if startled by a headline on the state news page. "It's kind of a long story . . ."

"Oh my, I wonder if we can still catch your mother?"

"Catch her? Doing what?"

"Going to the—You've got to put this in context, Willa." His voice was ambassadorial. In recent years, he'd taken to mediating between me and my mother, trying to make my practicality less alien to her and her politics less ridiculous to me.

"Put what in context? Is she in trouble? What's she done now?" I felt the strength drain out of me. I'd warned her till I was weary; I thought I'd made my point. "She's not getting herself arrested?"

"No. No. It's you, she's been worrying about you."

I ran through a list of worst-case possibilities. In any context involving me, could she be picketing anyone? Trespassing? Calling a news conference? "And?"

"Because she knew how happy you were about getting this job, you know."

"So what did she do?"

"She phoned you all morning, then she went by your place." He was hedging, soothing.

Arthur was making strangling noises. I glanced at him. He didn't seem to be choking on anything. I put a hand over my free ear to block out the sounds.

"Cut to the chase, Daddy, would you? She's not in trouble?"

"No. But she thinks you are."

I still didn't get it. Why was he so reluctant? "Oh, my God!" It hit me. "She's gone—"

"Well, because she was so worried. And he's the only policeman she really knows."

"Oh, no. Please."

Arthur's head lolled against the futon cushion, newspaper fluttering to his feet. He looked glassy-eyed. I hoped he wasn't about to fall asleep. If I understood my father, we would have to get the hell out of here very soon.

"She went to Don Surgelato." I waited for my father to contradict me. "Did she?"

"She was worried. She thought he'd have, you know, injury reports and the like."

I had fallen in love with San Francisco's Homicide Lieutenant once, stupidly and inappropriately. By the time I'd screwed up my courage to make a total fool of myself over him, he'd reconciled with his ex-wife. You haven't quite hit bottom until you've trekked to a man's house to declare your love and had an ex-wife in a bathrobe open the door.

I could have gone the entire rest of my life without hearing the name Don Surgelato again. "She really went there?"

"Again, Baby, context. She knew how much you wanted this job, and yet you didn't— Why didn't you go to work today? Why are you still home? You know, we called several times, but—"

"Arthur Kenna. He was about to get arrested, and the only thing I could think of to get him out of it was pretend to be his hostage." I never bothered lying to my father. He was shrewd and nonjudgmental, so there was no point.

"What?"

I was troubled by Arthur's posture. I hoped he wasn't having a heart attack.

"The police think he took a hostage, only they don't know it's him, they don't know it's Arthur. He's going to think the hostage was me."

"Surgelato will?"

"Yes. Mother's going to tell him I never made it to work, and he'll have heard the description of a short blond hostage in a blue suit, and he's going to know it was me."

"Why would you want to pretend you were Arthur's hostage? Am I hearing this correctly?"

"I've got to get Arthur out of here. If the police come to check on me—" It took me but a second to ponder this. "I don't want the police to see us together; we match the description of the gunman and his hostage—at least, I assume we do, since it was us. God, leave it to Mother to clown everything up."

"But she was only trying—"

"Is that ever the truth! I need to get Arthur away from here. And I'd better go with him." I didn't trust him not to go to the cops, but I didn't want to say so in front of him. "I don't have an explanation for being late—I'll get all flustered. I always act weird around Don, anyway."

"What happened with Arthur?"

"The cop thought he was holding someone at gunpoint. I had no idea what was really going on, so I pretended I was a hostage to get him—us—out of there."

"Does he know about Billy's sea wheat?"

"His what?"

"Billy Seawuit." He spelled the surname.

"Who's that?"

I noticed Arthur's eyes were shut tight. His shoulders were shaking.

"His assistant was murdered. I saw it on the Internet news this morning."

"Oh, no. I think he just found out."

I felt caught in an avalanche. I felt immobilized, everything around me collapsing.

"Your mother might not have found Surgelato in his office. I'll go right down there and see if I can stop her." A brief pause. "Willa, you're safe?"

I was startled. Did he believe Arthur had harmed his assistant? "Unless Mother has her way. Hurry up, okay?" An afterthought: "But Daddy, don't tell her about me and Arthur. She'll blab it, you know she will. She won't mean to, but she will."

"What can I tell her?"

I closed my eyes. I'd wanted this new job, I really had. "I can't think of anything. Maybe finding myself? Hint that I went off on some kind of midlife thing."

"She won't believe it. You're so responsible." He spoke the word almost apologetically.

"Tell her I broke under the pressure or something. If she believes it, maybe the cops will."

"Surgelato? Do you really think so?"

If Don had no further feelings for me, any reasonable explanation of my truancy would suffice.

I was surprised to hear myself say, "No. He won't believe I'm okay until he sees me."

"Maybe you'd better see him, then."

"I can't now, not with Arthur here. And I wouldn't want to"—I dropped my voice—"leave Arthur yet. Especially since . . . that other matter."

"Billy Seawuit? What a tragedy."

"Do you have any details?"

"Apparently he was shot Saturday. They found the body yesterday afternoon."

And I'd had a gun in my briefcase this morning. "Did they find it?"

"The body? Of course. It was down in—"

"No."

"Oh, the gun. No, they didn't."

Thank goodness I'd wiped the prints off before chucking it. "I've got to go. Don't worry." As I was hanging up, I added, "But put a muzzle on Mother!"

His snort reflected what everyone who'd met her knew: That was no easy task.

I crossed to Arthur. He was crying.

"I'm sorry, Arthur, but we've got to go right now," I told him urgently. "Right this very second."

He looked up at me. "Billy, my—"

"I know. My father just told me. He also told me"—I decided to make a long story short—"that the police are on their way over here."

"We've got to talk to them, Willa. I've got to find out about Billy—"

"Later. Right now, I'm telling you, I do not want us to get busted for what we did this morning, much less for other things we didn't do!"

He seemed prepared to argue further. I cut him off.

"I spent the two very worst months of my life in jail, Arthur, and I am not going back, not for a minute. So you have got to get up and come with me."

"Willa, no, I can't. I have to find out about Billy. We can simply explain—"

"I'll never forgive you if I end up back in jail, Arthur! You've got to come."

Whatever he'd been about to say died on his lips.

28

Tears still glinting on his creased cheeks, he rose from the chair like a gentleman.

I dashed into my bedroom, grabbing some jeans and a coat. Arthur followed me into the kitchen, where I turned off the coffee and ran water over the carafe to cool it.

I let us out the back door, locking it behind me.

All the way down the back steps, I considered our next move. Get my car out of the garage and drive somewhere? Or would Surgelato put out an all-points with my license number?

When we reached the breezeway door separating my landlord's yard from the street, I heard a car pull up. I imagined Surgelato in his big American car, my mother in the passenger seat.

"Come on," I said to Arthur, pulling him through the yard.

I led us over a flattened portion of my neighbors' fence. We'd leave through their breezeway.

I waited a few minutes before pushing through the neighbors' gate to the street. Maybe I was making too much of this. Maybe my mother hadn't reached Surgelato, after all. It would certainly be more convenient to take my car than not.

But when I peeked around the gate, I did indeed see Surgelato's monstrous purple sedan. He'd done my mother the courtesy—or been sufficiently worried by the hostage description—to come in person. In different circumstances, it might have gladdened my girlish heart.

I didn't see Don or my mother in the car. They must already be on the porch. I seized the moment to hustle Arthur onto the sidewalk and around a corner.

I yanked him into a dark little donut shop with a rear door. We were back to playing hide-and-seek.

CHAPTER FOUR

Somewhere between the donut shop and the corner of Haight and Ashbury, I had an unwelcome realization. Don Surgelato might have shown my picture to the Financial District cop. By the time Arthur and I reached the Panhandle, I'd had another: Billy Seawuit's murder might put Arthur's photograph in the news. I could only hope the cop had a terrible memory for faces.

In case he didn't, I wanted to get us out of the city, somewhere far enough to establish Arthur's alibi for this morning's incident. And I needed a place I could stay for a while, long enough for the cop we'd hoodwinked to blur my mental image into Anyblonde. A change of hairstyle had fooled him in the bank lobby. If he didn't see me soon, he'd grow uncertain of his photo ID. In the meantime, I'd work on my own "alibi."

Unfortunately, I needed a place I could stay for free. If I used my bank card or my credit card, Surgelato would find me. If Arthur used his, we couldn't claim he'd been elsewhere this morning.

We spent our pooled cash on BART tickets to Daly City, then bus tickets south. (I'd been afraid to take the Greyhound from San Francisco; afraid the cops were watching the depot.)

Arthur had suggested going to Santa Cruz, two hours away. I'd agreed at once. I had a friend—of sorts—there. He didn't usually care to admit it, but he owed me a favor. And I didn't usually care to admit it, but I trusted him.

So dinnertime found us, like thoughtless guests, on the doorstep of Edward Hershey.

It was a shabby doorstep on a hilltop of small Queen Annes with flaked paint and scraggly lawns. Edward's closed curtains sagged slightly. But his old Jeep gleamed in the streetlight and a kayak leaning against it dripped as if recently hosed down. The smell of chili engulfed us.

I knocked. I heard Edward shout, "Come in," and I knocked again. If someone was inside with him, I didn't relish a round-robin of introductions.

A moment later, Edward flung the door open. He was drying his hands on a half-burnt dishtowel, looking happy in sweatclothes and bare feet.

The sight of me wiped the pleasure right off his face. His thick brows went up, he took a backward step. "Willa," he said.

"Are you alone?" I asked him.

"Yes." His tone was guarded, if not downright suspicious. "Are you here . . . ?" He glanced at Arthur. "Is this a . . . ?"

"A visit? Yes." I took Arthur's arm, guiding him past Edward into a room that looked more like someone's garage than a living room. The wood floor had probably once been varnished, but it currently resembled a country bar's, minus the sawdust. Big rubber boots dripped in a corner near fishing gear. The sofas were covered with afghans that didn't quite disguise collapsed springs.

I heard Edward sigh as he closed the door. I didn't blame him.

The last time I'd arrived unannounced at his house, I'd reviled him thoroughly for involving me in a domestic dispute. I'd been particularly incensed that it involved his former girlfriend, a woman from whom he'd contracted herpes many years earlier. Unfortunately, I'd fallen hard for Edward around the time of their affair. Because of that, herpes was a problem we'd long shared. And I'd been very slow to forgive.

I had definitely brought it up a few times.

"Edward, I need a favor." I turned in time to see him look relieved. He was a private eye now; I'd asked him to track down an anonymous letter writer for me several months ago. "Okay?"

"Let me turn off dinner." He'd retained his macho good looks: fit, not quite handsome, slightly undergroomed. "Unless you'd like some fish chili?"

"Yes." Of that I was sure. "We haven't eaten today."

Edward's brows went up. He tilted his head, squinting at Arthur. Then his expression changed. "You're Arthur Kenna."

Arthur looked flustered, almost as if he wasn't sure.

Edward stepped up and began pumping Arthur's hand. "I read a couple of your books in college. I caught your TV programs." He flushed slightly. "I'm Edward Hershey."

"Oh, yes?" Arthur looked weary, distracted. All afternoon he'd wiped away tears, to the chagrin of our fellow Greyhound passengers.

When Edward turned back to me, he was considerably more gracious. "I've got plenty of chili. Come on in the kitchen so I don't burn it."

We followed him into a room larger than the living room and twice as cluttered. A Formica table was spread with newspapers, documents, and fishing lures. An ancient claw-foot stove had bubbling pots on two burners.

Glancing frequently at Arthur, whom I guided to a wooden chair, Edward poured the contents of the one pot into another.

"We're in trouble, basically," I informed him. "We need a place to . . ." *Lie low* sounded a little melodramatic, but there it was.

"What kind of trouble?"

I hesitated. I had no choice but to trust Edward, but it didn't come easily. I'd spent a dozen bitter years not even speaking to him, followed by a few years of sporadic fighting with him.

As briefly as I could, I told him what had happened. He watched me intently, smiling only when I explained my mother's role in our flight.

"Okay," was his matter-of-fact response. "I've got a place up in Boulder Creek—bitty little cabin, but it's stocked. It's yours as long as you need it."

For the first time all day, I felt my shoulders relax.

I should have known it was just too easy.

CHAPTER FIVE

It turned out Edward hadn't oversold the cabin. It was bitty, all right. But his idea of "stocked" turned out to mean that it had bottled water, a couple of sleeping bags that stank of mold and wet animal, some canned soup, a freezer full of fish, and a naked light bulb suspended from the ceiling. It looked like someone had built a tool shed in the middle of nowhere and then forgotten to add the house.

It took over half an hour on winding mountain roads to reach it, though; at least we weren't in danger of accidental discovery. I'd let Arthur ride up front with Edward, and I'd stretched across the back seat, vaguely listening to Edward ask about Arthur's work. His voice quiet with fatigue, Arthur rambled about longhouses, dug-out canoes, and totem poles. Neither man mentioned Arthur's odd morning or murdered assistant.

I was surprised, when we pulled into the long gravel road to Edward's cabin, to hear Arthur say, "It's fitting we came here."

"Really?" Edward sounded surprised. "I'd have thought the opposite."

"Fitting" in terms of what, I couldn't imagine.

When we went inside, I noticed a hamper of unfolded, but seemingly clean, sweatclothes. I asked to borrow some, then headed for the bath.

As I closed the door, I heard Edward return to "the problem of being here right now."

But I was more interested in the problem of not having had a moment alone all day. I stood in Edward's rustic shower examining mildew patterns and trying not to think. I stayed there, cherishing the solitude, until the water ran cold.

When I came out, Edward was putting away a pocket notebook and pen. Arthur sat in a rickety wooden chair, shoulders drooping, staring at his knees.

"Why don't I make you guys some tea or something?" Edward sounded troubled. I knew the feeling.

He stayed with us another half hour or so. He made tea, swept the place out, unrolled sleeping bags, broke up some nasty spider webs, and showed me where everything was—the last taking maybe thirty seconds. He seemed inordinately proud of the fish carcasses in his freezer.

I must have looked as unhappy as I felt. As he said good night, Edward did the unexpected: He gave me a brief squeeze, promising, "I'm on it."

I was startled. We'd squandered little good will on each other over the years.

"I'm booked tomorrow, but I'll try to get up here if I can," he continued. "Wish this place had a phone. But you can always call me from town—just follow the road down."

I thanked him. Arthur did, too.

After he left, Arthur and I lapsed into tired silence. We soon turned the light off, lying side by side in our sleeping bags. We might as well have been on different planets.

Arthur wept quietly, presumably over his dead assistant. I didn't cry, but I certainly mourned the blow to my career.

I had no idea how to explain this failure of professionalism to Curtis & Huston—or to future employers. My one consolation was that, since I hadn't begun the job, I wouldn't have to list it on my résumé. I wasn't actually worse off than I was last month. Except that I'd lost a wonderful option.

Arthur suddenly spoke. "It's uncanny how often the universe will build an unexpected carriage of experiences to take you where you should be."

"You think this"—I could barely restrain my scorn—"is where we should be?"

"Oh, most definitely. Can't you feel it?"

I could feel the hard floor beneath my sleeping bag. I could feel dust and grime clog my nostrils and tighten my lungs. I could feel a half-dozen insects—imaginary, I hoped—crawling on my legs.

"Feel what?" I asked.

"The spiritual power here." His tone said, What else? "You know, our gods used to be part of us, part of where we were, the very ground, the greenery, the vicissitudes of climate. We were all aspects of the same grand something; spirit, soil, and flesh. But in postulating a heaven, we moved God into the manor house, we turned Him into an absentee landlord. It allowed us to despoil, to pave over, to exploit and ignore—after all, God didn't live here with us; and we could expect to move in with Him, one day."

When I didn't respond, he continued. He'd been a lecturer at Yale too many years to stop mid-thought.

"Our political structures were basically feudal: Pharaohs and princes and emperors lived in palaces, and so must God, you see. We took the earth's spirit and banished it into the clouds. And in the process, we lost our fellowship with nature, our very sense of consanguinity. But there's tremendous spiritual magnetism here, Willa. Modern religions—including science—insist we ignore it. But you feel it, don't you?"

"Magnetism?"

"A feeling of power and communication from the land. From woods, sea, open space."

"Well, no."

"Really?"

"I'm a city girl, Arthur. Golden Gate Park's as far out into the country as I ever get." And its most powerful communication so far had been rollerbladers mowing me down.

"Ah, but you haven't really seen these mountains yet."

That was true. We'd traveled unlighted roads, the trees in the Jeep's headlights telling me only that we were on forested terrain.

"When you see it, you'll experience it. You'll understand about Billy Seawuit." I could hear his quiet sniffles.

"I'm sorry, Arthur."

After a few minutes, he pulled himself together. "Well, perhaps he'll speak to me again. At least we've come to the right place."

I hoped he didn't bring up fate's carriage of experience again. To me, it felt more like we'd been thrown aboard irony's paddy wagon.

CHAPTER SIX

I awakened first. My body screamed at me, angered by the absence of foam or cushions. Then my nose twitched with the stench of Edward's bedding. I opened my eyes to find dust motes and cobwebs glowing surreally in a shaft of light from an uncurtained window.

Arthur lay snoring in his bag, his face tranquil, his mane of gray and white hair tousled.

It was dreary in the cabin, chill with the damp of a cold forest. I climbed stiffly out of the sleeping bag.

I showered, wishing I had clean clothes to get into. (Edward's sweats were too big to wear outside.) I poked quietly through the cupboards, praying for coffee. I found none. My luck was worse than I'd supposed.

Edward had left us all the cash he had—eighty-seven dollars. I grabbed three twenties and stepped out into a gray morning made gloomier by tall redwoods and firs.

I found myself in thick woods carpeted with oak

leaves and evergreen needles and vines sporting purple flowers. Fallen logs hosted huge colonies of mushrooms and furry lichens. The air smelled of cold mud and pine trees.

I started down the gravel path leading away from the cabin. A creature darted in front of me, stopping in apparent surprise when it saw me. Twenty yards ahead, a mountain lion stood watching me.

It was skinny, small; not, I felt, a threat. I was surprised to feel no fear. Before it ran back into the woods, it engendered in me a feeling of good fortune, of a special day. Perhaps I was braver than I'd supposed.

I walked along in better humor.

A series of trails eventually led me to a paved road. Another half-hour's walk took me into a mountain community consisting mostly of hardware stores and coffee shops along a small highway.

I went straight into a restaurant and tanked up on java. I warmed up, apologizing to my bones for their hard night.

I was ready to go find a grocery store and head back to Arthur when a group of men entered.

"Hey, Mary," a man in a leather hat said. His tone was coy, as if the greeting carried years of prior teasing.

"Now, Louis," the waitress replied.

She handed the men menus, asking, "You still working on your bug zapper over there?"

When she brought me my check, she said, loud enough for them to hear, "They're making a computer that can sniff out moth smells. Just what we need in this world, huh?"

I hoped my lips were smiling. The rest of me was

panicking. Computers that could detect pheromones were under development by one of Curtis & Huston's clients. Cyberdelics (as the firm was called) was doing interesting stuff in search of future applicability. I'd met two of its designers during one of my interviews.

I doubted they'd remember me after so brief an introduction. But I didn't make eye contact on my way out.

The street wasn't very busy, but the traffic was fast. A road sign read HIGHWAY 9. Beneath that, someone had graffitied "From Outer Space," presumably to echo the B-movie title *Plan 9 from Outer Space*.

I passed a hardware store, a used bookstore, a crafts gallery. I found myself staring into a hair salon with two chairs and a longhaired man flipping through a magazine.

I whipped my hair over my shoulder, clutching its outdated length in my fist. I'd wanted to feel it again, all that hair, to feel it and remember. But even nostalgia gets old.

When I walked out of the salon, my hair barely reached my shoulders. I had bangs. I searched for my reflection. Asking to have my gray covered. I'd chosen a darker shade than my natural.

For twenty-five bucks, I was a different woman this morning. I hoped Edward didn't mind the loan. God knew, he'd often wished for a change in me.

I hadn't walked ten more feet down the street—the highway, I should say—before I saw a storefront with windows completely painted over in balloony letters reminiscent of sixties posters and the *Rubber Soul* album. They spelled out: CYBERDELICS. A note pinned to the door read, "Out to breakfast. Find us if you can't wait." Apparently, I'd happened into *the* break-fast joint.

I hurried past. Another few paces put me in front of a place called the Virtual Garage, which I knew produced virtual reality hardware and software. It shared a wall with a gallery displaying computer art and quantum physics books. Posted on its door was a list of upcoming local multimedia events. It was as long as any list in San Francisco.

I looked up and down the highway, confirming the boondocks tininess of this place. Judging by the number of stores here—four or five blocks worth—I'd be surprised if it served more than a few thousand die-hard mountain-dwellers. Why would so many of them be multimedia buffs?

I wandered to an organic market, stepping over lounging dogs to get inside. Standing at the register with my basket of fruit and bread and coffee and juice, I took a map from the top rack of a paperback turnstile.

Boulder Creek, I saw, was miles up the mountain from Santa Cruz. It was remote, certainly, surrounded by parkland and timber companies. But it was close to Silicon Valley, far closer than San Francisco was. Depending on the condition of the roads, I'd guess it took only as long to drive to San Jose from here as it did to drive to Santa Cruz.

I dropped the map into my basket.

I'd spent a little time in San Jose—as little time as possible, in fact. It was a flat, hot shrine to suburban strip malls. If I were a graphics designer, a computer artist or engineer, I'd rather live in the mountains and commute down when necessary. But I'd never have guessed the commute was so convenient.

By the time I left the market, the restaurant coffee had kicked in, cheering me. I was enjoying the strangeness of my unexpected new hairstyle. I was seeing new sights.

Maybe in my heart of hearts, I was happy not to be lawyering this morning. I was happy to be out in the world, not trapped at a desk.

I walked back up the town's only business street. I passed the Cyberdelics group leaving the restaurant. They stared at me curiously—I doubted they had many strangers in town—but didn't seem to recognize me.

Anonymity was a wonderful feeling. There was no possibility of running into my parents here, no need to chat with street people I'd come to know by name, no chance of small talk with someone I'd gone to law school with, no reason to worry about how I looked, how much friendliness I could muster, how much change I had in my pockets.

Just when I was ready to do something wild—break into a smile perhaps—I saw a stack of pamphlet-thin newspapers outside a drugstore. The headline read, LOCAL MAN MURDERED. Beneath it was a black-and-white photo of a handsome man with long black hair. It was captioned, "Billy Seawuit, recent to BC, killed in Bowl Rock."

I put my bag of groceries down and stared. No wonder Arthur felt we'd come to the right place, that he could "speak" to his murdered assistant here. No wonder Edward Hershey felt it was, on the contrary, the wrong place for Arthur to be.

It was where Arthur's assistant had most recently lived. It was the site—somewhere in these mountains—of his murder.

In delivering Arthur from the police, I'd brought him to the scene of a worse crime. If the man with the scarf had been trying to frame Arthur by handing him the murder weapon, I'd simultaneously foiled the plot and breathed new life into it.

I stared at the newspaper, feeling it must be impossible. I reviewed recent reality: It was Arthur who'd brought up coming to Santa Cruz. And I'd jumped at the suggestion; Edward lived here and Edward owed me a favor. Now I realized Arthur had wanted to follow up news accounts of Seawuit's murder.

I hadn't thought to question Arthur's motives. I hadn't thought to ask where Seawuit died. I'd blown my chance to cheat irony.

Of all the luck: Edward having a cabin here. But he was an outdoorsman, a hiker, a sportfisher, a rock climber; I supposed it made sense. Irony always did.

Even encountering Curtis & Huston's clients made sense, now that I knew Boulder Creek was half an hour from the heart of the computer industry.

What I didn't understand was why a scholar's assistant would come here.

As if in response, the opening sentence of the newspaper article read: "Billy Seawuit joined our community last winter along with famous mythologist Arthur Kenna, best known for the public television series *Violence, Myth and Culture*. The pair were hired as consultants by local computer firm, Cyberdelics."

Billy Seawuit had come here to work for Cyberdelics? Doing what?

I skimmed the rest of the article. Seawuit was known to be a totem pole carver from Canada. He was found dead in Bowl Rock on Sunday. Police were withholding details pending further investigation.

A clerk stepped out of the drugstore. "Did you want that?" she asked me.

"Yes." I handed her two quarters, and she handed one back.

"Did you know him?"

"No. Did you?"

"I wish. They say he was something. But Toni and Galen kept him pretty much to themselves. Either that or Toni shell-shocked him. That's where he was staying, at Toni and Galen's."

"Shell-shocked him?"

"Just kidding." She glanced away, an uncomfortable crease in her forehead.

I waited, hoping she'd elaborate. She didn't.

"How did he die? Do you know?"

"We heard he was shot."

"Definitely murder?"

"If he was inside the rock." She nodded. "I mean, nobody's going to mistake you for a wild boar or whatever in there." She waved to someone down the street, muttering, "Asshole." Her eyes continued following the person to whom she'd waved. "Are you new in town? Or just up to hike Big Basin?"

"I'm visiting a friend for a couple of days. This caught my eye." I waved the newspaper, not wanting to introduce myself. "Do you have many murders up here?"

She laughed. "Oh, you've heard that 'murder capital of the world' stuff, haven't you?"

I shook my head.

"Back in the seventies. There was some dumping of dead bodies here back then. Then the Trailside Killer did in all those hikers, so they started calling it that. But no." She sighed, looking down at Seawuit's photo.

"It's been a couple of years since the last one. Not counting the dump-offs."

I tried to smile thanks for her words of comfort.

"No, really, don't worry," she added. "We have more mountain lion attacks up here than murders!"

I walked on before I lost all courage. I thought I heard her snicker.

CHAPTER SEVEN

"**W**hy didn't you tell me this was where he was murdered?" If I sounded shrill, I couldn't help it.

Arthur, his chin stubbled and his hair wet from the shower, blinked at me. "But that's why we came here," he said.

"No. No, it isn't. This is the very last place we should be."

"But how odd, Willa. That's not what you said yesterday."

I groaned, brushing off a wood chair at a plank table. "Yesterday I didn't know this was where Seawuit died."

Arthur winced, then began going through the grocery bag. "Then I don't understand. Why did you want to come?"

"It seemed like a good hiding place."

"But there was no reason to hide. Not by then."

"Are you kidding? Our faces were still fresh in that cop's memory. Of course there was reason to hide. Especially you, Arthur." I knotted my fist into my bangs—the very reason I'd let them grow out. "The point was to take you where you could establish an alibi."

He seemed pleased to find orange juice in the bag. "We'll do that this morning if you like. There are people here I'm anxious to contact."

"Don't you get it, Arthur? Yesterday someone tried to hand you what was probably the murder weapon. Now we've brought you to the scene of the crime."

He suddenly looked perplexed.

"You can't deny there's something fishy about a man handing you a gun then screaming his head off." It struck me that Arthur resembled a blend of my parents. He had my mother's scatter-shot goodness, and my father's calm intellect. Maybe that's why I wanted to protect him; I'd been protecting my parents all my life. "We'll figure out later where to say you've been. But for now, don't talk to anyone, okay? Don't let anyone see you around here."

He stood there, carton of orange juice in hand. "Your hair," he said.

"I ran into someone who might recognize me." Which brought me to the real question: "What were you and Seawuit doing for Cyberdelics?"

"I wasn't doing anything at all. Billy may have been lending respectability to the project, but I don't think so. It's called TechnoShaman; a way for computer users to access nonordinary states. They say computers are becoming more like drugs, you know, and that drugs are becoming more like computers."

"Huh?" I couldn't begin to imagine what that meant.

"Technology keeps striving to provide a psychedelic experience—graphics, special effects, a certain freewheeling, mind-expanding quality. And recreational drugs are being designed to stimulate precise impulses, to amplify comprehension. For example, the so-called smart drugs."

"Okay." That would do for now. "Did Cyberdelics contact you guys? How long had you been here?"

"Galen Nelson, the owner, met us at a conference on shamanism. He persuaded Billy to come. He offered what they call a mother-in-law unit behind the Nelsons' house—excellent access to Bowl Rock. I visited him there. I'm sure they'll have a great deal to tell me."

"I'll talk to them, Arthur—without telling them you're here, without telling them who I am. We need to keep you out of this for a while, for both our sakes." I put my hand on his arm. "If the police find you, they find me, too. And it's too soon for them to see us together. If you don't stay out of sight, you put us both at risk. You mess up my future, too."

There wasn't much he could say to that, which is why I made a point of it.

"Well," he conceded, "there are other, more authoritative voices here."

I shuddered to think who he had in mind. "Such as?"

"The place itself."

I was relieved. He could talk to the trees all he wanted.

He set the juice down, looking suddenly bereft. "And Billy himself."

I sighed.

"We've come to the right place for a reason, Willa; you'd agree with that?"

"In a way." My ignorance was most of the reason.

"We've come here to do the right thing."

"What right thing?"

"Listen to Billy, and to the mountain. Find out what happened and what they want done about it."

That wouldn't have been my first guess.

I handed him a glass.

He held it in one hand, the juice in the other. "We'll take a walk this morning." He gestured with the juice, spilling some. "I'll introduce you to the Great Mother."

I smiled. Lawyers are rarely introduced to the Great Mother on a work-week Tuesday morning. Nor would most of them welcome it.

I made Arthur temper his enthusiasm long enough to have breakfast. Even so, he talked more than he ate. Between sips of juice and distracted bites of sweet roll, he set out to tell me how he'd met Billy Seawuit.

"Almost fifty years ago, I searched for insight in southern places; I'm not sure why. First I went to the Amazonian tribes, including the Juavaro. I spent the questing part of my youth south of the equator. And then I sacrificed my middle years to academia, endlessly recogitating things I'd already done and was finished with." He stared thoughtfully into his juice. "What a sad waste of experience scholarship is. The most valuable part of any experience is seeing for yourself. Academics are too quick to accept hindsight analysis over the continuing nuances of observation."

"Not everyone has a chance to make those observations, Arthur. A lot of people are grateful to you for bringing them yours, even if they do lose something. I wouldn't consider your teaching years a waste."

"A waste to me. I litanized my experiences to the point that I petrified them. I robbed them of the fluidity to carry me in new directions. But," he shrugged, "that was my choice. Or rather, my bow to the conventional wisdom. Then I saw myself becoming a sort of parrot of my younger self. In the field, I'd touched something universal. My teaching had become a Cliff Notes version of it."

He slumped in his seat, bags bulging beneath his eyes. Last night had been hard on me, and I was half his age. Watching him in the harsh light of an uncurtained window, I was more concerned with his health than his philosophy.

"Try a roll, Arthur."

After a placating nibble, he continued. "I'd already been south, and so I traveled north this time, into British Columbia and the Yukon. That's where I met Billy." His expression brightened. "By then, I'd concluded that vision questing had nothing to do with ayahuasca, nor yagé, nor Dr. Leary's LSD. The true purpose of the drugs was to induce a state of terror and profundity. No matter what you can achieve by praying or meditating . . ." He shrugged, roll poised halfway to his lips. "No one approaches meditation with knocking knees and fear in his heart. But you can't take a drug without facing danger and the specter of the unknown. And that's it, you see. You put yourself on the line. The shamans knew it with their ghastly rituals. They knew that the exotic and ancient places within us couldn't be reached cheaply and comfortably; that you can't unroll a little mat and safely mantra yourself there. But it's not the drug itself that's essential. It's the stake. Do you see?"

"I suppose." I'd been too recently in jeopardy to find glamour in danger.

"I had started out as an anthropologist and ethnobotanist, studying the relationship of plants to culture. But I had turned my experiences into an easy sort of chapbook, describing the mythologies of others without conveying the fearsome passages, the tumult and exultation of survival inherent in them. In the process of relating myths, I'd lost touch with their very source."

"The individual putting herself on the line?"

"What the individual finds when he's willing to gamble everything to listen to and be led by the universe. It's from that place that all mythologies unfold."

I liked to have a more detailed map, myself.

He put his hand on mine. "Across the globe, our stories are parallel, you know. Our myths resemble one another. Because their source is common to us all. You don't have to go out and buy *Bulfinch's Mythology*, nor do you have to apprentice with a Juavaro storyteller. If you're willing to surrender control over your very life—and thereby your intellect, your expectations, your limits—if you're willing to take that journey to the source within yourself, the story is waiting there in richest detail. It comes from a vast elsewhere that we've lost the habit of accessing. We literally have to scare centuries of cobwebs out of our mystical machinery."

I supposed I couldn't keep skepticism off my face.

Arthur patted my hand. "Ah, all those years you spent among ideologues. I sound like them to you, don't I? But I'm not asking you to accept my view—that's why I stopped teaching. Science, religion, popular culture: they bludgeon us with a theory, a spin, a replacement for personal observation. Consensus trance, I believe they call it. And it becomes difficult to break free, to have one's own experience of anything . . . absent a profound internal upheaval."

"I hope you're not wishing that on me."

"I thrust it upon you yesterday morning, my dear." He attacked the sweet roll as if noticing it for the first time. "How good of you to bring me this. Billy used to provide for me, you know. Make sure I had my keys, put meals in front of me when I'd forgotten to be hungry." He looked surprised. "But that's what I started out to tell you: how I met Billy."

"Enjoy your breakfast, Arthur. We have all day."

"No, no. We have to get to Bowl Rock."

"It's not going anywhere," I pointed out. I entertained an optimistic thought: "Do you think you'll find something the police didn't recognize or understand?"

"Oh, yes."

"Botanicals? Traces of shamanic ritual?"

"The experience of the place itself."

To me this seemed a sentence fragment. But he appeared to feel it was a complete answer.

He stooped over his breakfast. "That's what I learned when I went north. I learned that a place can be as revelatory as any drug. A place can tear you from the safe coffin of your assumptions as dramatically as any chemical. I learned that from Billy Seawuit." He pushed aside what remained of the meal. "His magic will blow away everything you think you know about reality, Willa. I guarantee it."

CHAPTER EIGHT

"The earth used to be covered by redwoods." Arthur waved his arm at the dense growth around us. "Giants, three or four times larger than these young trees." The "young" trees were as tall as three-story buildings. "Now they exist only in certain parts of the Pacific Northwest. That's a very important and primal link for us. We've been educated to think of Africa and perhaps parts of ancient France as our cradles of civilization. But our link to the primeval goes back farther than that, to the first botanical habitats of the earth. That's why redwood forests speak to us in a way savannas can't."

I was aware of the smell of evergreens shading wet earth, the sting of cold mist on my cheeks. I felt an invigorating freedom, probably because I was truant. But if the redwoods were "speaking" to me, they were being far too subtle.

"This particular area is a power spot. If you can survive your most basic emotions, you can feel its history. It was flung up out of the ocean in a vast upheaval hundreds of millennia ago—very recently, geologically speaking. In eroded areas, it's common to find fossilized shells. It must have been quite a sight, an entire ecosystem of sea creatures and vegetation lying here for however long it took water bacteria to develop a land version. Imagine the ground slowly desalinating in the rain until it could sustain plant life, then giant sequoias moving across it like a green glacier, making shade for ancient horsetails and ferns."

"What killed the rest of the world's redwoods?"

"The Ice Age. They can survive anything now and again, but for frequent or persistent cold, you need hemlock, spruce, cedar. Ah, the ancient cedars of the Northwest . . . the fragrance! No smell satisfies like cold cedar forest. We're all Kwakiutls at heart."

I had to smile. I wasn't sure what I was at heart, but Kwakiutl wasn't even on the list.

"What's that?" I spotted something with a bright pattern under a tangle of shrubs.

Arthur stopped, walking closer. "A bedroll. You do see them up here. Perhaps the hard economic times . . ."

He walked abruptly on, as if embarrassed to find something so depressingly usual in his power spot. He took a left at the head of a trail barely wide enough for one. I hoped he knew his way around. I hoped we weren't going to get lost in the woods. This environment might speak to my primeval soul, but my chilly body didn't want to be lost in it.

I knew we were getting close to Bowl Rock when I saw a snippet of yellow plastic police tape caught in a blackberry vine.

Somehow that shiny yellow strip, not six inches long, brought it home to me. More than Arthur's tears, more than this morning's newspaper account, this accouterment of disaster stopped me in my tracks.

I hadn't known Billy Seawuit, thank God; I'd been spared the pain of surviving him. I didn't want him becoming real to me now. I felt, as usual, that I had enough problems. But I'd never known the universe to agree.

I picked up the strip of yellow tape and stuffed it into my pocket.

I glanced at Arthur. His shoulders rounded, his steps slowed as he continued. I caught up quickly. It was too late to worry about sparing myself pain; and it seemed unworthy in the face of Arthur's.

A few more steps took us into a clearing shagged with shrubs and vines and redwood saplings. Where the clearing met deeper forest, a boulder, roughly egg-shaped and as tall as a person, nested in a rut of smaller rocks and mossy mud. Alone at the edge of the clearing, it almost appeared deposited by a giant hand. The seam of stones around it gave it the look of a jewel in a setting. Even its color, yellow-beige with subtle reddish patterns, made it look otherworldly.

Arthur stared at it, then raised both hands as if saluting it or waving it back. He closed his eyes and stood motionless a moment.

He started toward it, then stopped. He turned toward me. "They'll have removed everything?"

"The crime scene tape is down, so yes. They've removed everything they think relates to the . . . to it." But they wouldn't have washed away blood on the rock; they'd have photographed it and walked away. I wondered whether to say something.

Arthur had crossed to the other side of the boulder. Within seconds, I could see no part of him. I knew the rock obscured him, but I felt a surge of panic, a frantic need to see he hadn't been swallowed up.

I was startled to hear Arthur's voice raised in song. It wasn't like anything I'd heard before, somewhere between a dirge and a chant. I couldn't understand the lyrics. It might have been Native American, a repetition of syllables like *wa* and *nee,* deeply sad and resonant.

I crossed to the other side of the rock, stopping in shock because Arthur wasn't standing there. I was struck by an unreasonable fear that he'd sung himself into some other dimension.

What he'd done was climb inside the boulder.

I could see why it was called Bowl Rock. From this side, it had no top. It was like an egg lying on its side with half its top, this back half, sheered away. Inside, it was thick-walled but hollow, the opening just large enough for Arthur to lie semisupine as if in a bathtub.

I looked in at him. The sun filtering through treetops bathed him in fluttering shadows. His eyes were closed tight and his body trembled, either because he "felt" Seawuit's presence or because it was cold in there. Dark tracings of moss and lichen started beneath Arthur, disappearing where the hollow stone arched above him. I could see dried blood behind his head.

I backed away, not wanting to interrupt his song. I waited at the fringe of the clearing for over an hour, until the cold and the eeriness of the ceaseless chanting overcame me. I decided to leave Arthur there. Whatever he was doing must be important to him, part of his grieving. No one would lie atop bloodstains singing himself hoarse if it weren't.

I walked back to the cabin, relieved when I could no longer hear the *waa oo ah waa nee* of Arthur's grief.

CHAPTER NINE

I waited hours for Arthur to return. I considered going back after him, but I thought better of it. It would take more than half an afternoon to blunt his grief.

Out here with no phone, no computer, not even a radio, my options were narrow: I could sit around or I could walk back into town. I decided against leaving Arthur a note. If by mischance it was found, it might incriminate us both. As I'd waited for him, he could wait for me. I wouldn't be gone long; long enough to call Edward from a phone booth. Long enough to drop into the Cyberdelics office and strike up a conversation.

The afternoon had grown warmer, buzzing insects catching shafts of light through trees. The trail smelled of warming pine needles. My feet, in leather flats, alternately kicked up dust and squelched through mud, depending on how shady the spot. The walk seemed longer this time. The novelty of not working—especially after five months of unemployment—was wearing off fast. On the other hand, I'd have to be much more bored before longing to write a brief.

Again I walked through downtown Boulder Creek. It certainly lacked the urban trappings: no street people or street music, no fine suits or prissy accessories, no jockeying traffic or swearing pedestrians, no neon windows, no bas relief or flashy architecture, no Asians or blacks, no SE HABLA signs. It looked like what it probably was: a shady mountain village on a minor highway, a community where people knew one another and found few occasions to dress up.

I stood before Cyberdelics' sixties-poster window. This was the anomaly. Not many mountain villages could lay claim to two computer design firms, both famous enough for me to have heard of them.

Taking a deep breath, I stepped inside. A heated conversation ceased. Four startled faces turned toward me. A statuesque blonde whirled with the drama of a cyclone and rushed out a back exit. One of the remaining three, a gaunt dark-haired man, scowled, watching the door swing shut. The other two glanced at each other. I'd seen these three at the restaurant, and I'd seen one of them briefly at Curtis & Huston. I hoped their glance had nothing to do with me.

No one spoke.

I'd expected to enter some kind of foyer or reception area. I'd been prepared to ask to speak to someone. I hadn't expected to walk into what was obviously a workroom, with computers scattered over several long tables, monitors and VCRs mounted on wall brackets, keyboards on people's laps, candy wrappers and wire snippings strewn across the floor, soft drinks nestled between cable wires and silver envelopes of computer chips.

I hoped they didn't build machines for sale here. They might literally have bugs in them.

"I'm sorry," I faltered. "I thought this was a business office."

"Didn't we all," one of the seated two said dryly. He was fortyish and paunchy, in jeans and a sweatshirt, his thinning hair caught in a ponytail. He stroked his graying mustache, regarding me with sharp blue eyes.

"What can we do for you?" The gaunt dark-haired man—whom I'd seen at Curtis & Huston—stepped toward me, scowl still in place. He buffed his short beard with his knuckles.

"I . . . I wondered if you needed any employees?" And here I'd told Arthur he didn't need to worry, that I'd be able to get information out of these people.

"No." His tone invited me to leave.

"Do, um, any of you know of a place for rent up here?"

"No," he repeated.

The back door was kicked noisily open. The blonde reentered as forcefully as she'd gone. She stood for a moment, looking larger than life in her tank top and jeans, sweater tied around her waist. Then she strode across to the dark-haired man and smacked him. He reeled, falling against a table right beside me.

"Jesus!" The paunchy man leaped to his feet. "Toni, what are you—"

She lunged again, forcing him to quit talking and jump between them.

The fourth person sat passively, watching. He looked young, barely out of his teens, and none too bright despite the expensive computer clutter around him. He neither intervened nor showed surprise.

The big blonde was screaming, "Don't you lie to me, Galen. Don't you ever lie to me again!"

"Goddamn it," the man in the middle insisted. "He's not lying."

Galen didn't seem to have anything to add.

I was alarmed by the tangle of bodies leaning over the table just a few feet from me. The brawling blonde looked angry enough to strangle both men—and me for an encore. I tried to back away.

A nearby chair tripped me up. I overcompensated to keep myself from falling, accidentally brushing the woman's arm.

Surprised by my touch, she struck out absently, swatting my face as if I were a bothersome mosquito. I felt a hot stab of pain in my nose. I blinked away tears, trying to stay upright.

The group staggered left, bumping against me. I managed to keep my balance, making my way to the opposite side of the table.

From here, I could see red streaks on the blonde's arm. I stifled a scream, thinking one of the men had scratched her.

But I quickly realized the blood was mine; it had gushed out of my nose. It was dripping onto the table. The woman had given me a nosebleed.

When she noticed the mess on her arm, it momentarily derailed her fury. She rubbed it, smearing it onto her hand. The paunchy man pushed her away from Galen.

Galen carped, "Get a grip, Toni!"

"Look what she did." The young man pointed at my nose.

"I'm okay," I assured them. Blood streamed down the hand I'd raised to my nose. "I used to get these as a teenager." At every demonstration where my face contacted a police baton.

"It's not broken?" Galen's tone told me I wouldn't be very popular if it was.

I felt the bridge. Damn, this had been a trying couple of days. "I think it's okay."

The blonde's voice was tremulous. "Look at this. Look at my arm."

"Well, if you'd control your—"

Galen's advice was greeted by a look so patently furious he turned away.

The paunchy man sighed. "We've got a sink and some tissue. Come on back with me."

"Okay." My voice sounded nasal. The man led me to a corner behind a screen. I saw a rather unprivate toilet, seat up, a sink, and a table with a coffee urn.

"My name's Louis. Hi. Sorry about your nose."

I ran water, washing blood off my face, my shirt-sleeve, my hand. "I'm . . ." I hadn't thought this through. I didn't want to give my real name. "I'm sorry—did you say Larry?"

"Louis." He handed me a stack of paper towels. "I wish I could tell you things aren't usually this crazy around here. Well, maybe this is a little out in left field, even for this place."

"I wouldn't have walked in like that if I'd known— I assumed you had a front desk."

"We don't get many walk-ins. You're looking for work, you said?"

"Mm." I blotted my nose with the towels.

"We're not that kind of company," he apologized. "We're more like, oh, I guess you could call us a design team, a think tank, something like that. We don't interview people. Ever. Occasionally, some fool of long acquaintance is compelled by the forces of destiny—and Galen—to join us.''

"Oh." I tried to sound like a disappointed job-seeker. I sounded like a dumb kid with a head cold.

I could hear Toni lecturing Galen: "If you want to know what the truth is, I'll give you a goddam dictionary, because your idea of the truth is—"

"Toni." Galen's voice carried a backlog of frustration and defeatism. "Must we do this now? Must we do this over and over and over?"

"Yes! Because I'm that angry, Galen. You want me to put it away. Well, I put it away every single day, don't I? Every day I live with you."

"No, you don't."

"And there it is the next morning bigger than ever, bigger than both of us, bigger than this mountain."

"Then what the hell, go ahead and feed it the relationship, feed it your sanity," Galen replied. "But we can't keep taking time to let the world revolve around you, Toni. We've got serious work. Could you try to be a little cognizant of what we're trying to do here?"

Within seconds, she was running past me and Louis, my blood still splotching her arm. She slammed out the back exit again.

Galen stepped behind the partition. "Are you all right? Is it broken?"

He had streaks of blood across his cheek. Toni had slapped his face with bloody fingers.

"I don't think so," I replied. "I've gotten these before."

"When strangers punched you in the nose?" He had the pale skin, aquiline nose, and pronounced cheekbones of a medieval portrait. He looked like some brooding, disinherited younger son. "That was my wife."

"Oh." I wanted to add, I'm sorry.

"Why don't you come and sit down. Aren't you supposed to tilt your head back or something? Do you want coffee or—"

"Yes! Please." I was used to a lot more coffee in the morning.

I followed him back around the partition. He pointed to the young, golden-haired man, now tapping at a keyboard. "That's Jon."

Without looking up, the man corrected him. "Jonathan."

Louis rolled a chair over. I sat in it. The blow to the nose had dulled my wits. I needed to offer a name, but I hadn't thought of one I liked. "I'm . . . Alice."

"In Wonderland?" Jonathan laughed, Beavis-like, at his own joke.

But he was right about the name's genesis. It didn't say much for my imagination. I was determined to do better for a last name. "Alice Jung."

"Well, young Alice," Galen said, inverting the name he thought he'd heard, "you certainly walked into round one—or, more accurately, round one hundred."

"Galen." Louis settled into a chair. "Dirty laundry and all that?"

"My dirty laundry, as you call her, just socked Alice in the nose, Louis."

Louis merely shook his head.

"Tell us again what we can do for you, Alice."

No one seemed very anxious to get me the coffee they'd offered. And I hated to say I was looking for work now that I knew they never hired. Nor could I think of any clever pretext.

I pretended to be troubled by my nosebleed.

Louis sat forward, obviously expecting me to say something. Galen looked merely ironic.

"I guess, really, I was hoping to talk to you. I was, um, looking for a job. But I'm also freelancing, hoping to get an article into *Mondo"—Mondo 2000, the* hip cybernetics magazine—"about your project and some others like it."

Galen frowned. "There are no others like it, Alice."

His repeated use of the name struck me as patronizing. Maybe his wife had her reasons.

"Digital Group," I said. There were myriad businesses with those words in their name. Surely one of them was doing something arguably of the same type.

Galen's frown lifted. "That's airy-fairy bullshit. A bunch of FX crap for Hollywood."

I raised my brows as if I knew better.

"Don't write about us yet." Louis rocked in his wheeled steno chair. "When we're sure we have a product, we'll call you."

"By then, there'll be more interesting trends."

"No there won't." Louis seemed certain.

"My angle is that computers are becoming like drugs, and drugs are becoming like computers." I quoted Arthur, hoping it made me sound informed.

Jonathan looked up from his keyboard.

"Wouldn't you say so?" I pressed on. "That we don't want to take the risks associated with ayahuasca or LSD, so we've turned to computers?"

"Maybe that's what the glossy magazines would say." Galen crossed his arms. I noticed he was completely dressed in black: shoes, jeans, shirt, belt. "But as Louis pointed out, we don't discuss products in development."

I sensed a big hook coming to pull me off stage. "Billy Seawuit believed that risk is the most important precondition for that kind of experience, didn't he?"

Galen's posture sagged. He turned away.

Jonathan stopped what he was doing and stared at me.

Only Louis seemed unaffected. "The precondition for what kind of experience?"

Arthur had told me the name of the program. Was it CyberGuru? No: "TechnoShaman."

That got a reaction out of Louis. "How did you find out about that? Did Billy tell you?"

"Kind of." I felt sleazy, to say the least. "I came up here to interview him. I was told I could find him through you guys."

Louis's eyes narrowed. "Why didn't you ask for him when you came in?"

Because I'm not that quick-witted, alas. "Actually, if you'd had any kind of job available, I'd have jumped at it."

"Frankly, Ms. Young," Galen turned, standing very straight now, "I don't believe you came here to talk to Billy. Who sent you?"

I could see I'd walked into some sort of mine field. "No one. I'm freelancing. And I was told about this, um, being a power spot, that's all. I thought I could pay for the trip here with an article."

Louis shook his head. "If you'd like to be contacted by our attorneys, fine. Lie to us some more."

"This is really bullshit." Galen nodded without pause, nodding and nodding. "Damn you people! Who sent you?"

You people? Who could he mean?

"I'm not with anybody. If I can't get work in the

field, I thought I'd freelance. Billy Seawuit was supposed to be here teaching about power spots, so I came. I know this area got cast up out of the ocean millennia ago, and that . . ." I ran out of steam. It's exhausting—and creepy—to lie so elaborately.

Louis said to Galen, "That does sound like Seawuit."

"Can we see some ID, please?" Galen remained unconvinced I wasn't one of "you people."

"I'm sorry I bothered you. Obviously I've done something gauche here, which I didn't mean to do. Could you just let me know where to find Billy Seawuit?" I was desperately uncomfortable, more than ready to leave. Earlier, I'd referred to Seawuit in the past tense; had they noticed?

They all watched me. In silence.

I'd come for information. I had to try. "He's supposed to be staying with someone here?"

"Is this a sincere question?" Louis asked.

Had they seen me reading the morning paper out in front of the drugstore earlier?

I felt thoroughly ashamed of myself, embarrassed by my insensitive gambits. The need to confide my perfidy almost overwhelmed me.

But I said, "Yes."

Galen sat down with a sigh. "He was killed sometime Saturday. He was found on Sunday."

"What happened to him?" They'd expect me to ask. "How did he die?"

"He was stabbed."

"Stabbed?" This time my surprise was genuine. We'd heard he'd been shot. I assumed I'd thrown away the murder weapon. I'd fretted incessantly over whether I'd wiped away every trace of fingerprints. "Stabbed? With a knife?"

Galen nodded. "Presumably. They didn't actually find the weapon. But he was . . ." He stared into the middle distance.

"He was slashed," Louis said quietly. "Practically disemboweled."

I guess the last two days got the better of me. I started crying. I hadn't even met Billy Seawuit, but his manner of death suddenly became the last straw.

I got up and walked out.

I hadn't made it half a block down the street before Toni Nelson ran up behind me, taking my arm and stopping me in my tracks.

I was overloaded, didn't want to deal with her now. I wanted to go back to Edward's cabin, take a hot shower, and pretend I'd had a lobotomy.

Toni said, "Your nose looks better. I didn't mean to hit you."

I was still carrying the bloody paper towels. I stared down at them. I'd forgotten about my nose.

She linked her arm—now in a fisherman sweater— through mine. She started us walking again. "Where are you going? I'll come with you partway."

"I was going to take a hike."

"I'll show you a good one."

She must have been five-ten to my five-two. And determination added to her stature. For the moment, I walked along with her.

Our growing silence was less than companionable, at least on my part.

I asked, "Are you a computer designer?"

"I'm an artist." Toni Nelson's voice was unthinkingly, almost regally blunt. "I met Galen when he needed some art to digitize for one of his programs. He's good with the mechanics and the conceptualization, but he's not artistic. He'd seen my work at Menzies." She pointed toward a tiny gallery down the street.

Her face, blue-eyed and bow-lipped, was as sweet as a doll's—when she wasn't pitching a fit or smacking strangers in the nose.

We traversed the main street at quite a clip. She steered us up a road with a sign giving the miles to Big Basin. We were heading in the exact opposite direction from Edward's. If we walked far, I'd be a mass of aches and tight tendons tomorrow. I was about to demur when she spoke again.

"I've made a garden trail on our property. A work of landscape art. Only no one ever walks it but me. Galen moved up here because he's antisocial, basically, not because of the scenery. When I met him, he lived in a studio with almost no windows." She looked down at me. "He was rich. I lived in a garage, but not because I didn't want a house. Our business— mine and my ex-husband's—went bust." She shook her head wonderingly. "Can you imagine living up here, and not noticing?" She waved her arm at the scenery. "Look at all the greens—every shade you could mix. And the smells. Can you imagine becoming an expert in nasal ganglia, in the way we smell, without snorting this up like cocaine?"

I caught the scent of warming fields, of tall grass and wildflowers and manure.

She watched me, apparently satisfied that I was making more of an effort than Galen.

We veered into the woods, taking progressively narrower paths. She seemed lost in thought, paying little attention to the scenery she'd just accused her husband of ignoring.

I began to worry: Would I be able to find my way back to Edward's before dark? I didn't want to test Arthur's theory about enlightenment through terror.

As we rounded a bend, I saw a house. Its appearance was so sudden it might have sparkled into being a moment before. The path was in solid wooded shade, but the house was in a tiny clearing, at this moment dazzled with afternoon sun. It was two-story, of chicly stained wood, with a wraparound deck and a profusion of hollyhocks, gladioli, and other tall flowers. It was as splendid as a *Town & Country* layout.

I stopped, unaccountably afraid of the place. Maybe it came of being marched here by someone who'd recently socked me in the nose. I felt like Gretel, getting her first glimpse of the witch's house.

"Everything bloomed when Billy Seawuit came. Everything. The bulbs weren't ready. They shouldn't have bloomed yet, but they did."

"An early spring?" I didn't know anything about flowers; but I didn't want to believe they bloomed magically for certain people.

She walked swiftly, leaving me to trail behind. She was quite a sight: big-boned, big-hipped, big-chested, striding along in perfect fitness, not overweight but decidedly large in her jeans and bulky sweater. Her hair streamed behind her, partly caught with a ribbon, partly trailing like that of Venus on a half shell.

I followed, feeling like her small, drab echo. Perhaps that was why Galen Nelson seemed so reserved and self-contained. Maybe he'd faded by comparison to his wife.

When she reached the sunny clearing, she beckoned impatiently. "Come on, we don't have much more daylight."

When I caught up to her, she walked me alongside the house, past more hollyhocks and gladioli. Behind the house was a tiny bungalow. Beyond it, flowering shrubs framed a winding path. It looked like a Middle Earth poster.

Toni Nelson stopped, touching the bungalow wall. "This is where Billy stayed."

I hurried closer, looking in through a window.

"You won't see anything," she told me. "Nothing that belonged to him."

"Did the police take his stuff away?"

"No." She stepped up beside me. "Galen took it, he took it all." Her eyes burned with anger, her cheeks flushed. "He denies it. He says Billy didn't bring anything. What a lie!" She leaned her forehead against the glass. "I saw those things, I handled them. I just wanted to touch them again."

"Is that what you were . . . talking to him about? Just now?"

"No." She didn't elaborate.

Through the window, I could make out a small room, its drywall unpainted and its plywood floor partly hidden beneath throw rugs. It was sparsely furnished, with only a duffel bag to show anyone had occupied it.

"Is that Billy's duffel?" I wondered.

"Just his clothes and some books. But where's the rest of it; that's what I want to know. Where are the rattles and drums and carving tools? Where are the cedar blocks? The notebooks?"

I scanned the room again. "In a cupboard?" But I didn't see any. "A closet?"

"No. I've looked everywhere! I've torn Galen's room apart. They're gone."

"Could I . . ." I hated to be pushy, but this might be my only chance. "Could we look around?"

"I told you! There's just his clothes and some books. The police went through them, then Galen packed them up." Again, her voice deepened. "But Galen hid the good stuff."

"Before the police saw it?"

"Yes. Everything the police found here is in that bag. But there was more. Billy had more. Galen swears he didn't. He swears I didn't see the things I know I saw. He's such a liar. He lies constantly."

"You actually handled the other things? The drums and notebooks and all that?"

"Why?" She tilted her head mistrustfully. "Why do you ask about them?"

"Only because you brought it up." I stifled an urge to protect my nose. "Are you sure the police didn't take them? For their investigation?"

"I told you: Billy's things weren't here then. Galen already hid them. If they're found, he'll say he didn't know about them, that he never noticed them here. But it's a lie." She turned to me. "He denies things all the time, out of habit."

"Habit?"

"Like a politician. He's so careful, so stingy with what he knows." Her shoulders rose. "Because everyone wants TechnoShaman."

"I guess he has to be discreet," I agreed.

"No! No, really. What's the point?" She chewed her lower lip, pale brows furrowing. "Why should he tiptoe around doing things at night when he thinks I'm sleeping? Why should he keep the office in town when everyone could come here and be more comfortable? If he doesn't trust me, he should just say so." She stood taller, suddenly haughty: "He thinks he's hiding something from me!"

Didn't she have anyone to talk to up here? Why unload on a stranger?

I wished I could think of a way to take advantage of it. "I guess it's hard to keep computer technology secret."

She smiled as if I just didn't get it.

I waited a polite moment before changing the subject. "Would it be all right if I went inside?" I tried to think of some pretext. I was researching guest houses? I appreciated a good drywall? "Um, to use the facilities?"

To my relief, she strode to the unit's front door and flung it open.

I followed her in.

The room was hardly large enough for a sofa and a rocking chair. A clock radio sat atop a lone end table. A waist-high refrigerator and a toaster oven took up most of the counter space beside a sink. An open door showed a closet-sized bathroom, bare of toiletries.

I went in and washed away the last traces of my nosebleed.

When I came out, I crossed to the duffel bag. It was unzipped. I could see clothing and the spine of a trail guide.

"See?" She sounded irritated. "His things are gone."

I decided to interpret this as a green light to look

for myself. I squatted in front of the duffel, quickly rummaging through it.

I felt a psychic jolt, touching Billy Seawuit's clothes. I'd watched Arthur's heart break because Seawuit would no longer wear these jeans, these shirts. A scent of moss and trees and winter rose from them.

"Come on," Toni snapped. "I want to show you."

With a last look around the room, I followed her back out.

I assumed she wanted to begin showing off her landscaped walk. So I was surprised when she led me into the house proper. We went through an oiled wood kitchen into a bright living room. But we didn't make it to the couches and chairs. We went down a staircase.

It was dark downstairs despite daylight windows. It was one huge room, apparently as big as the whole ground floor. It contained an eccentric arrangement of monastery couches and coffee tables, the latter strewn with computer parts. One wall was covered with masks, most of them Pacific Northwestern, most of them looking like pictures I'd seen of totem poles. An assortment of drums, African or perhaps Native American, were clustered beneath the masks. Dried herbs hung upside down from ceiling rafters. The room smelled of them and of cedar paneling.

Three large tables in the center of the room were crowded with computer peripherals, most of which I didn't recognize. Some looked like they belonged in biology or chemistry labs. Several steno chairs were clustered nearby.

Toni Nelson followed my gaze. "This is where it's really happening. TechnoShaman. This is where it's coming to life. It's like a child's being born, something completely new with a life of its own, its own reason for being." She stepped closer, fixing me with a wet-eyed stare. "It's not like a computer program, it's not a servant. It's going to be a master, a teacher, a portal. It's going to recognize our needs—smell them. It's going to understand our environment by scent in a way that even the finest dogs can't." She sounded like she was reciting a speech.

No wonder Galen attempted to keep his computer business secret from her. Or was she sharing only common knowledge, the gist of their company brochures?

"Have you ever noticed a sand dune," she continued, "how it takes its shape from the wind? That's how our perceptions work on us. But the computer won't be limited by that. It's going to look behind it all, go outside of it."

"In what way?"

"Billy had a term for it. But his terminology was quaint. Maybe that was his strength. He didn't have to create new metaphors as he went along."

I was surprised to see tears slide down her cheeks. She hurried away, crossing the room. She walked to the drums, tapping each in turn. "Drugs, drums, chanting. Now computers."

"Is that what TechnoShaman is going to do? Put people into some kind of a trance?"

"No. It's going to go directly to that other place, that nonordinary state, for them."

That didn't jibe with Arthur's theory that jeopardy was essential, that risk was the vehicle. But I'd certainly prefer to bypass danger and let my computer program obtain enlightenment (or whatever) for me.

"And it's going to use pheromones and scents?"

She nodded, in no way acknowledging the strangeness of it. "Watch," she said. She crossed to the nearest of the tables, to a computer with a row of hard drives and other devices behind it. She turned it on. "It takes a while to load."

"How long did you know Billy?"

"I don't believe time is linear."

Her lunch dates must love that about her. "Did you meet Billy recently? Or your husband met him?"

"Galen makes it a point to be everywhere and meet everybody without noticing a thing about them or giving anything back for what he sucks away." Beside her, the computer screen lit with graphics that looked like shadows dancing on a cave wall. "He sucks nutrients out of people's heads and leaves them like Louis."

"Louis, the man with the mustache?"

"Louis, the corn-husk doll Galen bats around when he runs out of mice." She bent closer to what must have been a twenty-inch monitor. "Okay, you don't believe me? Watch. No hands." She raised her hands overhead. "It's been syncopated to my scent. The interface is so small you can't even notice it; but I have to be within three feet of it." She made sure I was looking. "It can only do two tricks right now. It can do this." The images on the screen suddenly stopped moving. "It can pause when it recognizes me."

My "Wow" was sincere. "Can you unpause it?"

She clicked a key. "I have to do it manually. But watch again. Second trick." She scowled at the screen of shadows dancing on a cave wall. It suddenly went blank. "That's beta-wave technology; it's been around for a while. We've probably done as much experimenting with it as anyone—well, except maybe my first husband, but he went belly up. This is about the most anyone's been able to do without a headset."

"You mean, you stopped it just by thinking?"

"That's right. Eventually, computers will respond to a whole range of thoughts. You might have to have a technician fine-tune your interface with the machine, but you won't need a mouse or any of that crap once it's done. Right now, a few computers can interpret some brain waves with the right hardware connection to your head. But we've been able to get this computer to do it without any device on the user. It interprets beta waves as a 'stop' command. It's a beginning." She hit the keyboard again, bringing back the dancing cave shadows. "I did this piece of artwork. I do them the old-fashioned way—oil pastel, chalk, ink. Galen's people can animate in cyberspace, but they can't seem to come up with the original objects, the things they fly around behind your screen. I do those for them, and they use them as models or scan them in. So you see, I'll be the one who benefits from this."

I shook my head to convey lack of comprehension.

"Well, they don't have the artwork in their heads, so they'll always need me for that. But if they make it possible for what's in my head to appear on the computer, I won't need them, will I?"

"I guess not." In however many decades that might take.

"If I didn't need Galen . . ." Her eyes narrowed and her lips pursed. "I'd burn his house down and I'd kill his children. Close-mouthed, lying, selfish . . . playing keep-away, king of the mountain."

I didn't know if she meant her husband or his children. Either way, she didn't have much regard for their privacy. Or mine, for that matter.

"I'd track them all down, all his children from all his alliances; and I'd kill them, every last one of them."

Jesus, how many children could the man have? He didn't look a day over thirty-five.

The computer screen went black again. Toni Nelson frowned. "It does that sometimes," she said. "It misinterprets."

Misinterprets murderous rage for "stop"? I guessed that could be inconvenient for her.

"Here, you'll like this." She stepped behind a semi-circle of sofas. The wall was lined with cupboards.

She flung open two huge cabinet doors.

I was shocked to see a vast collection of moths, big ones with ferny antennae and little ones both drab and colorful. Most were pinned to white backgrounds, but some fluttered in small cubicles, trapped behind glass.

"For the pheromone research," she said. "Did you know that one invisible pheromone particle a mile away is enough to draw a moth? That's how sensitive these computers will be."

"I've heard something about that." This aspect of Cyberdelics's research was no secret in nerd circles— or local breakfast spots.

"The government's forever trying to seduce us with grants to build computers to lure crop-eating moths." She stepped closer to the floor-to-ceiling moth zoo. "I wonder what kind of information they're sending to other moths? When you think how little one particle a mile away is, it makes you laugh at fax machines and e-mail."

"I suppose so."

"Imagine if your e-mail could find you by scent. All you'd have to do is walk up to a computer, and it would recognize you. Without you even tapping a key, it would summon your messages like a female moth attracting mates."

Through the basement's daylight windows, I could see the afternoon begin to fade into evening.

"One more thing. Look at this." She crossed to another cupboard, yanking it open.

I steeled myself, hoping not to see some cute little animal trapped inside.

What I saw looked like a brown wall with profuse tracings in no particular pattern.

"It's too dark, isn't it?" She reached behind her, throwing a switch that bathed the wall with light, seemingly from within.

"It's an ant farm!" I couldn't believe anyone would build a floor-to-ceiling ant farm ten or fifteen feet long.

"Ant society is completely organized around pheromones. Ants smell what to do and where to go and when to do what. Their life is one hundred percent governed by it. They're a living computer program."

She pressed her cheek to the glass. "You can feel them in there. You shouldn't be able to, but you can. They're like a circulatory system. They make the wall feel alive."

I nodded uncertainly. Her face against the ant farm made me itch.

"I'm not sorry I showed you this!" She sounded defensive, as if we'd been arguing about it.

I did my best to smile. I was ready to get the hell out of here.

"I'm just showing off Galen's children."

I felt a chill of fear, recalling her desire to kill his offspring.

I fell prey to paranoid dread: Did she consider me a substitute? I glanced over my shoulder and up the stairs, wondering if I could outrun her.

"These are his babies." She sighed. "But we still need daddy."

A polite expression did not come easily. "Gosh, it's gotten so late." I started backing up the stairs, saying, "Well, I'd better . . ."

"Our walk—"

"Another time," I called down the stairs. "Thanks."

I dashed out of the house as resolutely as Gretel, all but running back into town.

CHAPTER TEN

The walk back to Edward's cabin, though fraught with worry that I'd lost my way, was nevertheless spectacular. It had been a wet winter, and every patch of unshaded ground was covered with emerald grass and yellow wildflowers. Fruit trees in rural yards had begun to flower. If indeed Galen Nelson failed to appreciate these visual riches, it was a shame.

It was growing dark by the time I reached the woods, but I could still make out twiggy plants with hot pink blossoms, madrone shoots hung with bell-shaped buds, and profuse ground covers dotted with flowers.

I stepped into Edward's cabin with the last of the twilight glowing behind a tall horizon of ragged treetops.

There were no lights burning in the cabin.

"Arthur?" My voice squeaked with worry. "Are you here?"

I clicked on the bare bulb, casting the shack into stark light. There was no sign of anything having been moved since I'd left. A dishcloth hung over the faucet, cups were upside down on a towel beside the sink, a broom was propped in the corner, the sleeping bags were rolled up, the table was wiped down. I'd felt a little like Snow White doing chores I often ignored at home. But apparently my prince had yet to come.

I hoped Arthur hadn't lain chanting in that rock all day. He'd be stiff with cold, well on his way to wearing down his resistance to illness. Worse, his assistant had been murdered there. Maybe the motive had nothing to do with Arthur. But if it did, he might be next on the list. He might be a sitting duck.

I sat and worried for a while. Every sound outside seemed huge, too loud for mere night life, certainly Arthur returning. But the wind had come up, rustling leaves and making branches creak. I stood on the porch with the door open, hoping enough light would pour out for me to see into the woods. But it barely illuminated the porch. I went back inside.

I waited another hour or so. I argued with myself. I wasn't Arthur's parent; it was silly to pace and fret as if I were. I had parents of my own to worry about, I didn't need to expand the scope.

Except that Arthur was old and skinny, and who knew what had happened to Billy Seawuit out there in the woods.

Edward had shown me where he kept the lanterns, cheerfully telling me his power failed frequently. I got one out and wasted ten minutes examining it, making sure it had plenty of kerosene, that its wick was in place, that the handle was clean enough for my dainty fingers. Mostly, I hoped Arthur would return and spare me the necessity of going out looking for him.

It was nerve-wracking at first, walking the narrow

trail with hardly enough light to see fifteen feet around me. But my eyes got used to the dark. There was a half-moon hanging directly above.

Oddly, I noticed more about the path tonight than I had this morning. The moonlight caught dew on ferns, the tall heads of occasional irises, the gloss of wet leaves. It also disguised steep drop-offs into tangled gullies, forcing me to slow down. Just before reaching the clearing around Bowl Rock, I stopped. I heard piping, thin breathy notes as of some reed instrument.

I got scared, recalling the bedroll I'd seen in the brambles, recalling Arthur's statement that homeless people camped here. I turned off the lantern. I stood motionless, my heart pounding, contradictory fears taking hold of me: men with guns, with knives, mountain lions, bears, even witchcraft.

The wind stirred tree limbs, making cracking, rustling sounds. I stood stiffly, listening with everything I had, trying to reassure myself the sounds were random and natural, not footsteps.

But there was no explaining away the piping. Someone was playing a sad tune on some kind of bamboo whistle, that's what it sounded like. And barring a trick of the wind, the person was close by.

I moved cautiously toward the clearing. I broke twigs, I nearly stumbled, I almost cried out when I turned my ankle. But the music continued without error or pause. If the piper heard me, he didn't stop to listen more carefully.

When I reached the outer rim of trees, I could see him. He sat atop Bowl Rock, his back to me, his legs apparently dangling into the bowl. The moonlight traced the tangled curls of his hair, glinted on what looked to be hair on his naked back. In fact, from where I stood, I could make out no hint of clothing. Shivering in the evening chill, I watched a naked man play some kind of flute-pipe in the moonlight.

He had wide shoulders, a big head with a mass of untamed hair. He was no one I'd met here, no one I'd seen; that was apparent to me even from the back.

What was he doing on Bowl Rock? Playing a musical farewell to Billy Seawuit? Was this some kind of New Age rosary?

Or was it a return to the crime scene?

I began backing quietly away. I hoped to God Arthur wasn't still lying inside the rock. I hoped this piper hadn't done something to him.

I was too unnerved to go find out. I turned and ran.

Moments later, I switched the lantern back on so I could run faster. I hadn't waited long enough: The music stopped abruptly.

The air was filled with the echo of a bellow, a vast release of air and emotion. To me it sounded feral, angry. I ran like hell.

I thought I heard crunching behind me. I turned the lantern off and continued running, hoping I could keep to the path and not crash into some sudden gully.

I got so frantic I started trying to scream. I expelled huge sighs, somehow not able to put my vocal cords into it. I felt like I was in a nightmare, running through dark woods, trying and trying to scream without being able to.

By the time I reached the cabin, my calves were cramping, I had a stitch in my side, I was crying, and my lungs burned.

I finally remembered how to use my vocal cords when the cabin door swung open.

I thought for an instant that it would continue to be my worst nightmare, that I'd look through the lighted rectangle of open door and see the naked piper there.

I almost collapsed when I saw Arthur.

"Willa!" He came dashing out to meet me. "My dear! What—?"

"Behind me," I bleated.

Arthur put a supporting arm around me, keeping me steady on my feet. He looked over my shoulder, scanning the woods.

"Hurry. Inside," I begged.

"I don't see anything." He made a startled noise when I broke free and dashed into the cabin.

"Hurry," I begged again. But when I looked out beyond him, I didn't see anything moving, anything out of the ordinary.

Nevertheless, I beckoned him urgently, slamming the door after he entered. I slid the dead bolt into place and made a round of the windows, looking through each of them.

I could see no one out there. But I imagined the man lurking in the trees, and I started shivering.

And here I'd nearly convinced myself, based on facing down a scrawny cougar, that I was braver than I'd previously suspected.

I sat at the table, hugging myself while Arthur knelt beside me. I was, at best, a city girl, at worse, a wimp.

"There's a man out there," I panted. "I think he was chasing me."

Arthur looked troubled. "I came in not half an hour ago. I didn't see anyone."

"Came in from where? Where were you all day?" I couldn't keep petulance out of my voice. If he'd returned sooner, I'd have been spared all this.

"Out at the rock." His tone said, *Don't you remember?*

"You spent all day there?"

"It hardly seemed a moment." He smiled sadly. "It wasn't long enough, I'm afraid."

"It was almost too long, Arthur. I went out to look for you, and I saw a naked man sitting there."

My statement obviously shocked him; he rocked off his haunches, losing his balance.

"On Bowl Rock?"

"Yes. A wide, hairy, naked man playing a flute or something."

Arthur cupped his head in his hands. "Oh, no. No."

"Do you know him? Who is it? He scared the—"

Arthur sat up. "You're *sure* he was playing a pipe?"

"Of course I'm sure. Some kind of reed instrument."

"Might it have been panpipes? Reeds cut to different lengths and lashed together? Did it have a rather high-pitched quality?"

"Yes. Reedy, high. You're right. It sounded like the Peruvian instrument."

"Panpipes," he confirmed.

"Only it wasn't a Latin American tune. It was more of a . . . lament or something. He was sitting right on top of the rock with his legs dangling into it."

"I wonder." Arthur looked pale and unkempt, none the better for his day inside a rock. "I wonder if he waited for me to leave." His eyes filled with tears. "It would be too bad to have missed him by moments. After staying the day long."

"You were waiting for him?"

"No, no. Not necessarily. But it would have been magnificent to encounter him."

I scooted my chair back a few inches. "I didn't find it a bit magnificent."

"But you don't know what a rare thing it is to see him, my dear."

"See who? Who is he?"

"Pan."

"Pan who?"

"Pan the demigod of Greek mythology. Billy stayed here in part because of the rumors."

I shook my head, hoping I was hallucinating this conversation. "What rumors?"

"That Pan wasn't killed, as the myths imply, but that he was banished here, cast deep into the sea. Diana couldn't kill him, you see; that's what we think. There's been a rumor circulating for a few thousand years that Pan pulled the ocean floor up with him; that he spent the millennia quietly husbanding it, mourning Syrinx. Forsaking revenge as his firmament of gods and goddesses faded from universal consciousness. He was marooned here, in a sense, by the changes in our mythology. By Christianity."

"Are you crazy?" He couldn't possibly be suggesting I'd encountered the demigod Pan. Could he?

"Billy learned this is one of the few regions on the planet that fits the profile. It rose from the ocean bottom for no discernible reason, you see."

"You're talking about a Greek myth?" If my tone didn't tell him I thought this was ridiculous, I'm sure my face did. "Are we really discussing this?"

"Not just Greek. Pan is the European emblem for the first shaman. Pan didn't belong in Olympus, the world of the gods; he was half goat, you know. Nor was he fully of the earth, but he chose to work his magic here. The parallel to Kwakiutl myth is striking.

And Billy felt a presence, a powerful shamanic impulse in this land. A shaman generally feels that on his own land, the place of his own generational roots. So he was mystified—until he heard the rumors."

"The rumors that Pan wasn't dead?" I'd been thinking of Arthur as merely overeducated and eccentric. Now this.

"Well, no. Those rumors date back to the Greek texts. I meant the rumors here, among the locals."

"That a demigod hangs around in these woods?"

"Yes. There are many accounts of hearing his music, reports of sightings."

"You told me yourself a lot of homeless people moved up here when things got tough." I felt like I was explaining reality to an overimaginative boy.

"But the music and sightings go far back into the recorded history of the area. Costanoan Indian oral tradition also mentions it. According to Awaswas and Zayante legend—"

"Arthur, there are probably kabillions of legends about the woods here. That always happens, right? People tell spooky stories over and over because they're good stories?" Here I was explaining the origin of legends to the world's foremost mythologist. "Maybe your work has kind of, I don't know, opened your mind a little too much? It's like lawyers who get so caught up they start believing law is the most glorious achievement of—"

"No no no. The interesting thing about myths, Willa, is that they come from a universe within us, yet they connect us to experiences far outside our ordinary reality. It's like the flying saucer mythology, you know. It used to be that people saw visions of nymphs and classical beings. Then, they saw elves and sprites and goblins. Later, they saw the Virgin Mary. Now, they see flying saucers."

It was my turn to cradle my head. "Are you saying they're all equally imaginary or that they're all equally real?"

He crossed his legs comfortably, as if delivering a lecture at Esalen. "They all provide sensory proof that the establishment—science, now; the church, in earlier eras—can't explain everything. We simultaneously dread this and hope so. Today, for example, we have thousands upon thousands of reported UFO sightings each year. But if they are appearing so frequently, why do they always leave us with empty hands and blank film?"

My patience was stretched thin. But it did feel good to be safely inside, debating something as academic as UFO sightings. "Okay—why?"

"If you're not willing to dismiss thousands of contactees as liars, you're only left with one explanation. Not objects traveling impossibly fast through space—they couldn't *always* get away in the click of a shutter—but rather objects manifesting and demanifesting out of another dimension."

"Oh." I couldn't keep all my scorn out of that syllable.

"We're probably dealing with an other-dimensional phenomenon that can manifest literally as anything—elves when that's what we are prepared to see, the Virgin Mary when that comports with our mythology, spaceships after all the nineteen-fifties movies. It pops out at us from its own dimension as whatever we expect to see, as our currently appropriate embodiment of otherworldliness. It thumbs its nose at the prevailing orthodoxy, prying open our minds as best it can."

"That's what you think Pan is?"

"Here, yes. There's a tradition of believing him to be here. There's a tradition of sighting him and hearing his music."

"But I didn't know about the tradition. So why would I see him?" I shook my head. "He was real. And he wasn't a demigod."

"Of course he was real. And it's irrelevant that you didn't know about the tradition. The other-dimensional, whatever it may be, is in the habit of taking material form here as Pan; not as the Virgin or as a UFO or as the Loch Ness monster. In these woods, when it appears, it appears as Pan. It's been doing so as long as anyone remembers."

"Arthur, local legends aside, there's a naked man running around these woods. Maybe the police don't know about him and haven't questioned him." I leaned forward in my chair, watching his haggard face. "And he's obviously wigged out, or he'd wear clothes at night. He might be crazy enough to have killed Billy."

Arthur slumped, rubbing his knees as if they ached. And well they might, after a day inside a damp rock. "It could certainly have been a person you saw out there. It's not impossible that someone would be naked in the woods, playing pipes. But I offer this thought: Why is it more difficult to believe in something people have been seeing and describing for hundreds of years?"

"Because I personally have never seen a UFO," I pointed out. "Or an elf, or the Virgin Mary."

"You've never seen the wind or a magnetic wave or an electron, either. You have only indirect evidence and the word of those you consider better informed than yourself."

"Well, I did see this man. And he didn't have—"

"Goat legs? But you didn't see his legs, did you? They were dangling into the rock. That's what you told me."

"He was definitely a man." It was a measure of how tired I was, no doubt, that "Pan's" broadness and hairiness should suddenly strike me as beastlike.

"And another thing: your reaction to him, Willa. Judging from how you looked when you got here, I'd say you panicked."

"I thought he was chasing me."

"But that's the very essence of the word, you see. Pan, panic. He gives rise to it. That surge of terror when one encounters him in the woods: That's the origin of the word."

"Arthur, somebody got killed out there. It was dark and spooky. It doesn't take a demigod to make someone panic in those circumstances."

"And the music? Was it something a man would play?"

"Yes." But it was unlike anything I'd heard before.

"It's rare, you know, not to hit a false note on pan-pipes. They can be quite squeaky if you're not adept."

"Let's change the subject." I'd lost my adrenaline. I was getting cranky. "Why did you stay out at the rock all day? That might not be a good idea. People could be going there to check it out now that it's been in the papers."

He nodded, looking away like a bad child.

"Tell me."

"I came to briefly and saw a woman staring down at me."

"Who?"

"Nelson's wife. Thea or Terry, I believe."

"Toni. I met her." I touched my nose, feeling for swelling. She hadn't mentioned seeing Arthur, not to me. But she might tell her husband. She might tell the police. "Damn. Did she say anything?"

He shook his head. "She looked in at me, then went away."

"Do you think she recognized you?"

"My impression is that we were both in other worlds. That we registered each other's presence without squandering much consciousness on the encounter."

I rose, crossing to the sink to pour myself some water. Damn Arthur and his unsquandered consciousness. I needed a straight answer.

"So you think she looked at you without necessarily realizing who you were?" I was trying to hope.

"I think she was as far away as I was."

"Which was where?"

"I was journeying."

I was almost afraid to ask. "Journeying where?"

"To the lower and upper worlds."

It was all I could do not to walk over and slap him. I'd had about as much mumbo jumbo as I could handle. I came presaturated from living with my parents.

"You know about shamanism, Willa?"

"Not really." Shamanism had few political overtones. Otherwise, no doubt, it would have been as much a part of my upbringing as Trotskyism.

"It's a surprisingly direct route to another dimension."

I didn't respond.

"Perhaps another night, when you're not so . . .

tired, I'll attempt to take you, shall I?" His tone was cordial, conversational.

"Take me where, Arthur?"

"On a journey. It's not difficult, you know. Most people never try it, they simply pooh-pooh it. It's ironic to live in a culture that scorns a personal experience of the supernatural while believing in the Eucharist."

"Well, I don't believe in that, either."

I turned toward the sink, rinsed my glass, then splashed water on my face.

When I finished toweling my face, Arthur said, "I had a remarkable revelation when I was in Bowl Rock, Willa. I felt an iciness in my abdomen as if I'd been hollowed out. I had an impression of Billy . . ." He blinked away tears. "I would say disemboweled rather than shot. If I didn't know otherwise."

Until this afternoon, I hadn't known Billy Seawuit had been stabbed. And theoretically, Arthur hadn't known.

Either he'd lied to me about his level of complicity or he'd found some other-dimensional informant.

I could believe his hocus-pocus, or I could believe he'd lied to me.

"The people at Cyberdelics told me Seawuit was disemboweled, not shot."

Arthur's face crumpled. He began to shake.

Overloaded and confused, I left him alone. I went into the bathroom and stood under a hot shower.

Perhaps if I made it through the night without seeing a UFO or the Loch Ness monster, the rest of this would seem manageable again tomorrow.

CHAPTER ELEVEN

I awakened to the smell of fresh coffee and the sound of clattering dishes. For a few seconds, I willed myself to ignore my grieving bones and the perfume of sleeping-bag filth. I tried to believe I was at my parents' house, about to be pampered with espresso and their latest health-food chaff.

I sat up, knowing that I wasn't home, but taking cheer in imminent caffeine. I looked around, expecting to find Arthur. Instead, I saw Edward Hershey crouched before a cupboard, frying pan in hand.

He cast me a quick, over-the-shoulder glance. "Up and at 'em," he said in his deep, I'm-a-jock voice.

"What time is it?"

"Seven A.M."

I made a sound indicating how I felt about seven A.M.

He snickered. "I gather the years didn't turn you into a morning person."

"Where's Arthur?"

He turned to face me, still crouching. "What did

93

you do to your hair? Scared the crap out of me—I come in here and find a brunette in my cabin."

"I ran into someone I'd met before." I felt silly saying so, but, "I'm in disguise."

"Will it wash out?"

"Forget my hair."

He grinned. "Okay, Natasha. So you don't know where Arthur is?"

"No."

"But he was here last night?" He waved the frying pan toward the other sleeping bag, unrolled and still rumpled.

"Yes." I climbed creakily out of mine. Had I really spent my youth gypsying around to demonstrations? I must have had more yielding bones. "He spent all day yesterday out at the rock where Billy Seawuit died. Edward?"

Edward rose from his crouch.

"Edward, how did Seawuit die?"

He averted his eyes. "The news said he was shot."

"Did the police put out a call for information? Ask people to phone in with tips?"

"Yeah, I think they did. What are you driving at, Willa?"

"I think Seawuit might have been stabbed, not shot. Did the news reports mention a particular caliber of weapon?" I surveyed the stove for coffee. Seeing a pot, I stepped straight over to it.

"It may have." He watched me pour coffee into one of three cups he'd set on the counter. "What's up?"

"The person who handed Arthur a gun, he must have heard Seawuit was shot. But maybe that's not true; maybe the cops just want to weed out false tips."

"Maybe they do." Edward sounded noncommittal.

"But bullets can be traced. It wouldn't do any good for someone to hand Arthur any old gun. Everybody knows that. Every guy, anyway." I watched his chest expand as if he meant to pound it, Tarzan-like. "So why are you asking about Seawuit getting cut? What did you hear?"

"Do you know the people at Cyberdelics?" When he shook his head, I explained, "Seawuit was working on a project with them. They told me he was slashed. Pretty much disemboweled."

Edward scowled. "How did they know that?"

"I assume the police told them."

He crossed his arms over his chest. He was un-shaven this morning, in a flannel shirt and jeans jacket: the Marlboro Man. "But you haven't had confir-mation."

"Well, maybe in a way. Although Arthur can be pretty out-there." I sipped coffee, surprised to find it strong enough. "He spent the day inside the rock where Seawuit died. And he came back here con-vinced Seawuit was disemboweled, not shot."

"Convinced by what?" Edward's tone was guarded, if not outright suspicious. "Blood patterns on the rock?"

"No." I felt a throbbing in my temples. "No. In fact, when I looked inside the rock, it seemed like the stains were behind where Seawuit's head would have been."

"So the blood stains suggest a shot in the head. Why would Arthur think he got disemboweled?"

"He had a vision."

Edward squinted. "A vision? Like Elvis at Lourdes or something? That kind of vision?"

"Basically. He didn't 'see' the murder. But he felt,

I forget how he put it, a hollowness in his abdomen. It made him think Seawuit was disemboweled."

Edward put down the frying pan and poured himself a cup of coffee. "If Arthur knew that, he didn't find out from any vision. You know where he was before you saw him in the city?"

"No."

A surprised glance. "All this time, you never asked?"

"I've had a few things on my mind!" I hated being made to feel like a dummy—especially since it happened fairly often. "Besides, I knew you guys discussed it." When I came out of the shower Monday night, Edward was putting away his notebook.

"Yesterday evening, for instance. You two sat here for hours and it never came up?"

"Let's just say we were covering other ground." I finished the coffee and poured another cup. I was almost awake enough to shower. "I've known Arthur since I was a teenager. If you're thinking something sinister, forget it. There's just no way."

"I wouldn't take too much for granted if I were you." Edward looked as cynical as years of private detection would make a person. "For one thing, I happen to know Seawuit *was* disemboweled. Or at least, cut deep and long." He mimicked stabbing in and pulling down. "Enough for . . . some organ spillage, shall we say?"

"Please. No details." Not at seven in the morning. "Why didn't you tell me? Why so damn cagey?"

"I wanted to know how you found out first."

"Why? You know I didn't kill him."

"But I don't know Arthur didn't." He raised a hand

to shush me. "I'm supposed to believe he learned about it from sitting in a rock?"

I wanted to defend Arthur, but there wasn't much I could say to that. "Okay, so who told you?"

"I am a private eye. I do know how to get hold of police records."

"How long have you known?"

"I checked yesterday morning."

I must have glowered ferociously; Edward made a cross of his index fingers, stepping back. "What was I supposed to do—send you a carrier pigeon?"

"So," I said grudgingly, "where was Arthur last weekend?"

"He was here—early Saturday, anyway. He and Seawuit did some kind of dawn ritual thing together. Arthur had a rental car; says Seawuit loaded his trunk up; was going to meet him in San Francisco midweek."

"Ah ha!"

"Ah ha, what?"

"Toni Nelson—wife of the guy that runs Cyberdelics—she thinks her husband made off with Seawuit's stuff." Some or all of it might be in Arthur's trunk. Should I tell her? "Seawuit was staying with the Nelsons."

"Oh." He didn't seem to find this as interesting as I did. "Anyway, Arthur *says* he left here before ten, then stopped someplace called Fern Grotto, just north of Santa Cruz. The problem is, he didn't get into San Francisco, didn't get checked into a hotel, till Saturday night."

"So no alibi."

"No alibi."

"That doesn't mean you should suspect him. Arthur's not like that." I'd lived with him these last two days. I'd seen him wracked with grief, not guilt.

Edward didn't say anything. He put the frying pan on a burner and turned on the gas.

"What time was the body found? Who found it?"

"Someone phoned 911 from BC, from a phone booth. Sunday, a few minutes after noon. Said he found it when he was hiking. Didn't identify himself; hasn't come forward."

"Seawuit was inside the rock all night?"

"Yup."

"Arthur would never have left him like that." I repeated, "He's not that kind of person."

Edward dropped a dollop of butter into the skillet.

"You're going to say something snotty, aren't you?"

"What I'm going to do," he corrected me, "is fry us up some eggs and spuds. Then, we'll take a hike to Bowl Rock and look for Arthur."

After a moment, I said, "I'll be out of the shower in five." Why argue with breakfast?

Half an hour later, I was stuffed with scrambled eggs and home fries—Edward had obviously acquired cooking skills in the many years since we'd lived together. We set out toward Bowl Rock.

It was a cool, misty morning. Trailside leaves cupped moisture, sprinkling us as we brushed against them.

"How long have you had this cabin?" I asked Edward.

"Year or so. It's important to get up early if you fish—saves me a drive. The place was cheap enough."

Six hundred square feet of raw wood, with indoor plumbing as its main selling point: I could believe it had been cheap. "Have you mingled much?"

"With the mountain folk? Nope. Defeats the purpose of getting away from it all."

"You haven't heard about Pan?"

"Pan? Spanish word for bread?"

I took that as a no. "The goat-footed demigod. Arthur says there's a local legend about him."

"Hm." He swatted some shrubbery, raising a spray of dew.

"I saw a man last night sitting on Bowl Rock playing panpipes."

"What are panpipes?"

"You know, they're shaped like a little xylophone, only they're hollow reeds tied together. You blow into them."

"Okay, panpipes."

"I don't know if he chased me or I just"—I didn't want to use the word *panicked*—"freaked out. He was sitting with his back to me, and he was undressed." Trying to be delicate, I'd implied nearby clothing. "He was naked, with his legs dangling into the hollow part of the rock."

"Well, be careful. The woods are crawling with weirdos—homeless, tweaked, survivalists, local militia, mushroom hunters. There are self-proclaimed tribes living like gypsies from one state park to another. And lots of bikers, Harley-Davidson types—they love the winding roads."

We continued in silence. The sky was white above dark treetops. The ground frequently plunged into lush ravines, some with streams trickling through them.

"It wouldn't be hard to live out here," Edward mused. "Plenty of fresh water and edibles—fish, game, berries, miner's lettuce, 'shrooms. It's damp, but it doesn't freeze very often."

I glanced at him, striding comfortably in his boots. At least I'd thought to grab jeans and a warm jacket before fleeing my apartment. No use being jealous of Edward's hiking duds; I could be worse off.

"The police must have combed the woods looking for witnesses and suspects."

"I imagine so. That doesn't mean they'd find any. The folks who live up here know the land, know where to go to keep out of sight." He grinned at me. "I could find them," he boasted.

"You know these woods that well?"

"Pretty well. I know where some of the favorite campsites are."

Though it was the last thing in the world I wanted to do: "Maybe we should talk to them. The police might have missed something important, something that could exculpate Arthur."

"You're assuming he's a suspect."

"They've got to be looking for him."

"Speaking of looking for: You made the TV news. They've got police drawings." His grin broadened. "Not much of a likeness of Arthur, but pretty close to you. They didn't mention you by name, so they're keeping it under wraps about you not showing up for work. Probably the thing with Judge Shanna works in your favor. If you'd been Miss Predictable, they might have broadcast your photo."

"What 'thing' with Judge Shanna?"

"Quitting on him twice in two weeks for no known reason."

No known reason! He, better than anyone, knew why I'd quit. The favor I'd done Edward, intervening in a family squabble, had resulted in Judge Shanna recusing himself from a big case. My rapport with the judge went downhill fast from there.

"Then there's—" Edward glanced at me. I must have looked angry. He stopped talking.

I walked in silence. Unfortunately—or fortunately, in this situation he was right. If a woman with a perfect résumé failed to show up for work on the morning a hostage fitting her description was taken, the police might be more concerned. But I had a history of short-lived jobs. And I had quit my clerkship early and often.

"It's probably because of my father," I insisted. "I talked to him on the phone; he knows what happened. He probably told them I'd had my doubts about starting work, something like that."

"Mm-hmm." Edward's tone was a little too neutral.

We stepped into the tiny clearing around Bowl Rock. I heard no chanting, none of Arthur's *waa oo ah waa nee* this morning.

I crossed quickly to the other side of the rock, looking into its bowl. It was empty.

Edward stepped up beside me, touching the encrusted red blotch near the bowl's edge.

Then he hoisted himself up, sliding into the rock. I noticed he was careful not to touch the dried spot.

Edward stood inside, bending to avoid the rock's eggshell curvature. He leaned back as if to rest his hips against the bowl's rim, bracing himself with his hands.

"Maybe Seawuit stood so he could greet whoever was walking up; maybe he was already leaning against this spot. Either that or he stood up when he got knifed. He must have turned around and tried to climb out, leaving a big old blob of blood and guts right here." He hopped out of the rock.

He stood a long time looking in.

I looked in, too. Other than the big splotch, it was hard to tell the difference between the rock's crevices and mosses, and other, possibly nefarious, stains. Edward touched a couple of spots, then walked around the rock.

"They probably swatched off some of the little splashes. And organ matter in the big patch." He was behind the rock now, hidden by the curved canopy top. "You ever have a hankering to be a detective, Willa?"

"No." I'd had my Nancy Drew moments, but I'd bungled them, and in retrospect, they hadn't been much fun.

"Well, you want to give me a hand, anyway?"

I had a long history with Edward, resulting in a hard-won distrust. But I am not completely petty. He'd made me breakfast, and he'd paid for my haircut, after all.

I went around to where he crouched behind the rock. He looked up at me.

"Basically, I want to trace arcs around this rock, going back and forth over the ground bit by bit. I want you to start on the other side and do the same thing."

"But we'll be covering the same ground."

"That's right. With luck, if I miss something, you won't." He shaded his eyes against the bright white sky. "You with me?"

"Okay."

I crossed to the other side of the rock and began a slow arc, at times passing Edward and at times opposite him as if we were locked in some mating ritual.

I had the pleasure, as we neared the edge of the clearing, of shouting to him, "Found something."

"Cheap shale arrowhead?"

Rats, he'd seen it. "Yes. Aren't you collecting this stuff?"

"No. Just looking at it. Leave it where it is so the cops can come back and find it, if they get the urge."

"Have you found anything else?"

"Plenty of stuff. I doubt any of it's important. I'll take you back around and show you when we're done." There was a certain pompous pleasure in his tone.

But true to his word, he walked me back through the clearing, stopping at various locations. Edward showed me wood shavings, a beer tab, a knotted string, a tiny rusted bell, a squashed spoor, and something that looked to me like a tiny dirtball but he thought might be a blood drip.

"But," he grinned, "you did spot the arrowhead." Leaving me no time to reply, he continued, "Of course, that probably found its way here after Seawuit died."

I tried not to look impressed. "Why do you think so?"

"Because it's too big for the cops to have missed."

"What about the other stuff? Do you think any of it's important?"

"I didn't know Billy Seawuit, so I have no idea." He seemed cheerful enough about it. "Any thoughts where Arthur might be?"

"I don't even know the possibilities. He could be . . . flying around in a UFO. Although I hear they don't stop here."

Edward looked at me askance. "They don't?"

"No. The other-dimensional whatever manifests as a demigod here." My turn to look at him askance. "And you call yourself a detective."

CHAPTER TWELVE

On our way back to the cabin, I showed Edward the spot where I'd found the bedroll. It was gone now.

"We should talk to some of the people who live out here in the woods." I faintheartedly hoped he'd disagree.

"Okay. Halt. We'll double back to the clearing, take a different trail. I'll show you one of the favorite camps. You wearing good shoes?"

"Good for impressing a new boss on the first day of work."

"Babe shoes, huh?"

"Don't call me 'babe.' " What happened to the politically correct youth I'd lived with all of eight months?

"I was talking about your shoes. At least they're not high heels."

The terrain on the other side of Bowl Rock was rough and lovely, with a stream defining a steep gorge, and the mix of redwoods, fir, and pines giving way near the water to oaks and alders and vast patches of manzanita and monkey flower, all identified for me by Edward. Where the trail ended at the stream, we followed its muddy, log-littered path until we picked up another trail.

I wasn't used to getting up at seven. I wasn't used to long hikes before lunch. But it's difficult to complain in front of someone with a history of poking fun at you.

Finally, when my shoes were as muddy inside as out, when my jeans were stiff with dirt and stitched with brambles, Edward slowed to a cautious pace. He motioned for me not to speak, though I'd been lost in a fantasy of comfort and sleep for the last twenty minutes.

I caught up to him. We'd taken a trail through sparse forest to an area of spiky, tough-leafed shrubs. Through an opening in them, I could see movement. Someone in a white shirt was moving first in one direction, then another. Because of the bushes, it was impossible to tell what he was doing.

"I'll do the talking," Edward said. "Hey, friend," he shouted. "Coming up to you."

I could see the wisdom in not interrupting hermits without calling out a warning.

We crashed quickly through the bushes, not allowing the person time to run off.

He looked surprised, half-crouched as if he'd wheeled around when he heard Edward's greeting. He was skinny, perhaps in his late twenties, wearing jeans and a too-small blue vest over a big, dirt-streaked white shirt. A canvas hat trimmed with ribbon and feathers was pulled low over his shaved head.

Around him were all the comforts of home: a lean-to made of sticks and green garbage bags, several buckets full of water, a pile of potatoes, a stone fire ring beneath a drying rack hung with meat strips.

The man straightened as he assessed us. His shoulders relaxed.

"Hi," he said.

"Hi, there." Edward's tone was friendlier than normal. "I've got a little cabin up here; I fish. This is my . . . babe. How ya doin'?"

"I'm getting by." He looked pathetically thin, but his grin seemed happy. "You're out for a hike?"

"Nope," Edward admitted. "Fact is, I've had some problems at the cabin. Have you seen anything weird going on up here the last few nights?"

The man squinted, turning his head to look sideways at us. "No."

"I'm not up here to accuse anybody. I'm here to reassure her." He nodded toward me. "That there's no bogeyman, you know? But she thinks she saw a guy with a knife one night, a naked guy with a flute another night, an Indian guy, too." Edward shrugged. "Doesn't sound like any of the regulars to me."

The man looked relieved. "No. I haven't seen anybody like that."

I disobeyed Edward. "Have you heard music playing at night? Panpipes?"

"A syrinx?" The man shook his head.

"A what?"

"Pan was chasing a nymph named Syrinx. When he caught her, she turned into reeds; you know, that grow in the ground. Pan cut some and made the pipes." The man smiled, showing dark teeth. "That's what the pipes are called. A syrinx."

I was surprised he knew that. I wondered if he'd

encountered Arthur, if Arthur had burbled it to him. "Where did you hear the story?"

He seemed surprised by the question. "My father teaches literature at Rutgers. He used to tell me and my brother classical stories when we were kids. My brother's an engineer now. I'm a bum. Go figure." He laughed, a quiet *hee-hee* that shook his shoulders.

"You lived out here long?" Edward asked him.

"Here or someplace like it, pretty much since I was eighteen. I like Canada way better than here, but it gets cold up there. I stay down here almost till summer. It's way prettier up there, though, way prettier."

"Really?" I tried to keep my tone conversational. "I heard this was some kind of power spot."

The man waved away the suggestion. "You hear a bunch of New Age crap around here. All I know is, it's the prettiest spot this far south. But it doesn't compare to what you get in British Columbia or the Yukon."

Just what Arthur had said. "A friend of mine was down here from British Columbia," I pushed on. "Billy Seawuit. Did you know him?"

"Nope. I don't get in much."

"He was a Native American. I thought you might have run into him."

His brows went up. "I wish I had. What tribe?"

"Kwakiutl."

"Oh, man. I've been all up and down Vancouver Island. If you see him, tell him to come up and visit me." His thin face, made smaller by stubble instead of hair, expressed a goofy enthusiasm that made him look like a kid.

"Sure."

"You want some jerky?"

I looked at the strips of meat hanging over a ring of cold stones. Flies buzzed around them. "No, thanks."

We left him to his one-man village.

When we were out of earshot, Edward commented, "There's a fair number like him on this mountain—probably on any mountain. Hermits, survivalists, neo-natives, didn't get socialized into city life, or even town life. Assuming he's being straight with us."

"He filleted that jerky with something, Edward."

"True. I looked around, hoping his knife would be sitting out, but . . ." A moment later, he scoffed, "A power spot? What the hell's a power spot?"

I explained about this land having heaved up out of the ocean and the gradual movement of redwoods across it. "Somehow that translates into a person feeling greater shamanic power here."

"I had to ask."

"Arthur's into this stuff."

"I had him pegged for more of an academic type," Edward observed. "More of a classics scholar."

"He is—or he used to be. He's at least four people rolled into one. But this shamanic power spot stuff is new, since the last time I saw him. Maybe Seawuit got him into it."

"Too bad. Sounds like a no-brainer to me."

"How come we're going this way?"

"Talk to a family of mushroom pickers. I saw them up here last weekend. They usually camp in their cars for a week or so; they might still be around."

We pushed our way through more chaparral plants. It took a few minutes to reach anything resembling a trail.

Edward spoke again. "So this power spot business,

and sitting in the rock all day chanting . . . you think the old guy's Alz'ing?"

"As in Alzheimer's?" I wanted to leap to Arthur's defense, as I usually leapt to my parents'. I wanted to say, what's wrong with an adult being . . . eccentric? But Edward knew my parents, knew what a lot of trouble they'd been to take care of.

"It must have occurred to you he might not have been handed that gun? Maybe he did try to hold up that guy in San Francisco."

"No. I can tell you that much: Arthur was more surprised than anyone to be holding a gun. I could tell from across the street that he wasn't intending to use it as a weapon," I insisted. "You think I'd go throw myself in front of him if I thought he'd shoot?"

Edward shrugged.

"I'm not suicidal."

"I'm just saying, as a judgment call—"

"It was right! I was right." God, the man annoyed me. "I have good judgment." If I'd had my law degree handy, I'd have brandished it as evidence of my practical nature, proof that I was not my mother's daughter.

We stayed in chaparral, dusty and full of meanly barbed shrubs, until we reached a dirt access road. Edward crossed to the center of it, scanning each direction, his hand shading his eyes like the Deerstalker.

"They must be gone, following the mushrooms."

"How big a family?"

"Two preteen boys, an older girl, a mom, and a dad; illegal Cambodians; supposedly came to visit relatives, then melted into the forest. I guess they make enough cash doing this to support themselves during the dry season."

"Well, unless Billy Seawuit was picking their mushrooms—"

"There were a couple of shootings north of here over mushrooms. Pickers have their territories. It's a cash crop, same as pot. Hell, chanterelles are eighteen bucks a pound at the supermarket. And there's a mushroom up here the Japanese will pay four hundred dollars a pair for."

The woods were a busier place than I'd supposed. "What next? I'd love some lunch."

"You want to go tell our friend you changed your mind about the jerky?"

Edward always did find himself very cute.

Before we reached the cabin, purely by accident, we spotted another encampment.

Edward whispered, "There's two of them. You better stay here. Keep your eyes open."

He crashed swiftly through the brush and into their camp. I was tempted to follow. But I had the impression Edward wanted me to watch his back.

I shifted so I had a better view. Two middle-aged men stared up at him from a ground tarp. They'd had recent haircuts, and their clothes were nice and warm and clean-looking. There were backpacks beside them and thermoses between them.

One man leaped to his feet.

The other said, as if giving him a cue, "Great day for backpacking."

"You drive down from the city?" Edward sounded casual, neighborly. I gave him points. "Lousy weather up there lately."

"No, we're from Watsonville. Getting away from the wives."

"Corporate retreat?" Edward laughed at his own

joke. "Have you been out here awhile? A couple of nights? I'm looking for a buddy I hope didn't get lost."

"You lost someone on a hike?" The seated man did all the talking. "That could be bad news. Although there are lots of trails; your friend should be okay if he stayed on them."

"I'm hoping he's just late getting started. I thought he'd be at my place by now, but maybe he got hung up en route; that's possible, too."

"Still, you have to look."

"That's right," Edward agreed. "It's a little early to call the rangers and all that, but . . . You guys been out here a night or two? Seen anybody?"

The standing man finally spoke. "No."

"What does your friend look like?" the seated man asked.

Edward answered, "Burly guy. Plays the panpipes when he hikes."

"Well, we just started our little trip," the seated man said. "Just about to have some lunch and push on. But if we see your friend, we'll tell him you're worrying about him."

"You must have trail maps on you," Edward observed.

The standing man sat back down, exchanging a glance with his companion.

"Could you show my friend where he is, how to get into town? If you see him." Edward continued to sound casual.

"Will do," the man said.

"Thanks." Edward crashed back through the shrubs, collecting me and hustling away from their camp.

We walked in silence for a few minutes, then Edward stopped, motioning me to stand still. He listened for a moment.

"Good." He took a deep breath, then exhaled. "I was afraid they didn't buy it. I was afraid they were going to follow."

"Who were they? They sure didn't look like the backpacking type."

"No. They sure didn't."

"What are we going to do about them?"

"Not much we can do. If we phone in a tip to the cops, they'll be all over the woods: They might find Arthur," he pointed out.

I frowned over my shoulder, trying to devise a plan. We'd come to gather information from the human fauna in the woods. But we hadn't asked these men anything.

"But shouldn't we bring up Billy Seawuit? Or something?"

Edward shook his head emphatically. "They don't have rifles, they don't have fishing gear; they're not your usual guys on an outing. They're not dirty; they haven't been out here long. And I don't like it that they're so close to my cabin. But I'm not going to go ask them questions that let on I'm suspicious. What's the point? Best case, they lie some more. Worst case, they pull out guns and blam."

Edward walked on. I had no choice but to follow my guide. I hadn't even realized we were near the cabin.

I didn't have to keep my mouth shut, however. "But you agree those guys aren't who they say they are. We should do something."

Edward sighed, stopping again. "I did do something."

"All you did was chitchat. They could be knee-deep in all this, and we'll never be able to produce them." I imagined myself in court, trying to introduce evidence that the woods were full of strange characters, any of whom might have killed Seawuit. "Do you think . . . ?" Again I cast about for a plan. "Could we try to trick those two guys into touching something? Get their fingerprints?"

He snorted. "Like I've got me a fingerprint lab at home."

He started walking again.

I didn't. "Edward!"

He turned. "I told you: I did do something." He motioned for me to catch up.

When I reached him, he opened his hand.

I was surprised to see a cigarette lighter-sized object there. Bending closer, I recognized it.

"A camera?" I looked up at him.

He smiled. "Just like a real private eye."

"I didn't see you use it."

"Oh, that would have been brilliant. Hold it up to my eye and say, 'Smile, lying scum.' Of course you didn't see me use it."

"Are you sure you got pictures?"

He waggled his eyebrows. "They might be vampires; no soul, no image."

"Vampires," I reminded him, "don't manifest here. Pan does."

CHAPTER THIRTEEN

When we got back to the cabin, there was no sign of Arthur having returned. Our cups and dishes were still stacked in the sink, the portion of breakfast we'd set aside for him was still uneaten.

"Where could he have gone?" I couldn't keep worry out of my voice.

"Kids today," Edward agreed. He crossed to the kitchen sink and started washing his hands, splashing water over his face. "How 'bout we go into town for lunch?"

I wanted to groan; I was hiked out. I wanted to sit and languish. As hungry as I was, it didn't match my exhaustion.

"We'll take the Jeep. I'll take you for a drive after."

"Perfect." I emptied my shoes of dried mud clumps and a cascade of dirt. "You didn't bring extra socks, did you?"

"We'll get some provisions."

"Socks, underwear, T-shirt. Okay? I'll pay you back when this is over."

"We'll get our film developed. You'll love the back views of you crouched down looking for evidence," he promised.

His ratty old Jeep seemed the height of luxury after wooden chairs and way too much walking in city shoes. It was also a treat to see the world more quickly.

I was surprised how close to town Edward's place was—by car. The cabin seemed so lonely, so remote, and yet it was an easy drive to the supermarket.

In exchange for the ride, I was able to take Edward to *the* hip restaurant.

Ever skeptical, he looked at its plank exterior and general air of a run-down saloon. "This is your idea of happening?"

"I ran into the people from Cyberdelics here."

"Since when do nerds know the hot spots?"

"They're not unmitigated nerds. One's kind of a hippie-nerd, another's a surfer-nerd." I wasn't sure how to describe Galen Nelson.

We pushed through the restaurant's screen door. A big-screen TV, mounted high over the bar, showed a grainy, washed-out commercial, the sound muted. A few languid flies buzzed over green vinyl tablecloths.

Couples in flannel shirts occupied the window tables. A few men with bill caps were seated at the counter, giving the waitress their orders. On the walls, beer ads jostled chess tournament sign-up sheets and missing dog notices.

In the back corner, because we'd spoken of the devil, were the three men from Cyberdelics. Their conversation stopped when we approached. I stopped, too. I wasn't sure if our meeting yesterday had been friendly or hostile. My predominant memory was of being smacked, then swooped away, by Toni Nelson.

Finally, the man named Louis said, "Hey, Alice." A leather cowboy hat was tilted back on his head.

"Hi." I elbowed Edward, hoping he'd registered the phony name. "I guess I found the best restaurant in town?"

Galen looked grumpy, not acknowledging me. But the youngest of the three men—Jonathan—laughed his goofy laugh.

Jonathan said, "They have chili fries."

Even chili fries sounded good to me after a mountain hike.

"Mind if we join you?" Edward asked, in no way consulting me first.

Galen raised his brows, still saying nothing. But Louis said, "Sure. Pull up a table."

Edward, showing off, lifted a two-person table with apparent ease, depositing it at the end of theirs.

The waitress stepped up then, looking alarmed. "Hey—don't break anything!" She picked up a catsup bottle that had rolled to the floor.

She looked Edward over. "You need a menu, Samson?"

"Naw—I'll try the chili fries. And a cheeseburger," Edward replied. "The diet plate."

I pulled up a chair, accepting a menu.

"You want me to bring everything out together?" the waitress asked. "Or you fellows going to scarf down like hogs while these people wait for theirs?"

"Hogs," Jonathan answered immediately.

And, a few minutes later, he proved to be distinctly hoglike in his eating habits.

While the three dove into burgers and chili fries,

116

Edward did something I wasn't able to do. He bonded, guy to guy.

It started with his gesturing toward the big-screen TV. "The Niners looked pretty good last season. But I don't know about that play-off game."

"Young still chokes in the big ones," Louis agreed. "He's no Montana."

Galen raised a brow. "The offense is ragged. You can't blame Young for that."

While I looked over the menu, they made puppets of saltshakers and spoons, showing how "play-off" plays should have gone.

After I ordered, everyone looked a little ill at ease: A female was among them. In the nineties, one couldn't simply ignore a female. The football players turned back into cutlery.

I changed the subject. "A friend of mine was telling me about the Pan legend up here."

Jonathan nodded emphatically. "Yeah. I've seen him." He colored, glancing at his companions. "No shit, I have."

I sat forward. "When?"

"End of last summer. I was up near Skyline where the meadows are, and I saw him running like the fastest thing you ever saw, just ripshitting downhill through a meadow. It was a trip!"

Galen broke his silence to say, dryly, "What makes you think it was Pan?"

"He was naked." Jonathan seemed to believe that settled it. "Hairy fuck. Way past wild. Definitely Pan."

"There are probably more than a few naked wildmen up here," Louis pointed out.

"You ever seen any?" Jonathan countered. "Besides in the mirror?"

Louis laughed, his chili fry poised halfway to his lips, dripping red grease.

"I saw him last night," I told them. "It really scared me. I'd never heard the legend. I didn't know what to think."

"Well, I wouldn't be persuaded by the wives' tales." Louis spoke with his mouth full. "I'd be careful."

"Did your guy have goat legs?" I asked Jonathan.

He nodded. "Yeah, what a trip."

"If you saw him in a meadow in the summer," Galen observed, "the grass would have been thigh high."

Jonathan nodded again.

"How do you know he had goat legs if he was in thigh-high grass?" Galen demanded.

"They were so hairy. You could tell. The sun was all absorbed into the hairiness."

Galen shook his head, going back to his lunch.

"I couldn't see his legs," I admitted. "So I guess I can't be sure it was Pan."

"You can be sure it wasn't." Louis smiled.

"Well, who knows?" Edward chimed in. "Nobody would believe a person could make a computer turn off with thought waves, either."

I'd described my afternoon with Toni Nelson to Edward. God, the man was indiscreet.

The temperature seemed to drop twenty degrees.

Edward continued, "I've heard that's what you guys are into."

"Where did you hear that?"

"From Alice here," he said, hardly missing a beat.

If I'd had my lunch before me, I'd have dumped it over his head.

"Your wife told me," I confessed to Galen. "After I left yesterday."

"Toni told you that?" Galen asked calmly.

"Uh-huh."

Louis watched him, brows raised as high as they could go, beagling up his forehead. Jonathan continued eating as if nothing had happened.

"Well," Galen said, "Toni exaggerates. She conflates what we say about where the technology's going and what we personally are working on. She's not into computers. She's an artist."

"I thought her and Stu had a software company," Jonathan said innocently.

Galen looked annoyed, to say the least. "Stu is Toni's ex-husband," he explained. "The business failed."

I waited for him to say more. When he didn't, I asked, "Did she do any actual software designing?"

"A bit." His tone was clipped.

"But your computers don't respond to thought waves?" I tried to sound merely curious.

"No."

"Oh." Lie to me some more. "I knew it was too good to be true."

"Too good?" Edward said. "It would probably be a disaster—get your computer off daydreaming with you and who knows what it would do. Think what kind of e-mail it would send."

Jonathan smiled but didn't look up from his lunch. Louis said, "Talk about some flaming."

I had learned only last month that flames were outrageously rude or angry electronic mailings.

"Talk about your porn." Edward seemed determined to come across as a Guy guy. Or perhaps all traces of refinement had atrophied. You see a lot of that in former boyfriends.

The waitress brought my lunch and Edward's, giving Louis a chance to shoot Galen a look a lesser sleuth would have missed. (I'd have to quiz Edward on whether he'd caught it.)

"What do you do, um? Did we get your name?" Louis asked him.

"Edward Hershey," he said, sticking out his hand. "I'm an honest-to-God private eye."

That stopped every fork at the table.

"Are you on a case, Edward?" Galen asked him.

"Nope. I own a crummy shack near the creek. And this is my first year of decent fishing. You see the article in the *Valley Press* about the coho? Makes you glad we had a wet year!" He glowed with enthusiasm. "Or don't you fish?"

"Yeah, I fish," said Louis. He proceeded to cross-examine Edward about bait, lures, casting techniques.

They talked for a while—apparently, Edward was passing the test. I asked Galen if Toni was doing better today.

"You say she ran into you after you left?" Galen wiped his fingers on one of a stack of napkins beside his chili fries.

I nodded. "She apologized for the nose thing. She was very friendly about it. I was glad not to be left with a . . . strange impression of her."

I could see Louis's glance waver from Edward, see his slight smile as he eavesdropped.

"And she told you we were doing stuff with brain waves?"

Again I nodded. "And smells."

"Smells, yes," Galen admitted. "Basically, a circuitry model of our own nasal setup. We have nerve ganglia in our noses with jigsaw puzzle-type receptors to particular odor molecules. We figured out a way to mimic it with a combination of hardware and software. In theory, anyway."

Theory, my foot. They had several patents pending, or they wouldn't be discussing it.

"What would you do with the technology?" I couldn't decide if Galen was being forthcoming or simplifying most of the truth out of his description.

"We don't really have an application in mind. We don't have to—we'll license the technology out. I'm sure there'll be quite a few uses: smoke detectors, chemical reaction alarms, devices to alert health care workers when diapers need changing." Galen spoke matter-of-factly, pushing away the remains of his lunch.

His explanation was a far cry from Toni's description of e-mail following body pheromones rather than circuitry highways.

Their discussion of fishing concluded, Edward butted in. "Alice tells me you guys are the hottest of the hot. I'm kind of surprised you'll talk about what you're developing. Don't you have any problem with industrial spies? Or is that just Hollywood movie stuff?"

Galen's face pinched up as if his skin had shrunk. "I wish it were," he said forcefully. "Last year, we found one camping behind town. Can you imagine? Engineers sneaking around trying to break in at night?"

Edward looked duly astonished. "You hire security people? Just like the Silicon Valley boys?"

Galen grinned, the first truly pleased look I'd seen

on his Sheriff of Nottingham face. "We've rigged up our own system. It works, too."

"Ooo," Edward said boyishly. "Indiana Jones stuff, huh? Gizmo alarms?"

"No," Jonathan said breathlessly, "we leave Toni in the store at night. Heh heh. Heh heh."

Louis hid his smile behind a napkin. Jonathan oomphed as if he'd been kicked under the table.

Edward, of course, couldn't let it go. "A wild one, huh? My last lady, I could have entered her in a rodeo."

"She was that big?" I inquired.

I saw Galen gesture for the check.

This was my last chance. I turned to Jonathan. "This Pan character that runs around here? Has he ever done anything . . . violent? Hurt anybody?"

"So you don't believe he's a Greek god?" Louis sounded satisfied.

"He looked life-sized to me," I admitted. "He scared me. I just wondered if he's dangerous."

"Naked man running around the woods night and day." Again, Edward had to put in his two cents' worth. "I wouldn't get too relaxed around him."

"But the legends about him, do they report him actually doing harm to anyone?" Again, I addressed Jonathan. Edward would leave tonight, and I'd be in the middle of the spooky dark woods with a frail scholar twice my age. I didn't want to worry about "Pan" bursting through a cabin window.

On the other hand, he might be a welcome explanation for Seawuit's murder.

"I don't know much about the legends," Jonathan said, his youthful blankness unperturbed.

"I've heard about him, but I've never heard anything like that," Louis offered. "Just sightings. I don't know anyone who's gotten close to him. In fact, I'm not sure I know anyone who's actually seen him. Except you."

"And me," Jonathan added.

"And what were you on, Mr. Reliable?" Louis asked.

Jonathan flipped him off.

"What about Billy Seawuit? This man,"—I couldn't refer to him as a demigod—"do the police know about him? Is he a suspect?"

Louis shrugged. "We thought we'd be talking to the police quite a bit, but you know, except for right after they found the body, they haven't been back."

"They only talked to you once?" I looked at Galen. "They've also been to your house, right? I heard he was staying with you."

"They looked through his things. That's it."

"We called for an update this morning," Louis continued. "But they didn't seem in any hurry to talk to us again. It could be they've got a suspect in mind."

I wondered whether it was Arthur. I considered bringing him up. Edward jumped the gun.

"He was an assistant for that mythology guy, wasn't he? That PBS guy?"

"Arthur Kenna. Yes." Galen was starting to squirm. "We should get back. Mary! Check, please."

"I wonder what a mythologist's assistant does," Edward mused. "He wasn't here checking on the Pan legend, was he?"

Louis and Galen exchanged glances.

"No," Galen said. "Arthur Kenna was consulting with us. We like to use mythological 'wallpaper,' for lack of a better word, in some of our programs. Almost like old-fashioned dioramas, only inside the computer. As a setting for menus."

"Well, I thought . . ." Edward looked puzzled. "I thought it was the assistant that was working for you."

Galen nodded impatiently. "That's what brought him here. We asked Kenna to help us design the settings. Seawuit came with him and stayed on."

"What kind of work was Seawuit doing for you? You don't suppose an industrial spy had a run-in with him?" Edward's chutzpah amazed me. But I supposed it was a necessity in his line of work.

"Stu's the one that had a fight with him," Jonathan said.

The waitress brought both checks then, though Edward and I weren't finished. In that moment of distraction, Louis signaled Jonathan, briefly making a *T* of his hands. "Time out": the only sports gesture I recognized.

Galen tossed two twenties on the table, then rose. Louis and Jonathan rose with him.

Galen would have ignored Edward's question and Jonathan's answer, would have said good-bye and walked out with his entourage, I was sure. But for one thing.

Jonathan said, "Wait a sec. I need to use the head."

Galen hesitated, as if looking for a way to say, Catch up, then.

Edward jumped in. "So your old lady's ex-husband—Stu, right?—he had a fight with Seawuit?"

"Just a rumor. If he did . . ." Galen was silent so long, I began to doubt he'd finish the sentence. "It wasn't just the divorce. They lost their business. Stu's not a bad guy, but that's a lot for anyone."

"Toni mentioned him," I put in. "She said he'd been experimenting with brain waves."

Galen's nostrils flared. His lips clamped as if in spasm.

"Yeah, right," Louis said. "To hear Stu tell it, he invented macaroni."

"What was his beef with Seawuit?"

"Chip on his shoulder." Louis shrugged. "Could be anything; you know the type. Like Galen said, it's hard to start all over again."

"But this industrial spying business . . ." Edward wouldn't let up. "You think maybe Stu's been spying on you—trying to get back at you?"

Galen shot him a withering look. "We're not hillbillies up here, we're not the Hatfields and McCoys. We're computer professionals."

Before Edward could respond, Louis changed the subject back to fishing.

I worked on my lunch, letting Louis talk trout while Galen stood stiffly by.

When they left, Edward leaned back in his chair, saying, "High five, girlfriend. That was *muy interesante.*"

"Are you taking Spanish lessons or what?"

"No way. *Yo hablo* already. You don't speak Spanish, you don't get much PI work, not around here." He attacked his burger. A few mouthfuls later, he added, "What do you think he's going to say to wifey when he sees her tonight?"

"Do you think those two guys in the woods were industrial spies?"

He shrugged. "I hope so. I hope they try to break into Cyberdelics: I want to know what the computer gizmo trap does."

"Do you think spies could have murdered Seawuit to keep him from helping develop TechnoShaman?"

"They'd be damn fools if they did. A computer product worth killing for?"

"You're being naive, Edward." I pushed my remaining crumbs away. I'd practically licked the plate. "I had to do my homework to get the job I just blew off. You wouldn't believe the incredible stuff computers can do now—they can create actors and movie sets out of cyberspace. No one's going to need Hollywood by the time they're done. Imagine how much money's going to be lost or gained in that transition. Or look backward: What if Apple could have had Bill Gates killed and kept Windows out of existence? You don't think they'd be way better off?"

"Okay, granted. Something as major as Windows or computer-made movies, that would get a few people excited. But this isn't really the big time, right? This is Boulder Creek."

"You've got that completely wrong. Cyberdelics is big enough to be treated like royalty by my law firm—ex-law firm. God, Edward, Apples were created in a guy's garage."

"True." He picked up the check. "You don't happen to know Stu's last name, do you?"

"No. Edward, if those pictures turn out, will you show them around?"

"To who?"

"To whoever could tell you if the men are industrial spies."

"Like there's a special bureau for that."

I sighed. "Can you do a computer match?"

"On my Bat Computer?"

"You must have some way to find out."

He shrugged elaborately. "Photo development person at the drugstore might recognize them." He checked his watch. We'd been told to return before one o'clock.

"Then why did you even take the pictures?" I snapped.

"Are you kidding? I've been dying to play with my new spy toy!"

I sat back, trying to relax. Maybe he did know how to find out who the men were. Maybe he was just too contrary to tell me straight out.

Information from Edward, I was beginning to realize, tended to come as punchlines at my expense.

CHAPTER FOURTEEN

We reached the drugstore at ten minutes to one, only to be greeted by a CLOSED sign. For the next ten minutes, I listened to Edward rail about "mountain hours" as he paced back and forth, pounded on the door, checked and rechecked the back entrance. Eventually, we ran our errands and embarked on a scenic tour.

We spent most of the afternoon on steep winding roads, Edward pointing out sights and landmarks. I could certainly understand Arthur's passion for the land, if not the full flaky extent of his feelings.

When Edward finally turned onto the gravel road to his cabin, I was feeling relaxed and satisfied. I had cash in my pocket, some thrift-store clothes, and groceries in a sack.

"What the—" Edward slammed on the brakes.

I came out of my cozy haze. "What?" But I saw the problem before the word left my mouth. There was a car parked in front of the cabin. A big purple Dadmobile. "It's Don Surgelato's."

Don knew my history with Edward. He must have gone to Santa Cruz to check whether Edward had seen me. He must have found out—from a neighbor? property records?—that Edward had a place up here.

"I don't see him in the car." Edward seemed to know the score. "He must be poking around the back. I hope Arthur stayed gone."

He gave me a light slap on the shoulder. "Get out. Hurry."

I got out, quickly taking cover. I didn't want Surgelato to notice Edward's Jeep had stopped. And I certainly didn't want him to notice me inside it.

Edward took off toward the cabin, Jeep wheels kicking up gravel and dust.

My first impulse was to dash away into the woods. It warred with my desire to linger, to try to get closer and see what Surgelato was up to.

I moved deeper into the woods, but tried to stay oriented. I stopped often to listen, in case Surgelato was lurking out here rather than waiting at Edward's.

It must have been around five-thirty. There had been plenty of daylight on the road. But the forest was one giant shadow across a floor of needles, leaves, and vines. I walked slowly, trying to keep the road to my left and the cabin up ahead.

I spotted a fallen log with a cozy-looking throw of lichen. I had a city-girl's aversion to sitting directly on top of anything green—it might have bugs or cause rashes—but I needed to choose a perch before it got much darker. I didn't want to wander too far afield. I wanted to stay close enough for Edward to find me if I couldn't find him.

I sat gingerly on the lichen. I looked way up to the

tops of the redwoods. I could see dark birds against the fading daylight. I tried to get comfortable.

Some people might have meditated. But I'd grown up with political activists; I argued with myself.

I'd sworn I wouldn't let my brain jump on the Surgelato hamster wheel again. I'd let him know I voted yes on a relationship. And he'd gone back to his ex-wife. Nothing had begun, so there wasn't much to miss. But I'd managed to get maudlin about it often enough.

I didn't want to speculate why he was getting personally involved in searching for me now. Maybe his wife didn't want to, either. But it hardly mattered: Surgelato and I had lost the moment. I just wished I hadn't been the last to know.

I watched the woods grow darker. I could hear the tapping of woodpeckers and the sound of falling pine cones. I didn't see any animals. Even on our hike today, I'd seen only jays and banana slugs. This would have been more reassuring if I hadn't seen a mountain lion Tuesday.

The gap between twilight and night didn't close, it slammed shut. One minute I was daydreaming, and the next, it was pitch black around me. The darkness made me claustrophobic, it seemed so dense and tight.

I took a few deep breaths. I wasn't far from the cabin. I could always scream.

A second later, I almost did. I heard voices close by. I saw a halo of lantern light and heard one voice clearly enough to keep me silent.

It was Don Surgelato, saying, "So no calls, no letters, no nothing?"

"Not since last time," Edward answered cheerfully.

"And that stuff in your car? It's for who, again?"

"You don't have to take my word on that, Lieutenant," Edward responded. "Ask anybody in town: I spent the day shopping with a young lady named Alice. I hope to reap the benefits this evening."

The lanterns weren't headed toward me; they were defining an arc closer (I thought) to the cabin.

"I still don't get why you'd look for her here," Edward said.

"I'm out of other places to look."

"So she didn't show up at work: She's not exactly career-oriented. She probably blew it off. She's probably off at some neo-hippie-yippie-ban-the-Republicans commune."

Surgelato's next statement wasn't audible.

"This wouldn't be the first time she played hooky." Edward's voice carried. "Ask Judge Shanna."

The last comment was maddeningly unfair—it was Edward who'd screwed up my clerkship with his "favor."

I remained there long after their voices and lanterns faded. Good thing, too. As I prepared to stand and stretch, I heard them again.

They'd circled back toward the cabin.

Edward was saying, "So what's the deal really? Between you two."

"There's no deal."

Edward's voice quieted to a confidential hush. I couldn't hear him anymore.

It took all my self-control not to jump out of concealment and pummel an apology out of Edward. Discussing my business, my private life . . . Long after I couldn't see the lanterns or hear the men, I fumed.

Eventually the night air cooled more than my anger. I wondered if I remembered the direction to the road.

I wondered if Edward would come shouting for me after Surgelato left.

Minor concerns came at me like a Greek chorus. Without visual distractions, my brain had time to amplify them.

For starters, where was Arthur? He obviously hadn't been at the cabin; neither Surgelato nor Edward had given the least hint of it. That left a hell of a lot of other places he might be. For all I knew, he was aboard a spaceship with Pan at the helm.

Most of the rest of my worries involved either insects or mad woodsmen. I wavered about which I feared most. I itched. I imagined loutish footsteps.

I alternated being scared and being bored. I wondered if this was one of those experiences where you think you've been out for hours and are annoyed to learn it's only been minutes.

I gave up on Edward finding me.

I walked cautiously, I hoped toward the road. A heavy overcast screened moonlight that had helped me last night.

I broke branches and tripped over a log. By the time I'd fallen a few more times, I knew it was a stupid idea. I picked myself up and sat on a stump, feeling welts rise on my scraped flesh.

I heard twigs crack, leaves rustle. After so many false alarms, I was rationing my adrenaline. But the sounds continued. Someone was out here.

I inhaled a scream.

To my shock, I heard the dark shape say, "Willa."

"Arthur! Oh God, thank God, you're the cat!"

He clapped my back awkwardly as I embraced him. "The cat?"

"You know, in horror movies? When the heroine

goes to check out a noise and something jumps on her?"

"And it turns out to be the cat, yes yes; so it does." Then, more concerned, "You're all right? Are you lost?"

"Maybe a little. Have you been out here all day, Arthur?"

"No. I was back for quite a long spell, but I saw a car coming—not Edward's. I thought you'd want me to leave. I was on my way back when I heard noises and saw you out here."

"The car was Surgelato's—same cop as at my apartment. I'm not sure if he's gone yet."

"Do you think we'd better wait awhile longer, then?" He disentangled himself from my needy embrace.

"No." I wanted to be inside. "Yes, we probably should." I didn't want to be inside with Surgelato, after all. "You want part of my stump?"

I sat down, leaving room for Arthur.

"You heard the piping?" Arthur's voice was agitated, boyish. "Wasn't it a miracle? Pitch perfect, flawless breathwork, a heart-rending tune."

"You mean tonight? You heard him tonight?"

"A short time ago. You didn't hear?"

"No."

"I've been wandering about"—his voice was hushed with the thrill—"hoping to encounter him."

"You wouldn't even be able to see him, not tonight."

"Oh, but I have a pocket light."

"You have a flashlight? Jesus, Arthur, let's use it."

"Certainly." He aimed a thin beam across the duff.

I looked at his hand. He was holding a tiny keychain light.

"I found it in a cupboard. I didn't want to waste the battery," he explained. "But perhaps my night vision's better than yours."

"It must be—you saw me, but I only heard you." I vowed to eat more carrots.

"I was given the gift of night vision by my spirit animal many years ago," he explained matter-of-factly.

I didn't even want to know the details. "Maybe you'd better turn the light off." I hated to do it, but, "We should wait here awhile longer; make sure Surgelato's gone. Then we'll turn it on and find the road."

"Fine."

The night seemed even blacker after the brief luxury of light.

"Oh, Jesus!" I grabbed his arm. The piping had begun.

"We'll signal!" Arthur sounded breathless, beyond excited.

I nearly crushed the hand that held the penlight. "No! No, Arthur, it's a man, not a demigod!"

"A man who's manifested here for at least three centuries?"

"Maybe something has. But not this guy. I've seen him."

"Listen to the phrasing," Arthur insisted. "We must speak to him."

"Please, Arthur—no!"

He wrenched his hand free, shooting a beam of light through the trees.

Immediately, the piping stopped. I thought I'd been frightened last night. Tonight took the trophy.

I heard twigs snapping, duff crunching. I heard footsteps too swift to be anything but a person running.

Arthur pointed the beam in their direction.

Oh please, let it be Edward, I prayed. Please oh please oh please.

I was drenched with sweat, heartbeats hammering my eardrums.

Even Surgelato. Let it be Surgelato. I'd take prison over massacre by a naked demigod.

A figure came into view: broad, muscular, unbelievably hairy, totally nude, carrying only panpipes and a leafy tree limb.

Arthur had gotten his wish. Except for one detail: "Pan" had human legs.

Chapter Fifteen

Arthur's light froze on the legs. They were as thick as pine trunks, carpeted in curly fur that glowed red in the light. Though they assured me he was human, his legs told me nothing about his mood or intentions.

I grabbed Arthur's arm, jerking it upward.

In the instant before the light hit his face, I absorbed an impression of a very short man with a barrel chest and a lot of muscle.

His face was framed with matted brown hair, mostly shoulder length. He was dirt-streaked and ugly, with an overhanging forehead, a nose that had obviously been broken many times, and a reddish beard with bits of leaf caught in it.

But he didn't look murderous. He didn't look angry.

I kept the light on his face. I held my breath listening to him; listening for his first hint of movement or aggression.

He simply stood there, brows relaxed over his bent, flattened nose. His lips parted but he didn't speak.

He held a huge leafy branch as tall as he was,

braced on the ground like a staff. His other arm, massive with undefined muscle, hung limp at his side, pan-pipes dangling.

"Who are you?" Arthur's voice was surprisingly commanding. He sounded like a much younger, stronger man. Or maybe I just hoped so.

I expected the man to grunt, he looked so primitive. Naked, hairy, filthy, he looked almost Neanderthal. But the noise he made was not primitive. In fact, he had a British accent.

He answered, "I am Pan."

I almost got the giggles. He certainly wasn't carrying any ID.

I let go of Arthur's arm. The beam of light dropped again to the man's legs. But Arthur brought it back to his face.

"Pan?" Arthur repeated. His tone said he'd need to see goat legs before believing it.

"Pan."

"You"—Arthur sounded bewildered—"you play very beautifully, sir; very beautifully, indeed."

Pan nodded. He cast a glance at his pipes. "Shall I tell you what they wrote about me?" His accent was clearly British, but not English, maybe Irish. I didn't know my accents well enough to guess. But it was toney, for sure. Educated, precise, well-modulated.

"What they wrote?" Arthur's voice sounded calm, which calmed me, too. "About Pan?"

"Yes." Pan nodded his head. His neck was as thick as some men's legs. "I repeat it but rarely. Very. Very. Rarely."

I'd have tried to find an excuse—train to catch, car to wash—anything to leave now. But I was no anthropologist. To me, naked strangers meant trouble.

Arthur answered quickly, perhaps to forestall me. "Why, yes. We'd be honored."

A scream gurgled up my throat as Pan stepped toward us, his gait distinctly King of Siam. But the smell of him, as ripe as a musk ox, seemed to kill my vocal cords.

Arthur moved aside, shining his light on the stump. "Please take our seat," he said.

Pan nodded regally. Seeing him up close—a short, ugly man with no sign of hostility in his movements or gestures—I began to relax.

When Arthur sat cross-legged on the ground, I joined him, feeling a bit like a kid in a fairy tale: We'd found a troll, and he'd promised us a fable.

"We'd be very pleased to hear your story," Arthur reiterated.

I just wished he were upwind from us. I guess my reluctance was apparent to Arthur.

He nudged me.

I wasn't quite sure about this. If Pan went berserk, he looked strong enough to knock over a tree. But the light on his face showed a very tranquil demigod.

"Wouldn't we be very pleased, Willa?"

Arthur nudged me again. Maybe he thought it best to humor Pan. Maybe the anthropologist in him was curious. Maybe he thought Pan could tell us something about Billy Seawuit.

"Yes," I said, tepidly.

"You'll tell us how you came to be in this place?" Arthur suggested. "What you've observed here?"

"I would tell no one the truth, no one my very own story, because there is no one left in heaven or on earth entitled to hear it. But I will tell you what they wrote about me. I will relate to you verbatim the best account by a man."

"Ah," said Arthur, "we're to hear a recitation, then?"

"And perhaps afterward, I'll play for you," Pan promised.

The weak light from Arthur's penlight lit Pan's face like the glow from a dying campfire. I felt like a kid at camp about to hear spooky stories from a counselor. An unclothed, delusional counselor.

But Pan's voice was a soothing baritone, and it's somehow easier to trust a British accent.

He began sonorously: "The man ran naked down the tangled slope." He sounded like a poet reading Joyce. "His hirsute form broke a path in the tall, wild-flower-dappled grass. He ran swiftly, chest heaving, brown hair whipped free of its natural curl, slanting eyes half-closed."

Pan's voice grew hushed, he leaned forward, picking up momentum. "His lips curled in wicked anticipation.

"Stationary the man might have seemed ordinary, even ugly. He was too broad for his height and tanned to swarthiness. His sunburnt skin stretched taut along the planes of his wide cheeks, and his nose was large and bent, perhaps by well-deserved blows. The hair on his body and even on his arms and back was too thick, a wiry weave of golden and russet that softened his powerful chest and flanks to wooliness.

"But in motion," Pan continued, "the man rippled like a cheetah, sprang like an ibex over the land."

He paused for effect.

"The land: clearings of wild radish and grasses blowing to seed, mixed forest of live oak and fir and madrone in flower, cool pine summits, fairy rings of redwoods tall in their bark like dowagers in mink, and here and there, tucked in creaking groves and sunny clearings on the slopes, a few rough houses, built without government sanction by men who did not care to be governed."

I heard Arthur's, "Ah."

"And from the occasional peak," Pan's voice swelled, "from the rare clearing, there, away to the west, catching the sheen of afternoon sky like silver lamè, the Pacific Ocean.

"The man stopped, tensed to stillness. He sensed that the woman was near, and he inhaled slowly. Among the meadow smells—beaten grass warming in the sun, the faint perfume of nearby manzanita blossoms, of distant pines and salt sea—among the meadow smells there lingered a sense of her, not precisely her scent, but the merest inkling. The man's shoulders drooped, and he lifted a short-fingered hand to his eyes."

Mimicking the man of the story, Pan lifted his (indeed short-fingered) hand to his eyes. He kept it there for a few more sentences:

"Behind the hand, thick straight brows knotted and drew close together. His mind's eye saw another meadow, far away, shimmering under a turquoise sky. At the meadow's foot there rustled a glade fed by a hyacinth-bordered brook."

He dropped his hand from in front of his face. He leaned forward, voice heavy with feeling. "In that meadow, Syrinx squatted over a rabbit hole in earnest expectation, slingshot braced against her bent knee. From a leather thong attached to her girdle hung two unfortunate relations of the rabbit pausing just beneath her in his tunnel."

Pan smiled suddenly, then continued.

"Syrinx strained to hold her lamenting muscles motionless. She was downwind from her prey; he would not take warning unless the faint rumble of her movement sent him scurrying back through his earthen sanctum. She could feel a drop of perspiration trace the cleavage between her breasts. It mortified her to kill this way, with the prey trapped before her, but she must have three rabbits for the Gods. If her sacrifice were scant, the Gods might shame her before the Huntress at the afternoon hunt.

"She imagined the cold blue eyes of the Goddess narrowing with disdain. She had seen that look before, when other dryads had let their prey escape through jinx or incompetence. The Goddess would turn those withering eyes on a frightened huntress, nostrils flared and thin mouth set in arrogant displeasure, and she would snap her fingers for the others to close around her. Then she would turn swiftly on her long, marble-hard limbs and disappear up a slope or into a copse, the others following quickly, casting fleeting looks of sympathy on the ostracized huntress. And it would be many hunts before the offending dryad would be allowed her place beside the others. And in the meantime there would be no meat for her because every creature would outrun her arrow and outfox her slingshot."

Pan's voice conveyed sympathy. And something more, a presage of danger?

"Suddenly the dryad leaped to her feet, golden hair tumbling free of the loose twist she had secured with a twig of myrtle. She had hunted too long to miss the signs: Something or someone was stalking her. She scanned the meadow quickly. It had been a hunter's feeling, a sixth sense, a sudden empathy with her prey. She began to back slowly toward the glade, where some naiad might help her.

"And then she saw him, up where the meadow crested and was crowned by a shaggy circlet of fluttering oak and olive."

His voice was remarkably expressive, almost enthralling. I found myself leaning closer, determined not to miss a word. And his next word was practically a shout:

"Pan! Broad and powerful and sexual, even in silhouette, arms akimbo and feet spread wide.

"Pan! Her sharp hunter's eyes squinted him into focus, and she caught the glint of large misaligned teeth gleaming in his rough face. For a moment she stood frozen with dread, as she had seen deer and rabbits freeze, eyes large and desperate.

"Pan. Trouble and dishonor and carnality. Melea the naiad had nearly died bearing his child, a hideous creature with the hindquarters of a goat.

"Not she! Not Syrinx, one of Diana's own huntresses! No God would profane her!" he boomed.

He put up his hand, wriggling his fingers. "Her fingers worked free the knot that held her girdle, and she felt the rabbits drop, then she turned and fled down the grassy slope toward the glade, hair streaming and breasts rising, frightened body glistening in the bright sun, legs stretched as long as an antelope's. But glancing over her shoulder, she saw the God closing the distance between them, saw his face turned comfortably sunward, like a man enjoying a race, and she knew she would only just reach the glade. If there was no one there to help her, the God would take her cruelly without a thought for her suffering or her future.

" '—Diana!' she screamed, nearly there now, nearly at the bank of the moss-green brook, 'Patroness, pity me!' " There was a throb in his voice. "And Syrinx felt a rough hand chafe the tender skin of her waist. Her toes began to falter in the damp, marshy earth of the brookside as the God caught her. She could smell the musk of his body as she choked in desperate supplication, 'Please help me, Goddess!' "

He let the plea hang in the night air.

"And in the next moment," his voice was grim, "her motion was arrested. She surged forward to escape, but her limbs would not carry her: She was rooted. She sensed that the God's formidable arms encircled her, but she felt nothing. She swayed in the breeze, blindly drinking earth-fragrant water through thirsty roots. She did not hear the raging bellow of the savage God.

" 'You, Virgin!' the God screamed," and indeed "Pan" screamed it. "He watched the Goddess come through a curtain of weeping willow that she parted with a deceptively delicate hand. 'What have you done to her?' He stared in horror at the stand of reeds he had been embracing.

" 'I've spared her your bestial embraces,' Diana said coldly, lids half-lowered over eyes that smoldered with contempt. 'As she begged me to do.' "

His voice trembled with the injustice of it.

"Pan took a step backward, away from the reeds. It was a moment before he could pull his astonished eyes away from them and say, 'So you'd do this to her?'

"The Goddess smiled slightly, her haughty face relaxing. 'I must teach you not to take my dryads.' "

Again, he gave us a moment to absorb the horror.

"Pan stared at the tall, long-limbed beauty, her body as white and strong as alabaster, her pale hair glinting silver in the sun, the thick cloak of weeping willow behind her. She was as beautiful as any Goddess, but she was the only one for whom he felt no sexual stirring. She reeked of celibacy and austerity, she brought death to woodland animals.

"He swaggered toward her. 'I've a mind to take you in her place.'

"The Goddess slid disdainful eyes over his short, hale body. 'You'll regret your impropriety,' she hissed. 'You forget who I am.' " He mimicked her voice as if it were a snake's.

"Pan lowered his face to glower at her." His voice became a resounding, angry thing: " 'And you forget who I am. You can't touch me, Virgin!' "

He waited so long, I almost prompted him to continue.

"Diana smiled her chilly smile," he said, finally, "and glanced at the stand of reeds that had once been a nubile dryad. 'No? Perhaps not previously. But I have a new ally.'

"Pan's eyes narrowed and flickered dangerous green-gold as he followed her gaze. Syrinx had been on his mind for months. He had tracked her relentlessly, hoping to catch her away from Diana and her frigid huntresses.

"The Goddess watched him and laughed."

His voice again rose to a feral boom: "This the God could not tolerate! He closed the space between them with an angry leap and noticed with some admiration that the Goddess stood her ground. She stood like statuary as he clamped her gossamered breasts to his damp body and reached a hand behind her head to press her face to his. She remained still and cold as his infuriated hands ravaged her, twisting her flesh between his callused fingers, parting the folds of her robe and forcing her legs apart with an upthrust knee. Then he knocked her off balance by wrapping one leg around hers and falling against her. As they fell, he found the soft dampness that was like a mortal woman's and entered it with the suddenness of a blow."

He was sitting forward, squinting as if lost in remembrance. I could see the muscles of his jaw working.

His voice hinted at feelings barely suppressed. I'd never heard such a fine storyteller's voice.

"Pan was buried alive then," he continued. "The earth sucked him in; he felt it clotting his mouth and ears, scraping his sightless eyes. He felt himself pulled deeper, felt the earth become colder, harder, crushing him on all sides, finally felt it throb with its own molten life until it seared him, twisting him and racking him and pushing him deeper and deeper until he lost consciousness."

His face was anguished. Tears ran down his cheeks. But he continued calmly.

"He awakened in this place, paralyzed with pain, when it and all the land around it still stank with floundering sea creatures. He raised his battered head to see a mountaintop just spewn from the ocean bottom, saltwater surging in thin sheets over its bloated clay."

"Magnificent!" Arthur commented.

Pan's voice was melancholic. "The man," he said

slowly, "scowling in this other meadow, found that the memory still rankled. Of a union with Syrinx might have sprung perfection; her delicacy and solemnity complemented his own character.

"As always, this reflection disturbed him. He sat cross-legged on the hillside, knees drawn up to accommodate his elbows. And in his hands," excitement re-infused his voice, "there shimmered into being a pipe made of several lengths of reeds, bound together side by side with tough threads stripped from another reed. The pipe he had fashioned himself, in frustrated homage, from reeds he'd found in his hand when earth and ocean spat him here, reeds he'd torn from the stand that had once been Syrinx." His voice was a sad hush.

"He played her obsequy on the pipes, finally laying moist lips to the huntress. And the union was perfection. From the instrument there floated a music both innocent and erotic, virginal and ardent. Naiads, so infinitely far away, lapsed from the brook to lay irises where Syrinx once stood, and in the sky, a cloud obscured the sun and cooled the afternoon, as the musician Apollo listened in grudging envy and chastened Diana with a nettled glance.

"And so through the millennia, as conifers began to share the land with chaparral, and chaparral gave way to meadowland, from the wildest peaks and the loneliest glades, the windsong of the reed pipe consummated an ancient longing.

"One hundred and fifty thousand years of husbandry turned ocean floor to meadow, but he never saw another to match the diligent Syrinx, with her air of vulnerable resolve. And he never forgot the Goddess who placed her out of his reach and caused his exile."

Arthur suddenly chimed in, "No, I should think not!"

But Pan held up his hand for silence. Head bowed, he continued.

"And one mild day, when the air was fresh with stirring grasses, the wind carried the piping through mountain thickets.

"In one of these, downhill from the man, a woman listened to the unearthly music. Her knife was poised above the rabbit hole. And she turned to hear his music. She looked upward, straining to see him."

His head snapped up out of its bow. "And it was Syrinx: Syrinx was here! The circle"—he made a circle of his thumb and index finger—"would close at last. And Diana . . ." His features twisted into a grimace. "Would writhe beneath them in their consummation."

Having earlier offered a premature bravo, Arthur sat quietly. We were like schoolchildren waiting for more story.

Instead, Pan raised the pipe to his lips and played the smoothest, breathiest piece of music I'd ever heard.

I watched him, trying not to be overwhelmed by pity. He was clearly an educated man, a brilliant tale-teller with a classically trained voice. He was also an exceptional musician.

And yet he lived naked in the woods, convinced this myth was biographical.

Arthur clicked off the penlight—something he should have done earlier, no doubt; we still had to find our way back to Edward's cabin. But I assumed his motive was to give the piping center stage.

We listened for five minutes, perhaps.

Then we heard Edward calling for us.

By the time Arthur fumbled the light back on, Pan was diving through the brush, moving as swiftly as any demigod I'd ever seen.

CHAPTER SIXTEEN

Arthur was on his feet, mouth open, arm stretched toward the spot where Pan had just been, when Edward came crashing toward us, flooding the area with lantern light. I jumped up.

Edward was panting; he'd clearly been running. "God!" He stopped to catch his breath, bending so his hand was on his knee. "Heard it! Heard the piping. See what you mean about it being spooky!" He panted some more. "What was going on? You're not hurt?" He straightened. "No, you don't look hurt. Hi, Arthur."

Arthur turned to him uncomprehendingly, as if he'd never seen a clothed man before.

"Was he here? Did he try anything?" Edward held the lantern closer to my face. "I thought you might be in trouble. I didn't know what I was going to find."

I had to shake my head to clear it. "Pan" had completely pulled me into his story.

"He was here. But we're fine. I . . . I don't know what to say about him." I glanced at Arthur, hoping he was feeling more articulate than I was. But he had yet to close his gaping mouth.

"Don't know what to say about him?" Edward repeated. "What does that mean? He didn't threaten you, right? You're both okay, right?"

"Yes. You don't have to keep asking."

"Could have fooled me. You're both acting drugged or something. What the hell happened?"

"He just sort of appeared out of the woods. He talked to us awhile—"

"No goat legs, right?"

"No goat legs. He talked about Pan, though. He obviously thinks he's Pan."

"Tell me you don't." Edward scrutinized my face as if searching for dilated pupils.

"He has a British accent."

"Welsh," Arthur corrected. "And then Oxford, if I'm not mistaken."

Edward's brows shot up. "What is he, some crazy Greek myth scholar?"

"I should think so," Arthur said. "In a sense, though, he is Pan. Didn't you feel it, Willa?"

"Yes." I wasn't totally sure I knew what he meant by that. But I'd certainly been lulled by Pan's tale, half-believing it, in a way. "He's got that Shakespearean actor voice that goes from quiet to thundering. He put a lot of feeling into it, that's for sure."

"More than feeling, Willa." Arthur clamped a hand on my shoulder. "It was possession. The myth took him over and became who he was."

"Maybe." I didn't pretend to understand delusions. Neuroses were more up my alley.

"One could almost say that type of quote-unquote madness is other-dimensional," Arthur mused. "Shamans were thought mad by the Europeans who first encountered them."

"So this guy talked at you? Told Pan stories?" Edward seemed confused.

"Yes," I reiterated. "And played the pipes for us."

"It was so perfect, every detail," Arthur stared at the stump Pan had occupied.

"What a waste of talent," I agreed.

"No no," he corrected. "I would guess it's the reverse: that madness sharpened ordinary talent into brilliance. Who could play the pipes so perfectly, with such inspiration, without first believing he was Pan? Who could live naked in the forest, yet be so strong and healthy?"

Edward snorted. "Let's go back. Your cop boyfriend's gone, so—"

"He's never been my boyfriend!"

"In fact, that's the very essence of the word 'inspiration.' " Arthur continued as if we'd said nothing in the interim. "It means, to have the Spirit blown into one. And that's exactly what happened to this young Welshman. He became inflated with Pan's spirit. That's why his words, his story, are so moving: To him they are real, so real he can pull us inside his vision with him."

"How long have we been out here?" I wondered. Mundane matters began competing with Pan for my attention.

"Couple of hours," Edward told me. "Not quite two and a half."

"Surgelato stayed this long?"

"Just about—the man's weird about you. He wouldn't take my word for anything. Insisted on tromping all around, asking me a zillion questions. I couldn't tell if he was worried or suspicious. Ten bucks says he's in town right now asking people if I went shopping with a brunette named Alice today."

"In a sense . . ." Arthur completed his thought, "madness is only a kind of unsanctioned inspiration."

"Yeah, well, let's go," Edward replied. "We don't want to be late to the Zelda Fitzgerald Fan Club."

CHAPTER SEVENTEEN

We recounted Pan's story—with far less aplomb—to Edward over canned beans and toast.

His reaction was, "He saw Syrinx here? Holding a knife over a rabbit hole?"

"I thought he said slingshot." But I wasn't sure.

"No no—unmistakably not," Arthur contradicted me. "It leaped out of the narrative—why a knife, you see? It should have been a slingshot, and yet it was a knife." Arthur pushed his beans away. He'd hardly eaten.

I wanted to urge him to have more, but Edward had already laughed at my "Jewish mothering" once this meal.

"Well," I conceded, "you're more used to oral histories than I am."

Edward stopped crunching his toast. "It's probably a waste of time, but let's take this Welsh guy at his word. Say he saw some woman with a knife. Who? Where?"

"Over a rabbit hole," Arthur mused. "I don't know if one could characterize Bowl Rock as a rabbit hole."

"It's a kind of hole," Edward said. "For the sake of argument, say a woman with a knife was poised over the rock's opening. Could this guy have seen her? There are hills above the clearing, but I doubt you can see Bowl Rock from any of them."

"You can," Arthur disagreed. "From one of them. But it's not simply that the rock is visible from Forty-eight Degree Point—"

"Forty-eight Degree Point?"

"I don't know what local name it might have. But it's roughly forty-eight degrees north, northwest of Bowl Rock, less than a quarter-mile distant. It has an excellent view of the rock."

"This is something people around here know about?" Edward sounded skeptical.

"Oh, I wouldn't think so. Billy and I were at great pains to map and document it."

"Document it? Why?" Edward sat back, picking up his bottle of beer.

"Because the rock was clearly placed in that spot. It could not possibly have occurred there naturally."

"I've seen big rocks on the mountain," Edward objected.

"But what you call *the* mountain is actually a few neighboring mountains. And there are vast geological differences from one to another. Boulder Creek is part of Ben Lomond Mountain, which is within the so-called Salinian block, a sliver of land bounded by two fault lines. The Salinian is comprised of rocks completely different from the melange surrounding it, completely different from Santa Cruz Mountain to the east and the marine terraces to the west. In fact, the Salinian block, Ben Lomond Mountain, is utterly exotic to California. That's what lends credence to the myth that it was suddenly thrust up from some mystical distance."

"Like Olympus?"

He smiled at me. "The geologists don't offer that hypothesis. But the fact is, they don't know why Ben Lomond Mountain rose out of the sea or why its composition is unlike that of the terraces beneath it or the mountain beside it. And with Bowl Rock, you have an isolated tufa—an unusual rock formation—in a part of the mountains where no other tafoni occur."

"A tufa?"

He nodded. "Have you been to Castle Rock?"

"No."

"It's about fifteen miles away, on Santa Cruz Mountain, atop the San Andreas fault. You see dozens of huge boulders there, honeycombed with nooks and caves. These are tafoni, a type created by conditions occurring only in a few places on the planet."

I wasn't in the mood for a geology lecture. "The point being, Bowl Rock shouldn't be here, it should be there."

"That's right. It undoubtedly came from the Castle Rock area." Arthur nodded brightly. "The question is, why was it moved here?"

"Well," Edward demanded, "why?"

"It may have been chosen because of its hollow egg configuration; we thought it likely. Why else move this particular boulder?"

"Why move any boulder?" Edward persisted.

"That's what we were trying to determine. Whether it might be another Sun Dagger."

Arthur did have a way of making one feel undereducated. "What's a sun dagger?" I asked him.

He looked surprised by my ignorance. I was relieved

to notice Edward didn't jump in with an explanation; I'll bet he didn't know, either.

"It's the most amazing ancient device for tracking solar and lunar cycles. It's in New Mexico, near Pueblo Bonito, but it predates the Navajo by centuries. Their oral history attributes it to a people—perhaps their forebears—they call the Anasazi."

"So this Sun Dagger is kind of a Stonehenge thing?" Edward's tone said, *Let's move along.*

"More sophisticated than Stonehenge—it not only tracks the solstice and equinox, but also a nineteen-year lunar cycle. It's a brilliantly precise alteration and adaptation of a natural butte."

"And you thought Bowl Rock might have been put here to track lunar cycles, too?"

Arthur nodded. "But a vantage point of some type would be necessary. Unless of course the portion of the rock that acted as a marker has fallen off or been knocked off. Or unless there was once a piece that fit over the opening. We simply weren't sure. We were checking various possibilities."

"When was the rock put here?"

"I would guess before the arrival of the Spaniards. They were brutal in their eradication of anything pre-Christian. And it would have been a project of many months to move a large boulder down the side of Santa Cruz Mountain and part way up Ben Lomond Mountain."

I sipped the beer Edward had opened for me. I hated beer, but there wasn't much else on the menu. I waited for Arthur to continue, but he didn't.

"So, anyway," Edward prompted him. "You found a spot above Bowl Rock where the Pan guy could have been standing and seen what he said he did."

"Yes."

"And he said he saw a woman with a knife."

"A woman who looked to him like Syrinx," I put in. "I don't know if there's a tradition about what Syrinx looked like, but Toni Nelson would be my idea of a dryad."

Arthur nodded his agreement. "Quite. Billy was extremely taken with the . . . classicism of her endowments."

Edward smiled. "I'll have to remember that line. What the hell is a dryad, anyway?"

"Naiads were water nymphs. Dryads lived on land."

"Were the two of them romantic?"

Arthur looked bewildered. "Dryads and naiads?"

"No. Billy Seawuit and Toni Nelson."

Arthur seemed a little shocked by the suggestion. "Billy was a guest on their land. I can't imagine him treating his host so shabbily."

"Even if it made his hostess happy?"

Arthur shook his head, unimpressed with the distinction.

Edward pressed indelicately on. "Let's talk about Seawuit. Are you sure he'd go for manners over lust?"

"You'd like to hear about Billy?" Arthur's eyes filled with tears. "He was the most powerful shaman of my acquaintance, and I've traveled the globe meeting many."

"Okay," Edward conceded. "But what does that mean? That he could go into a trance? Heal the sick? Talk to voices in his head? What, exactly?"

"He could enter nonordinary reality nearly at will, bringing back to this world whatever was needed from the other."

"Like what?"

"Like answers and treatments, advice, perspective."
A tear traced a crevice in Arthur's cheek. "Whatever
was requested or necessary."

"So he had a direct line to the . . . nonordinary,
you called it?"

Arthur nodded.

Edward looked at me. I'd tried to warn him.

"Would you like to experience it?" Arthur asked.
"It's no secret how to get there. Our culture, our religions especially, try to bar the gates, but it's quite
accessible. It's just that some people are natural shamans, they have a great soul capable of traveling far
and remembering much."

Edward sat up. "Are you saying you could take me
right now into nonordinary reality? Are we talking
drugs?"

"That's certainly one path, with the requisite terror
and uncertainty. But no. I was thinking of drumming."
Arthur wiped his tears.

"Drumming? Mickey Hart, Ringo Starr, Buddy
Rich—that kind of drumming?"

"Shamanic drumming."

"Toni Nelson has a whole wall lined with drums,"
I pointed out.

"Well, I'm a little short of drums," Edward said.

"Do you have a thin piece of leather? And something circular, ring-shaped?" Arthur made perhaps an
eighteen-inch circle with his hands.

"I've got chamois in my Jeep. And I've got a scoop
net. For fishing."

Arthur rubbed his hands together. "Perhaps. If
you'll get them for us?"

A few minutes later, we watched Arthur cut the
chamois, which I gathered was low-grade animal skin

used for buffing cars. He stretched it over the net ring. Then he punched holes in the edges with a knife, lacing it with leftover strips. He pulled it taut, then tied the laces.

He did it swiftly and expertly, saying, "It will lack resonance because it has no sides to generate an echo, but—" He tapped the skin: It definitely sounded like a drum. "If we could wrap a sock around a spoon for a striker?"

When we were done, Arthur held the "drum" by the fishing net handle, tapping it with the spoon-and-sock striker. It wouldn't have done for Buddy Rich, but it was almost passable.

"Let me explain to you what we'll be doing," Arthur said. "We'll turn off the lights and have you both lie down. I'll beat the drum in a precise, repetitive rhythm—a little faster than three times per second. The rhythm is fairly standard throughout the world, around two hundred and ten beats a minute. Different cultures having no contact or common ancestors all arrived at some variation of it. That's because it serves a purpose: It synchronizes the two hemispheres of the brain, making a trance state possible."

I was nervous. Reality was strange enough. Did I believe Arthur about the trance state? Did I want to enter one?

"Your task, after I begin, is to relax, and to try to forget your body and your surroundings. Try to visualize an opening."

"What kind of opening?" Edward wanted to know.

"Any kind that will allow you to enter. You'll be going to the underworld, so a fissure, a rabbit hole, a hollow stump, a lake, even a manhole—anything that might lead you downward."

"We're supposed to visualize jumping into a hole?" I didn't think I could do it with a straight face.

"Yes yes. Keep at it. If one hole leads nowhere, envision another. But you must keep at it, force yourself to burrow deeper and deeper. It sometimes takes a very long time and a great deal of determination to burrow to the tunnel," he explained.

"What tunnel?" I was having serious doubts—and I could imagine what Edward was thinking.

"You'll come to a tunnel. At that point, you're almost there. Go through it. You'll meet your power animal, your guide. It will take you for a tour. Let it talk to you. Ask it questions if you like."

"Are you telling us"—Edward's tone was contentious—"that shamans jump into imaginary holes and tunnel down to meet talking animals?"

"They also take voyages upward to meet their spirit teachers, which take human form. But yes, shamans across the planet have mapped two distinct realms, an upper and a lower—and their maps match. No one knows how many lifetimes it would take to explore it all, but some of it is charted. Healing and divinations are brought back. Power is restored to people, answers are provided to the worthy."

"You really believe this?" Edward wondered.

"Ask any field scholar, anyone who has directly experienced shamanism, whether there's a real power there, a real magic or whatever you want to call it. There's no doubt. Only a priest would tell you otherwise." He slowed down. "By priest I mean a functionary of a dogmatic religion. It's a priest's role to act out a ritual and to substitute his ritual for your direct experience."

"So priests bad-rap shamans, but scholars don't."

Arthur nodded. "The aborigines in Australia are able to track movements of fellow tribesmen no matter how great the distance between them. They know when harm has befallen a kinsman hundreds of kilometers away, and they know his location. It's not because they have maps or stick to particular routes. It's because they have access to a shared shamanic reality in which these things are known to all." His eyes were bright. "And I would defy you to find even one Australian anthropologist who disagrees."

I was tired of discussing it. "Let's just do it, Edward. Lie there and think about naked women, for all I care, okay? If we're going to try this, let's try it."

For all my practical and modern notions, for all my doubts, I found I was scared. I felt a kid's thrill that it might work and an adult's fear of what that would mean.

Not without wisecracks, Edward unrolled the sleeping bags and turned out the lights. We lay down.

The drumming instantly changed the mood. It wasn't just an auditory experience: I could feel the vibrations through the floor, throughout my body. They were stronger than I'd expected. As they rumbled through every inch of me, I became more willing to believe they affected my brain hemispheres.

I tried to do as I'd been instructed. All the while Arthur's drumming reverberated through the floor, filling my ears and striking my bones like a tuning fork.

I lay there a long time, squelching mental noise (especially the Beach Boys' hit, "Good Vibrations") and trying—very sheepishly—to jump into holes. Just when I'd decided it would be more fruitful to sleep, my mind's eye gave me a tunnel.

I never for a moment felt I left my body. I never lost awareness of being in a room listening to a drum being beaten. But I did feel as if finally, half dozing, I unhooked conscious control of my imagination, that it ranged freely because I'd dropped the reins. I felt as if I were allowing myself to dream while still awake.

When the drumming stopped, I was pulled out of a fantasy so colorful and, well, other-dimensional, that I didn't want to go.

"Wow," I said groggily. "It was like I saw—"

"No," Arthur warned. "Don't tell us. The animal you saw is your guide, yours alone. What's important is that you experienced something. You did, didn't you?"

"Well . . ." I wasn't quite sure. "I wouldn't call it a trance. It wasn't as real as a drug trip or as visual as a dream. But I imagined some places, yes."

"You didn't imagine them. When you go back, you'll find them as you saw them now. You'll begin making a map, as with any place you visit."

I was afraid to hear Edward's take on this.

"Edward?" Arthur asked. "Have we put the smallest chink in your skepticism?"

He didn't answer immediately. Then he said, "Yes and no." I heard him rise.

A moment later, the naked bulb glared above us.

"I guess I've got a better idea," he conceded, "of what shamans are up to. But I didn't trip out, myself."

"It's more difficult for some," Arthur said, shading his eyes. "We see video footage of tribal dances, the mask wearing, the trancelike movements, and we assume it's a ritual much like the consecration of the host in Catholic mass. But it isn't. You'll notice there's always someone drumming or shaking a rattle or rhythmically clapping sticks. The shamans in the circle aren't dancing, they're in nonordinary states, in another dimension entirely. Until our anthropologists understand this, their analyses will continue to be superficial. These people aren't in some mumbo jumbo discotheque they've gone someplace very real. We're the ones who've traded the universe away for one unremarkable myth."

Edward looked troubled . . . for someone who'd supposedly been lying there as sober as a judge.

"Billy Seawuit taught me so much." Arthur's voice cracked. "He took me places other shamans couldn't even imagine. He'd journeyed so extensively and returned with so much wisdom, so many answers."

"Including how to turn all this into a computer program?" I explained what Toni Nelson had said about computers journeying for us, bringing us the answers directly.

"It can't be done." Arthur looked aghast. "It's the soul itself—whatever you may think that is, whether the subconscious mind or the collective unconscious or the holy spirit—it's the soul that journeys. How can one send computer electrons out to do the soul's work?"

"You think Toni was lying? You don't think Seawuit signed on to help with this program?"

"Billy may have agreed to consult with them about TechnoShaman." Arthur pinched the bridge of his nose as if the thought were painful to him.

"But he didn't think it would work?"

"He had accepted the Nelsons' hospitality. He may have felt it necessary to answer their questions about journeying and, perhaps, even share his personal map. But when I visited him here"—tears welled up in his eyes—"it was to explore the potential new Sun Dagger. Or to discuss the sightings of Pan. Or to take care of mundane matters, the plans and correspondence Billy took it upon himself to help me organize. I am computer literate, certainly. But I am no computer mystic; I don't equate cyberspace with nonordinary reality. And I don't believe Billy did. Because they are not the same. It's the difference between Chartres and Heaven, between what we are able to create and the far greater thing we seek."

Edward sat at the table, beer bottle in hand. I lay on my side on the smelly sleeping bag, too tired to get up.

"He was a good-looking guy, Seawuit?" Edward wondered.

Arthur nodded.

"And he wasn't convinced this computer stuff was going to work." Edward waited for another nod. When he didn't get one, he continued. "Maybe he stuck around the Nelsons' for another reason. Maybe he was bonking Toni Nelson."

Arthur scooted his chair back, putting a few more inches between himself and Edward.

"Maybe Galen got jealous," Edward continued, "and knifed him."

"Or maybe her ex-husband did. Arthur," I said gently, "I know this isn't how you want to remember Billy, but . . . Did he ever mention having feelings for Toni?"

"No." Arthur shook his head. "He mentioned her in passing, of course. But she's a person of little apparent wisdom; I wouldn't guess her to be his type."

"But opposites do attract." Edward flashed me a broad smile. "Right, Willa?"

I wasn't sure if he referred to our years-ago affair or to my feelings about Surgelato. Either way, he was damned obnoxious.

"Did Billy ever talk about someone named Stu?" I wondered. "Toni's ex-husband. We heard he picked a fight with Billy."

"No." Arthur shook his head slowly. "No, I don't recall the name. And I certainly didn't hear about a fight." Again, he pinched the bridge of his nose. "Except within the context of his journeys."

"Maybe you assumed he was talking about a journey when he wasn't."

Arthur looked amused. "Struggles within journeys tend to be rather . . . titanic. So no, I don't think so."

"You know, we've got time enough tonight to go hang with the Nelsons," Edward pointed out. "Maybe get some details. Where to find Stu."

Since he seemed to be talking to me, I replied. "I don't want to see them. And I don't want them to see Arthur."

"You don't mind if we leave you here for a half hour or so, do you?" Edward asked him.

Arthur looked a little taken aback. "No."

"Well, I don't want to go," I repeated. "What would we possibly say to them when we got there?"

Edward guzzled the remainder of his beer. "We'll think of something. I want to see this place. See the famous dryadic Toni for myself."

"We don't have the slightest pretext, Edward."

"We'll tell them you saw this Pan character. You can go on about him. We'll say we wanted to warn them or something." He stood, looking cheerful. "It'll work. We'll make it work."

I almost expected him to add, It'll be fun.

I looked up at Edward, bursting with energy and cheer, a little tanked on beer. I felt wrung out, exhausted. Left to my own devices, I'd have lain down and mulled the waking dream Arthur's drumming had produced.

But it's useless to argue with someone whose energy far exceeds your own.

Before I could even try, Edward had taken my hand and yanked me to my feet.

"Good thing we bought you that party dress." He referred to the thrift-store jeans and T-shirt I'd changed into.

"I don't want to go," I repeated for the record.

But the record didn't do a thing to help me. Edward pushed me toward the door.

CHAPTER EIGHTEEN

Edward grinned at me when he rang the Nelsons' bell. I made sure my face told him I hadn't changed my mind about being here.

When Galen Nelson opened the door, his face mirrored mine. He pulled himself straighter, inhaling in a give-me-patience way.

Edward stuck his hand out for shaking. "Something's up. Do you mind if we come in and talk to you about it?"

Nelson might have said no to phony friendliness or a purported social call, but this left him at a loss. He shook Edward's hand.

Toni Nelson appeared behind him. "Who is it?" Her voice was soft with alarm.

Standing behind Galen, she looked enormous, taller and broader than him, almost flouncy in a multicolored caftan. She whispered something to Galen.

He muttered, "They say something's happened." To us: "Is that right?"

Edward said, "Yes. We're sorry to bother you. But,

Wil—Alice here had a hell of a scare, and we thought we'd better talk to you. Warn you."

In response to his nudge, I nodded.

Toni hugged herself, her expression guarded. Galen's was always guarded. It wasn't difficult to conclude we weren't welcome.

"Can we come in?" Edward asked. "It's important."

It was all I could do not to roll my eyes. Important to whom? Basically, Edward was bored tonight, and the Nelsons were our entertainment.

Galen shrugged, stepping aside to allow us in. Edward, his hand on the small of my back, gave me a push. Because Toni was slow to back up, I nearly collided with her. I offered a lame smile of apology.

Edward skirted past her.

It was a joy to sit in a warm room full of soft furniture. I sank into an armchair, wishing I could sleep in it tonight. The carpet was yellow-white, the furniture dark blue; it was cheerful. The walls were oiled wood with so many shuttered windows there was little room for art. I noticed a few small, precise drawings that looked more like symbols than scenes. I wondered if they were Toni's work.

Edward sat on a fat love seat, looking around the room. He seemed to focus on coffee-table objects—papers and books and a few remote control devices, though I saw no television in the room.

"Well," he said cheerfully. He watched the Nelsons sit opposite him on a sofa, two cushions between them. "Remember we were talking about this Pan character running around the woods here?"

"I wouldn't take Jonathan too seriously," Galen advised.

"Alice bumped into him tonight—Pan, I mean. I saw him, too. He's real, all right."

Galen looked at Toni. But the glance lacked warmth; it struck me as a quick check to see if she cared.

"You're not going tell us he's a goat man?" Galen said sourly.

"Who are we talking about? What about Jon?" Toni demanded.

"Pan." Galen's tone was arch. "Jon says he saw him, goat legs and all."

Toni stiffened. "Who's Pan?"

"The Greek god with the goat legs."

"Galen!" Her tone carried a warning. "Come on. Who are we talking about?"

"No, he's right." Edward sounded apologetic. "We were having a conversation over lunch about Pan, from Greek mythology. Alice was asking if anybody'd sighted him here. She thought she heard him playing pipes, thought she saw him the other day."

Toni's expression said, Lie to me some more.

"I didn't say he had goat legs," I hastened to add.

Galen seemed nonplused. "Are you mostly interested in the myth or in this person?"

"The person," I assured him. I tried to imagine myself dropping in just to chat about demigods. "I was taking a walk in the woods and there he was. He has a British accent. But he thinks he's Pan. He thinks he was banished here by the goddess Diana."

Galen shrugged. "Making him mountain nut case number two hundred and six?" He gestured toward the shuttered windows. "There are homeless people everywhere, and just as we tend to be more eccentric up in BC, our homeless are probably more colorful, too."

I looked at Edward. We'd pretty much exhausted our pretext.

Not as far as Edward was concerned. "He could be dangerous. You should take precautions."

"Did he threaten you in some way?"

"No," I admitted.

Again, Edward took the reins. "He mentioned seeing a lady here in the woods that he thought was his long-lost love from mythology. We're worried he meant you, Mrs. Nelson."

And indeed, sitting there in her colorful robe, hair tumbling almost into her lap, she certainly seemed a grander creature than my mortal self. I felt my hand stray to my hair. It had been as long and as blond as Toni Nelson's, but it had never made me look like Botticelli's Venus, not even close.

"Why would he think my wife was somebody in a myth?" Galen asked unchivalrously.

"We don't know that he does." I didn't want to scare them just because we'd needed an excuse to visit. "It's just that he said he'd seen Syrinx in the woods—"

"Syrinx being his mythological mate?" Galen wondered.

"Yes. And it occurred to us that she looks, you look, sort of like a Greek statue."

Toni Nelson didn't seem pleased.

Edward hastened to explain, "We thought we'd better mention it. In case it was a stalker situation."

I thought he'd gone too far. Nobody should have to worry about being stalked, not without evidence. And we were just blowing smoke.

Galen chewed the inside of his lean cheek, looking at his wife. He turned back to us. "Anything else?"

I glanced at Edward. Did he want me to bring up the knife?

"You wouldn't have some tea, would you?" Edward asked shamelessly.

Galen sighed. I was reminded of men I'd represented in L.A., Hollywood directors and screenwriters with egos the size of their incomes. They didn't bother hiding their smug unfriendliness, born of too many people jockeying to meet them, of having seen every ingratiating trick.

"Let's go, Edward," I said. "We've told them what we were going to tell them. Let's leave it at that."

Edward's brows rose. "I guess we're feeling a little unwelcome." Jeez, was that a catch in his voice? "Well, I hope we haven't taken too much of your time." But he was very slow to rise.

Nelson sat there impassively.

But Toni said, "Of course we have tea." She rose, surprising me by adding, "Why don't you help me, Alice?"

I shot Edward a glare that told him how little I liked this turn of events. But when Toni reached my armchair, I had no polite choice but to stand and follow her into the kitchen.

The moment we entered, she grabbed my arm and pushed me against the wall. "You're hiding something," she said. "What is it?"

She was so close I could see the pale down above her lip, the pores on her nose.

"I'm not," I lied. She was taller and bigger than many men, with an intensity that would have been frightening in a pip-squeak.

"Yes, you are!" She spoke each word as if it were its own sentence. Then, in a rush: "I know you are. What is it? It's about Billy, isn't it?"

"No. Pan. We came to tell you about—"

"No, you didn't. You came to invite yourself to tea." She scowled down at me, tilting her head from side to side as if examining a strange animal in its cage. "Your friend's a liar. And so's my husband. So we'll let them sit in there and lie to each other. And in here,"—her voice slowed to a patronizing singsong— "we'll tell the truth."

I considered calling out to Edward.

She leaned against me, burying her fingers in my arm. "Why are you here? Are you police?"

"No!" My denial had the authority of genuine surprise.

"So you're just a liar? You came here to lie to me again?"

Under the circumstances, it was a little hard to defend my veracity. But I managed another, "No."

"Did you know Billy?" Her eyes were bright. "Why do you keep asking me about Billy?"

I tried to recall whether Edward or I had mentioned Seawuit to the Nelsons tonight. I didn't think so.

I turned it around: "You have something you want to say? About Billy? About Stu and—"

"Were you with Billy?" Her tone was urgent. "Is that why? Were you his lady?"

"I didn't know he had one."

"Toni!" Galen called out from the living room.

She jumped back as if she'd been struck. "What?" she called back.

"Forget the tea."

172

I wondered if Edward had managed to get us kicked out.

Instead, the men pushed through the kitchen door. Edward was saying, "I didn't know you could even get it out here."

Galen, barely glancing at us, crossed to the refrigerator. He yanked the door open, pulling out two bottles of beer.

"You want some Rolling Rock?" he asked me.

"No."

He looked at the stove, brows rising, perhaps because the kettle wasn't on.

"Try it, Alice," Edward urged. "It comes from back East."

"I know." I also knew he hated the stuff when we lived together in Boston.

Judging from his grimace when he took a sip, he still did.

"So . . . you girl-talking in here?" Edward leaned against a butcher-block counter, crossing one booted ankle over another. "But I guess 'girl talk' is kind of a misnomer, since it's mostly about men—boyfriends, ex-husbands . . ."

Toni turned away, snatching up a kettle and filling it.

"Speaking of ex-husbands," Edward rambled on.

I cast him a startled look: How damn blunt could he be?

"You know, Alice, I just can't get used to the new last name," he continued. "I knew Alice by her ex-husband's name." To Galen: "Inconvenient all around, women changing their names. Especially if the new name doesn't sound so great with the first name.

Alice Young's not bad. I like your names together, Mrs. Nelson."

She didn't seem to care. "We were going to go downstairs," she said, not quite nonchalantly. "Alice wants to see the drums."

Edward gave me a congratulatory wink.

"Edward, you'll want to see them, too." My tone was as firm as I could make it.

He shrugged.

To avert the possibility of his declining, I added, "Especially after making your own drum tonight."

"You made a drum?" Galen didn't seem surprised. "What kind of skin?"

"Actually, chamois. First effort." He shot me a glance.

"Chamois? It must have sounded awful. Did you treat it? How did you stretch it thin enough?" Galen obviously knew his drum-making.

"I was just horsing around. Just laced it on a hoop and beat on it."

"I've got some very interesting ones downstairs." He seemed troubled. "But you know, I use it as a workroom, and I have things lying around there right now. Toni, why don't you take Alice down another time?"

"All right." She sounded matter-of-fact, still fussing with the kettle. "We'll join you in the living room in a few minutes." Turning to me, her face as blank as a lizard's, she said, "Come and check the selection, Alice." She opened a cupboard.

"You know," I said, "I think I'll have a Rolling Rock, after all."

Galen, still by the refrigerator, grabbed another bottle, handing it to me.

I twisted the cap off, avoiding Edward's eye. I took a sip. Rolling Rock hadn't improved one bit.

I preceded the men into the living room. I sipped bad beer while Edward and Galen chatted inconsequentially. Toni Nelson didn't come back into the room.

We left as soon as Edward finished his beer. But not before he'd exhausted his small talk.

Backing the Jeep out of the driveway, he was already complaining. "You couldn't hang out with Toni five more minutes? Get that last name? Act a little more sociable?" He sounded like a husband after a boring office party.

"Don't start!" I fell into office-party counterpoint. "She attacked me in the kitchen. Thanks a hell of a lot! I should have my head examined. Why did I let you take me to visit someone who bopped me in the nose the first time I met her?"

"What do you mean, attacked you tonight?" He focused on shifting gears. He was certainly not squirming with concern.

"Pinned me to the wall and snarled angry questions at me." In retrospect, and with a little beer in me, it made me mad. "She's really out of control! If I see her again—"

"What kind of questions?"

"If I was Billy Seawuit's woman."

"Whoa." That got his attention. "Good work, Watson. How'd you get her onto that?"

"I walked into the kitchen with her. Subtle, huh?"

"She asked you about Seawuit, then she pinned you?" He picked up speed, zooming through a corridor of tall trees.

"No. She pinned me and stood there looking all

scary. Then she asked why I'd come—if I was a cop."
That got a big laugh out of him. "Then she wanted
to know why we kept bringing up Billy Seawuit."

" 'We' meaning you and me? You and Nelson?"

"You and me."

"We didn't bring up Seawuit, not tonight." He
glanced at me for confirmation.

"I was having a little trouble contradicting her, since
I was squished against the wall. She was asking if I
was his 'lady' when you guys walked in."

"That's no lady, that's my fellow accessory after the
fact." It wasn't much of a joke, but he was right. "The
reason we came in, supposedly for beers, was because
Galen got very nervous. He was looking for a reason
to check up on her."

"And here I thought you were rushing to my aid."

"No way. I hated to interrupt—especially since it
was her idea to go off by yourselves. She obviously
had something to say to you."

"Do you think Galen Nelson wanted to stop her?"

"I sure do. It was a challenge keeping him out of
the kitchen long enough for something to happen."

"Luckily it didn't happen to my nose this time." My
shoulders ached from hunching up in fear. My legs
throbbed from too much hiking. And the beer was
making me queasy.

"When she asked if you were Seawuit's lady, was it
like, 'you, too?' "

"I don't know. Unlike her computer, I'm not a mind
reader," I pointed out.

"If you had to guess."

"I don't have to guess." But, having vented a bit of
crankiness, I couldn't resist adding, "She did sound
jealous."

"Then, voilà. Information and the pleasure of watching you try to drink a Rolling Rock. What more could a man ask of a social engagement?"

"What about now? What are you going to do?"

"Drive us back."

"I meant, are you going back to Santa Cruz tonight?" I was feeling apprehensive. And Toni Nelson hadn't exactly assuaged my fears.

"I was thinking about it. Look up Nelson's marriage certificate first thing tomorrow, get Toni's maiden name, find her divorce decree; get Stu's last name, address, all that. Maybe go talk to him."

We drove for a while. I tried not to admit how much safer (if more annoyed) I felt with Edward around.

"But what the hell," he said, finally. "Why break up a good party? I'll drive down in the morning."

CHAPTER NINETEEN

Lying on the floor listening to Edward snore and Arthur wheeze, I began to hope I'd been in hiding long enough. The policeman Arthur and I had eluded in San Francisco, his memory would have faded somewhat in three days. If I cut my hair shorter and bleached it back, I could claim I'd done it last week. Though no one would confuse me with Syrinx, it should distinguish me from the long-haired blonde hostage.

And to explain my absence, I'd say I'd needed time to think through a midlife crisis. That I'd spent a few days . . . That, of course, was my problem. Where could I possibly say I'd been? Meditating alone on a remote beach? Not likely, not without my car. Off on a tryst? The only man who might possibly have agreed to lie for me was Edward, and he'd just told Surgelato he hadn't seen me.

Plus, what would Arthur say and do without me?

He'd have to come forward regarding Seawuit's murder soon. He'd have to discuss his whereabouts.

And I just couldn't imagine him covering up these days with me, not very well. He'd slip up without meaning to or knowing he had.

The ideal—if one could achieve it without spending long nights on hard floors listening to Edward snore—would be to find out who killed Billy Seawuit. If that were established, no one would bother asking Arthur where he'd been. He wouldn't have to talk to the police at all.

And I would be free to offer whatever thin excuse I could devise for my truancy.

But for tonight, at least, circumstance left me no alternative but to lie awake listening to Edward imitate a pulp grinder. Except one.

I pulled my aching bones out of the sleeping bag and slipped into my shoes. I tiptoed over the two men, Arthur in his bag and Edward in a stack of blankets. Edward's keys were on the table. I picked them up and quietly went outside.

I was both relieved and irritated not to have wakened Edward. Some watchdog he'd turned out to be.

I unlocked the Jeep and slid into the backseat. It was much softer than the cabin floor, though it didn't smell any better and probably wasn't much cleaner. I locked myself in and lay down, tossing the keys up front. Night noises—cracklings and rustlings and whistling wind—couldn't keep me awake tonight. I conked out immediately.

I awakened at dawn, certain something was wrong. Raising my head only enough to see, I peered through the moisture-streaked windshield. Someone was outside the cabin. He was too bundled up for me to identify from the back. He was looking into the windows, creeping from one to another.

I watched, hardly breathing, though he certainly wouldn't be able to hear me. When he walked to the back of the cabin, I slid out of the Jeep, leaving the door ajar to avoid a slamming sound.

One nice thing about Edward's place: A few steps in any direction provided cover. I hid behind a bushy clump of redwood shoots.

The man came back around the cabin. He crossed to the Jeep. I thanked the Great Mother he hadn't checked it first. He tried the front doors. When he went to the back and found it ajar, I held my breath. Would he put his hand on the seat and notice it was warm?

To my relief, he merely reached in and unlocked the front passenger door. He took his time opening it, obviously trying to be quiet.

I still couldn't make out his features. From here, he looked bulky and short. He was white. He wore a cap and a padded jacket.

He leaned into the Jeep. I assumed he was checking the contents of Edward's glove compartment. He hunched over, and I had the impression he was jotting something down. Since I doubted he was leaving Edward a note, I guessed he was copying the car registration.

I was startled. Could he be a cop? But cops were supposed to knock and announce themselves, ask to see these documents. They might not follow the rules when it didn't suit them. But in this instance, it would certainly have been the easier path.

Was he a private investigator? He seemed to be investigating, after all. He didn't seem poised to break into the house, nor to steal anything from the Jeep.

He seemed to be doing what was necessary to find out more about their owner.

Suddenly he straightened, glancing at the cabin. He slipped something into his pocket.

I could see movement inside now, not what I'd have expected—not a figure rising and stretching, crossing to the bathroom. I saw a dark shape maintaining a crouch, creeping toward a window. Edward had been wakened.

The man crossed the gravel road, striding into the woods. He passed within ten feet of me. At last I saw his face. It was one of the two supposed backpackers from Watsonville, the ones we'd encountered in the woods yesterday.

Within seconds, Edward was out the cabin door, in hot pursuit. He wasn't being quiet. Apparently, he meant to collar the man, not follow him.

He zipped past me, turning briefly and meeting my eye. Unlike the man, he'd spotted me in the brush.

Since he was racketing along as noisily as a bear, I left my hiding spot and followed. I caught glimpses of both men running, the colors of their clothes popping in and out of view between trees. Edward was gaining fast.

Until he heard a gunshot.

At that point, Edward did a full-throttle reverse. If I'd been impressed with the speed of his pursuit, now I was amazed. Edward might have been an Olympic retreater.

The other man held his course, crashing out of sight as Edward doubled back.

A moment later, Edward almost collided with me.

"Come on," he panted. "Back. Back into the cabin."

He grabbed my arm, yanking it, pulling me along behind him.

The sound of our pounding footsteps and door slamming roused Arthur. He sat up, a shaft of meager light catching him by surprise. He blinked, apparently disoriented to see us up and out of breath.

"It was one of the men we saw yesterday," I told Edward.

"What were you doing outside?" he demanded.

"Sleeping in the Jeep. You snore."

"No, I don't." But he looked sheepish, as if he'd heard tell. "Did he see you?"

"No. I saw him walking around the cabin, looking in. I got out of the Jeep and hid. He copied your registration, I think. And he took something out of the glove compartment."

"Son of a bitch! My new toy."

I shook my head uncomprehendingly.

"My spy camera," he explained. "That's what was in there."

"He must have seen you when he looked in here. If he recognizes you from yesterday, the camera's going to make him think you took secret pictures of him."

Edward nodded. "Son of a bitch," he repeated. "What is he about?"

Arthur looked bewildered. "What? Who?"

"Someone just broke into Edward's Jeep," I explained. "A man we saw in the woods yesterday. He claimed to be a backpacker."

"Might he have been looking for money?"

"No." I was positive about that. "I watched him. He copied down Edward's name and address from the registration—or he wrote down something, anyway. It was clear yesterday he wasn't a backpacker."

"You seem certain his motive was sinister," Arthur noted. "Perhaps—"

"He shot at me." Edward liked having the last word.

"Ah." Arthur rose slowly, showing his age.

Edward began pacing, running his hand through his hair. "Okay, okay. He'll know I'm a PI because I put my business address on the reg. But he won't know I saw anything but his back today. He won't know I made him as the backpacker."

"You made him, Sherlock?"

He ignored my correction. "But you're right—he'll think I took pictures of him yesterday. That could be a problem."

He paced, looking around the cabin, shaking his head.

When he spoke again, he sounded more, not less, agitated. "How's he going to react to that possibility? Who the hell is he? That's the key."

I left him to consider it. I took dibs on the shower. Before I'd even shampooed, Edward pounded on the door, demanding that I hurry.

A few minutes later, I dabbed myself with a funky towel and put on another "party dress."

By the time I stepped out, the cabin had been cleared of our belongings. Neither Edward nor Arthur was inside. The Jeep's engine was running.

I joined them out there.

"He took the keys," Edward informed me when I climbed into the back. "You must have left them on the seat."

"How'd you get it started? You hot-wired it?" Just like a TV private eye; I was impressed.

"I keep a magnetized spare under the bumper."

As soon as I closed the door, Edward took off. "Either he took the keys because he doesn't want us leaving here—which is a pretty damn good reason for us to go—or he's heading down to my office."

"Is that where we're going?"

"Right now, we're going to a phone. I've got a friend who'll keep an eye on my office till I get a locksmith over there. Not that they'd find anything of interest to them, but I need to protect my client records."

"What about afterward? I don't want anyone to see me and Arthur together."

"Afterward?" He caught my eye in the rearview mirror. "I'll pop into a market and get some fixings. We'll have a picnic breakfast." He looked a little smug. "Then as soon as it opens, we'll go by the drugstore and pick up the film we dropped off yesterday. Stupid bastard wants to go shooting at me . . . well, tough *cojones*. I've got his picture, and I'm turning it over to the cops."

"Which cops?"

"The ones investigating Seawuit's murder. I won't mention you guys. I'll just say I snapped his picture because he looked suspicious. That he broke into my Jeep today and took a shot at me." He nodded. "That should get their attention."

"Do you know the cops investigating the murder?"

"Nope."

I sat back, watching the morning brighten. It was going to be a sunny day. "We can't stay at your cabin anymore, can we?"

"No," Edward admitted.

"Any suggestions?"

"Move into that shaved-headed kid's lean-to?"

"Ha ha." I knew better than to press him; I knew I'd get nothing but jokes. And I'm not at my best before coffee.

"You don't know how long the Nelsons have been married, do you?"

"I think she told me." I wracked my brain. "Two years?"

"Plus six months for the divorce, and let's guess six months single."

"What are you doing, Edward?"

"Say their business—"

"Toni and Stu's?"

"Yeah. Say it broke up the year they did. If I can find an old phone book, it might be in the Yellow Pages. Save me a trip to the county building."

"You don't know their business name."

"Process of elimination—there's only a handful of software designers in BC. With any luck, Stu's name will be in the ad."

"This is the person you believe fought with Billy?" Arthur asked.

"It's worth checking."

"Billy wasn't a fighter," Arthur assured him. "He was a healer, a shaman."

"He might have been backed into a corner."

"As he was in Bowl Rock?" Arthur stared out the passenger window. "But he didn't die fighting, did he?"

CHAPTER TWENTY

Coffee and rolls improved my mood. We ate beside a creek in a tiny clearing carpeted with oak and alder leaves. Fallen trees crisscrossed the water, creating small cascades and pools. Leaves collected in twirling eddies, breaking free when they reached critical mass. We watched a blue kingfisher dive into the creek.

Edward finally told us the plan.

"I asked the friend who's guarding my office to call and reserve us a cabin at one of the—well, they call them resorts, but they aren't much fancier than my place. The one I have in mind, the cabins are far enough apart you can't really see the other people. I'm having him take it in his name so Surgelato can't track us if he gets to missing you again . . . Alice."

"That's very nice of you." Arthur's manners were more polished than mine. "Would it have beds?"

Edward grinned. "Yup."

"And is it close to Bowl Rock?"

"Not as close as my place. But you could still hike to it." He looked at me expectantly.

"Thanks," I said.

"It's a two-bunker," he continued. "But that's okay—I'll need to go back tonight. I have to testify in a civil trial tomorrow morning; hopefully be done by noon or so."

"Is it really necessary to continue hiding?" Arthur wondered.

"Yes." I'd gone over it and over it in my mind. Until the police had a suspect in custody, we wouldn't be safe. "We can't keep it up much longer, but the longer we wait, the more likely . . ." I rubbed my forehead, trying to rid myself of a headache. "If nothing's changed by Monday, we'll talk about coming forward. We can't do this forever."

Edward gave me a tap on the arm. "Abby Hoffman held out ten years," he pointed out. "Had his nose surgically enlarged."

I didn't bother to respond.

"But he might have drawn the line at a Prince Valiant hairdo."

I continued practicing forbearance. "Shouldn't we go pick up those pictures?"

Edward rose, gathering our breakfast debris. "Arthur, I'm going to drop you off before we get to town—not a good idea for you to show your face. I thought I'd take you to the resort so you know where it is. Let you hike around, do your thing. It's on a piddley-ass creek about the size of this one—place is billed as a riverside resort. We'll meet you back there around check-in time, around three, show you which cabin's ours, okay?"

Arthur seemed about to suggest an alternative plan. Then he nodded.

By the time we dropped him off, I'd admonished him several times not to miss our rendezvous.

When Edward and I reached the drugstore, it was just opening. I strolled while Edward went inside and picked up the prints.

I could tell by his face, even at half a block's distance, that he'd gotten a good shot of the man in the woods. He pulled the pictures out, grinning, when I joined him. At that moment, someone hailed him.

We turned to find Galen Nelson striding toward us. Edward let the photos slide back into the envelope.

Nelson's brows were pinched to a tight line over his thin nose. He looked like a displeased monarch.

So his words took me by surprise: "I owe you an apology."

"I doubt that," Edward smiled.

"I didn't take your warning very seriously last night." He looked more angry than repentant. "But our place got broken into, our home. Some computer components were damaged downstairs."

"No shit?" Edward's shock was apparent. "Your wife's okay? Nobody got hurt?"

"No, we're . . . well, very shaken up. You can imagine. We were upstairs, but we didn't hear anything, we didn't hear it happen."

He seemed to find this startling, maybe galling.

"No alarm system?"

"On the house? Not much of one, not like the one at Cyberdelics. But I'll have top quality by tomorrow, I'll tell you that. I lost a bit of work!" His lip quivered under its trimmed mustache.

"Anything stolen?"

"No. Just sabotage. Except . . . possibly . . ." Nelson

looked troubled, at war with his own reticence. "I'm not sure; Toni misplaces things all the time."

"What's missing?"

"Probably nothing. Toni doesn't keep track of mere objects; she seems to feel artists shouldn't bother." He seemed too annoyed to elaborate.

"What object are we talking about?" Edward pressed him.

"If she'd go clear out her ex-husband's garage, she'd know what was downstairs and what wasn't."

"Tell me Stu's last name again?" Edward asked.

"Winsler."

"Well, here's something you'll be interested in." Edward spoke quickly—burying his question under new information? "Someone broke into my Jeep this morning. Stole my camera and"—he paused for effect—"took a shot at me when I chased him."

Nelson looked more than merely interested. He practically grabbed Edward. "What time?"

"Dawn."

"Have you been to the police?"

"Nope. I was waiting to pick up these photos." He held up the packet. "I recognized the burglar. I saw him in the woods yesterday."

Edward opened the envelope, Nelson and I hovering as anxiously as Oscar nominees.

He pulled out three snapshots—none, I hoped, of me bending over. Topmost was a slightly blurry one of the two "backpackers."

Nelson squinted at it for a moment. Then he looked at Edward. "Why'd you take this photograph?"

"I'm a private eye, remember? Alice got spooked by this Pan guy Tuesday night. I went out and snapped these yesterday morning."

"I thought Pan was . . . unclothed."

"So clothes make a good disguise. I wanted to ask Alice if Pan's one of these guys."

"Is it?"

"No," I answered.

"They didn't see you take the picture?"

Edward shrugged. "Actually, I'd guess they did. Considering this one"—he pointed at the stockier of the two—"broke into my Jeep and took my camera. Luckily, I dropped off the film yesterday."

"Let's go to the police." Nelson's tone brooked no argument. "This might help—" He'd fanned pictures, looking at the one beneath. "Wait a minute!"

"You recognize that kid?"

Nelson scrutinized the photo of the young man with the shaved head.

"It's Joel Baker. I'm almost sure." He looked at the third photo but seemed to find it of little interest.

I craned my neck for a better view: It was a picture of the wood shavings we'd found near Bowl Rock.

"Who's Joel Baker?" Edward was staring down at the photo, a shot of the man, his lean-to, and part of his meat-smoking rack.

"Without giving you his whole résumé—he's been a hacker, a designer, you name it—he's basically become an industrial spy." His lips crimped into a sour line. "At least, that's been our suspicion, our best explanation for how a few things jumped from one company to another." He tapped the photo. "I'd say this confirms it."

"How do you do industrial spying living in a lean-to in the woods?" Edward wondered.

"My gut feeling?"

"Go for it."

"You get Billy Seawuit convinced you're living like a Native American." He closed his eyes, taking a few deep breaths. "I never trusted that phony shaman." He spoke through clenched teeth. "I never trusted Seawuit. Goddamn Louis stuffed him down my throat—made me take him in. And Toni! Jesus, she thought he walked on water!" Again he tapped the photo. "Look at this hokey Indian crap!"

Edward seemed pleased, though he hid it when Nelson glanced back up. "And the other guy, the one who stole my camera, you don't recognize him, huh? Or his friend?"

"No." Nelson seemed reluctant to return the pictures. He glanced at the drugstore. "Do you mind if we take the film back in? Get a couple more sets made?"

Edward hesitated. "If they can do them same-day. They went and closed on us yesterday."

"They close early on Wednesdays," Nelson said absently. "Rhonda's daughter has treatments. They'll do them right away for me," he assured us.

"Look," I said, "you guys have your errands and I have mine." No way was I going to visit the police with them. "I'll see you later."

Nelson shook his head. "The police will want to ask you about Pan."

"Edward saw him, too."

Edward, never slow on the draw, said, "Yeah, that's right," though he'd had the barest glimpse and hadn't spoken to him. "Go ahead, Alice. Meet you back at the place."

I took off before Nelson could voice other obvious objections. As I rounded a corner, I thought I heard him calling me back.

I dashed down rural sidestreets. I seemed to be doing evasive maneuvers a lot lately.

I stopped when I noticed where my circuitous route was taking me. I was approaching the road leading to the Nelsons'. I turned back around.

Not soon enough. I heard a woman shout my name. I glanced behind me. It was Toni. Though she wasn't close, I recognized her size, her hair, her fisherman's sweater.

I picked up my pace, pretending I didn't hear her. But when she shouted again, she was obviously closer. In fact, she had to be running to have covered so much ground so quickly.

Maybe it was cowardly, I didn't care. She was too weird for me to risk meeting her alone.

I broke into a jog. I had visions of hurrying back into town and encountering Galen, of being trapped between them like a horror-movie heroine. I looked over my shoulder. Toni was running like an athlete, unself-consciously pumping every limb. The sight of it scared the hell out of me.

I took a sharp turn down a road I'd never seen before. (I wondered how many tombstones bore that epitaph.)

As I ran, my devolving brain fed me potential disasters: that Toni Nelson would claw at me, beat me with her fists, stab me with the knife that had disemboweled Billy Seawuit. It was countered by social shame: Jesus, here I was, a grown woman . . . running from someone who probably just wanted to tell me her house had been broken into.

Whatever the reality, another glance over my shoulder told me she was gaining fast.

I took off across a field and behind a house. Then,

because I didn't want to be alone with her in the middle of nowhere, I hesitated.

In my moment of indecision, she pounced on me.

She grabbed me from behind, saying, "What's the matter with you? Didn't you recognize me?"

There wasn't much point in being coy. "What do you want? Leave me alone!" I wriggled sideways in her arms, trying to see her face.

Either my rudeness made her angry or she'd started out that way. She'd scowled herself scarlet.

"Let go of me." I tried to bat her hands away. "You're always grabbing me."

But she didn't let go.

"Leave me alone." I struggled, but it seemed to make her more determined to keep me there.

"What's wrong with you?" she demanded.

"Wrong with me? I didn't punch you in the nose and pin you to the wall."

"I didn't punch you in the nose. And I didn't lie to you about who I am, either."

I froze for a second.

"I know a liar when I see one!" she continued. "Maybe Galen didn't recognize you, but I did."

I found my strength, wriggling free of a woman at least six inches taller and forty pounds heavier than me. I ran again.

I didn't believe her; didn't believe she'd been present the day of my interview with Curtis & Huston, the day I'd first seen Galen. I'd have noticed her, remembered her. But I ran anyway.

Whoever she thought I was—assuming her accusation wasn't generic—that person wasn't safe with her.

I made for the road this time. I wanted to be around people.

But a glance over my shoulder made it clear Toni would outrun me and overtake me before I made it.

I pushed the thought away—I didn't want to consider it. But I had to admit, and quickly, that I couldn't outrun her. I'd have to hide from her.

I veered off into a margin of oak and madrone. I was panting, nearly out of breath, my legs close to cramping. I was a good walker, but never a jogger, and it had been a tiring few days.

But I had to make it into deeper forest, I had to take cover, that was the most I could hope for.

I could hear her crashing along, not far behind. God, I hoped she wasn't a distance runner.

I grew hot in my sweatshirt. I heard myself gasping. I had to create enough of a lead to take advantage of a hiding place—*if* I spotted one.

Anger helped: Damn this woman. What did she have against me? Who did she think I was?

A second later she tackled me, sending me sprawling over dried leaves and clumps of bark and dirt, over prickly berry vines and sharp saplings.

Exhausted and in distress, I blurted out the babyish truth: "I hate you!" I cried.

Her voice had a similar sobbing breathlessness. "I hate you, too. You liar!"

Not since childhood had I had a fight that was based purely on antipathy and stress. We rolled and punched and cried and pulled hair. And I knew even as I succumbed that it was pathetic and stupid and fruitless, an embarrassment in every regard.

I just couldn't stop myself. She'd pushed me too far: I was willing to sink to her level. Hell, even lower.

Maybe there was more to it. I'd been frightened all week: running from the police; hiding in the woods;

startled by pipe-playing, Jeep-breaking, lean-to inhabiting men. I'd been forced to depend on Edward, a former boyfriend I'd barely begun to forgive. And I'd had to keep a tight rein on Arthur through all of it.

I transferred all my frustration and fury onto Toni Nelson. I lashed out at her, hitting her anywhere I could, rolling in the duff with her like an animal. Though I'd worried about running out of energy, I suddenly had an inexhaustible supply.

And her blows, though I registered their location and intensity, didn't really hurt. She wore a fanny pack facing front—that did smart when it burrowed into me. But I knew she felt it, too, so I didn't mind. In fact, I seemed to detach from my body, using it only as a vehicle to express a primal, generalized anger.

But even I couldn't remain irrational forever. There came a moment when self-knowledge reared its shamed face. Then temerity crept in, reminding me that the odds were against me, that I was going to get trounced, that there was no way I'd walk out of these woods the winner.

And then, with a sudden, swooping, almost Tarzan-like entrance, Pan was with us. He appeared out of nowhere—from behind trees, I later supposed—a blur of naked, hairy flesh. I didn't notice much more, didn't focus on his face. I watched his vast arm reach down and yank Toni off me.

I scooted back in the duff, so startled I couldn't wrap my thoughts around it.

Pan pulled her farther back, farther away from me, both his arms around her so she couldn't hit him. He lifted her off her feet so she had no traction, no leverage.

He'd seen her on top of me, and he'd assumed she'd

attacked me—which, in fact, she had. He'd freed me from her.

I watched him hold her as if oblivious to her wrigglings, too powerful even to stagger.

She still stared at me, hot-eyed, red-cheeked, not seeming to care who'd pulled her off me, ready to renew the attack.

She'd jump back on me if she got the chance, I was sure of it.

I scrambled to my feet and ran. Ran without regard to course or direction, without regard to anything but getting out of there.

I ran without concern for the stitch in my side or the hot pain in my lungs. I crashed over vines and through brush, doing a broken-field run around trees and stumps, down hills, and up seams of eroded dirt. I ran until I fell from exhaustion.

Somehow the terrors and worries of the last few days had crystallized into this one morning. I'd been running on fear, not real energy.

I lay on the ground in the middle of the forest, having absolutely no idea where I was. Every part of me hurt—my head, face, trunk, arms, legs, lungs, heart. I was so hot I thought my skin would blister.

I felt worse in repose than I had in motion.

I lay there groaning.

That's when it occurred to me: Maybe Pan hadn't been rescuing me. Maybe he'd seen Toni as his Syrinx; maybe he'd grabbed her to ravish her.

I sat up. He'd talked about spotting Syrinx in the woods. He'd talked about consummating an ancient longing.

Oh God, what if I'd left Toni Nelson with an insane rapist?

What if I'd run off—congratulating myself for having escaped—and all the while . . .

I struggled back to my feet, lurching along like a zombie. My calves were in spasm, my body was stiff.

I tried to scream "Toni," but it sounded more like croaking. I did better the second time, but I got no response.

I staggered around calling her name, fearing I'd run too fast on my adrenaline rampage; that she was too far away to hear me. Or worse, that she couldn't respond.

I was totally lost, not sure whether I was heading back or going in circles, never seeing a landmark to make me certain.

The forest seemed unique everywhere I looked and yet exactly like hundreds of other parts I'd passed through.

I tried to find traces of my passage: branches I'd broken, scuff marks in the dirt. But when I did see broken twigs or vines, I had no way of guessing whether I'd done it.

I tried scanning the sky, but I didn't know how to navigate by changing sun positions.

Finally, I sat back down, forcing myself to catch my breath.

I tried to reassure myself. "Pan" was really an Oxford-educated Welshman. When Arthur and I spoke to him, he'd seemed literate and restrained and perfectly gentlemanly, in his delusional way.

But I wasn't Syrinx, his long lusted-after, perfect mate. And unless I'd misinterpreted him, Toni Nelson was.

What if I didn't find them? How would I tell the police without revealing my identity? How would I avoid putting Arthur at risk; in effect, putting him in prison forever?

I started to panic. It would be far too late by then. I needed to find Toni now.

I forced my knotting muscles to bear my weight. I tottered on, screaming her name.

I could feel sweat or tears on my lips, taste it on my tongue as I called for her.

I couldn't stop: I'd abandoned her to a crazy man obsessed with the dryad he thought she was.

I pushed on, barely able to keep upright, my throat raw from shouting Toni's name.

It was the middle of the hot afternoon before I gave up. I sat in the breezeless woods, smelling the warm duff and evergreens, insects buzzing around me, birds hopping and pecking and flying from limb to limb.

It all looked so normal and benign. The great outdoors on a sunny, blue-sky day.

Except that I had no idea where I was. And no idea what might be happening to Toni Nelson because I'd abandoned her.

CHAPTER TWENTY-ONE

I wandered the woods, feeling desolate, unlucky, unworthy. I continued trying to console myself with Pan's fine accent, his obvious education. But I couldn't sustain optimism in the face of the worst possibility.

I grew to feel jinxed, lost forever. How big could the forest be? I had trekked through oak and fir forest, shady redwoods, now hot chaparral.

But I knew this was a mountain of parks and timberland with few pockets of habitation. Either I'd traveled deep into the wilderness or I was going in circles through the same near-city margin.

I walked and walked, dragging my frustrations.

I stepped through a scratchy stand of chaparral plants. I had no idea I would finally encounter a landmark.

I found myself before a lean-to of garbage bags and tree limbs. The shaved-headed young man we'd seen yesterday—and whose photograph we'd seen today—peered out at me. Judging by his face, he was far less disconcerted to see me than I was to see him.

"Howdy," he said.

I stood there, numb with surprise. "Hi." And then, because it might not be too late to help Toni Nelson: "That man we talked about yesterday? Pan?" Could I trust him? Did I have a choice? "He attacked the woman I was with." I had to try something, after all. Anything I could.

He stood, wiping his hands on his jeans. "Where?" he asked. "What can I do?" He looked bewildered.

"I don't know where." I gestured behind me. "I've been walking and walking, trying to find the spot again."

"You think . . . Pan?" He took off his hat, wiping his brow. His head was thoroughly stubbled. "Tell me what happened."

"The person who thinks he's Pan, he jumped out of nowhere. He grabbed her." Was it important to tell him we'd been fighting? "I ran away, and then I couldn't find her again. I still haven't found her. I don't know what he's doing to her."

The young man strode over to me. "You better relax a minute, have some water. Then we'll talk about where this was. Maybe I can get us back there. I know the woods pretty well; I've been living here a long time. Okay? So relax."

Living here a long time? Wasn't he supposed to be an industrial spy? Or was Galen Nelson wrong?

He produced a canteen. I drank from it.

"You don't look good," he observed. "Come on, let's get you into the shade. Let's relax a minute."

I let him lead me into his lean-to. I sat on a carpet apparently of rabbit fur. I looked around, noticing several things I hadn't seen yesterday: a small, leaf-lined hole full of water, some paperbacks, a store of tinder and a flinty stone, a few folded clothes. One of the paperbacks, I noticed, was open, spine broken.

He knelt. "Just relax a minute. You're probably dehydrated. It's a hot day, that can be dangerous."

I felt tears well up. I blinked them away. I could see by the fading daylight that hours had passed. Long, critical hours.

"I don't know, I don't know. He picked her up, and I ran off, and I just don't know. I don't know what happened to her. When I realized, when I stopped and turned around, I couldn't find the spot anymore. I couldn't find them."

"Start with Pan." He didn't look fully convinced I'd seen him. He kept looking at my cheeks and lips. "Have a sip of water, and tell me about him."

I took another sip. "Pan. Oh, God, let's see. We saw him in the woods, and he told us this long story about how he wanted Syrinx." I recalled with a start that this man had told us the same story. "Is that what Pan's mostly known for?"

"No." His eyes were pale green with the blackest of brows and lashes. His lean cheeks were tan, slightly paler where he shaved. "But it's supposedly why he ended up here on this mountain. It's a big part of the local legend."

"Oh," I said. "Okay. He talked a lot. He seemed obsessed with Syrinx."

"So you really saw him?" He didn't seem convinced. "And he talked to you?"

"He's a man with a British accent. He seems very well spoken and well educated. But delusional, obviously. Completely naked, plays the pipes, really seems to believe it's true."

"Well," the young man observed, "if he believes it

enough to live it, he's making it true. Maybe not for you or me, but for himself."

"That's why I'm worried. He said he'd seen Syrinx. And Toni looks like Syrinx."

The man looked skeptical. "Did he describe Syrinx?"

"No. Does the myth describe her?"

He shrugged. "Not that my dad ever mentioned. And this Toni? What does she look like?"

"She's got hip-length blond hair. She looks like a statue of Venus."

His brows shot up. "Is that the reason you think he meant her? Or did he say something?"

"No." I tried to hope. "I mean, he never mentioned her specifically. It's just she looks so mythological."

"To you. But you said yourself he's delusional. You don't know how he sees things."

I took another sip of water, touching my cheeks because he kept staring at them. My skin was hot even in the shade.

"I've known a lot of delusional people," he continued, as if that would console me. "There's no point in guessing what they think. You have to focus on what they do."

"He picked her up from behind. He has enormous arms. He's short, but he's massive. He pinned her arms and lifted her right off the ground."

"Is she small? Your size?"

"What's your name?" I asked him.

"Martin." He smiled. "Martin Late Rain."

"Is that your real name?"

"I took it when I lived with the Tsimshians. Not that they have that type of name, but . . . I get a little

202

tired of disgracing my father's name." He grinned. "So does my father."

"Joel Baker." I watched for a reaction.

"Who's that?" There was no glint of recognition in his eyes, no twist of displeasure on his lips, no tensing of his shoulders.

"Didn't you say that was your name? Yesterday?"

He shook his head. "You know, I'm thinking you should lie down. My first aid isn't the best."

"I'm okay. I'm okay. I'm just worried."

"What about your first impression—can you trust it? You ran, so obviously you thought he was . . . dangerous? Acting crazy? But maybe that was based on what he said about Syrinx." He shrugged. "I wasn't there. I'm not trying to second-guess you."

I didn't want to go into all of it—my fight with Toni, my impression Pan was saving me from her.

I was still touching my cheek. I suddenly realized what felt wrong about it. It had swollen where Toni hit me. No wonder Martin treated me as if I'd had a tough hike.

It was sympathy I didn't deserve: "I shouldn't have run off and left her."

"Maybe she got away from him. And you don't really know what he was planning. Maybe he wanted to talk. Maybe that was his way of getting an audience."

I accepted his solace because I didn't want to cry. I didn't want to waste the time.

"Try to visualize where it happened," he urged. "Maybe I'll know where it is."

I poured a little water over my hand, touching it to my face. "I was walking above town. I was on the street past the turnoff for Big Basin." Where Toni had taken me just the day before. Why hadn't I remembered? Why hadn't I avoided it?

"I know the one. Houses with meadows. Horses grazing."

"I didn't see horses. But I did cut through a meadow. I went behind a house, then I doubled back. I took a turn, and I headed for the woods—oaks and firs, I—we—hadn't gone far, not that far into the woods. But afterward I ran farther. That's when I got turned around."

"Okay, let's slow down. You went into an oak and fir forest. That's good. Let's just talk about what you saw."

It was difficult to recall details because I'd been running. I closed my eyes; I had to try—or be overwhelmed by guilt.

I began listing what I remembered, whatever appeared to my mind's eye. By the time I was through, Martin was nodding, looking excited.

"I think I know. I'm not sure. But I think I know because of the stumps."

"The stumps?" I'd described running through a forest of big trees and stumps.

"Yes. Private property is my plague, my scourge—I hate getting busted for trespassing. A lot of times you can tell you're on private land. If it's parkland, you have no cut trees. If it's timberland, you get clear cutting. But on private property, you have owners cutting here and there for more sun or for firewood or for a few extra bucks or whatever."

"Isn't there a lot of private property around here?"

"A lot of everything—protected land, state land, timberland. But it tells me the direction you took from the houses into the forest. I think."

He stood.

"You've lived here that long?" How devoted could industrial spies be?

"This is the fourth year I've come here. Canada's having a late winter, or I'd be gone already."

I tried to stand, but I got dizzy.

"No, stay. I'll go check it out," he said. "Not to worry. I'll be back." He frowned. "I can call someone for you. Go into town for you. You want me to do that?"

What was the name of the resort Edward had chosen? Should I describe it? Or would that put Arthur in jeopardy?

Martin saw my hesitation. "You can trust me." When I still didn't answer, he added, "I understand why you don't want to. I know what this"—he gestured at the meat-smoking racks, the campfire ring—"looks like to most people."

"Did you know Billy Seawuit?"

His expression brightened. I thought he was about to say yes—though he'd denied it yesterday.

Instead he answered, "Do you want me to call him for you?"

I shook my head. "No. No, don't call anyone. I'll come with you. I don't want to be alone."

"It's a ways. I don't know if you'll . . ."

"I'll be okay."

"If you want me to hurry, you'd better let me go alone," he pointed out. "You'll be fine here. You're welcome to some jerky. Although it's a little hard on the system if you're not used to it."

"You won't know if you're in the wrong spot."

"Do you really think you'd recognize it?"

He was right; I'd wandered for hours today not recognizing anything.

I could hardly bear the indecision: I didn't want to stay here, I didn't want to move.

"Can I be honest with you?" Martin said.

"Yes."

"You don't look good. You look pretty bad, in fact. If there's anyone I can call, anyone with an off-road vehicle? We could get them within three-quarters of a mile of here."

I stood. Everything ached. If I could just get back, find out about Toni, I'd spend the night soaking in a bath.

"I'm a fast walker," he insisted. "I could be back here in two hours. A little longer, if you want me to make a call for you. We could get someone here to help you."

Still I waffled.

"Even if there's no one you want me to call—or you don't want to give me a phone number or whatever—you'll be in better shape to hike out later. I can get you back at night, that's no problem. Night hiking's easy on a clear night like this."

I looked up at the sky. Sundown yellows mingled with evening blues.

I'd been running, fighting, walking all day, since maybe ten-thirty. He was probably right.

I described the spot for him again, everything I could recall about where I'd left Toni Nelson. "And you won't mind hiking me into town when you get back?"

"No, I won't mind."

"I'll be able to handle it by then." This was more for my ears than for his. "But you should call the

Nelsons. Call and see if Toni's home yet. If she isn't . . ." What if Galen Nelson was right? What if "Martin Late Rain" really was an industrial spy named Joel Baker? Would he call?

Or would he take off and leave me here?

"What's the matter? Person to person, okay? I know you probably live in some city, and you haven't been able to trust anyone for as long as you can remember. But this is the woods." He looked around. "The high chaparral. The way it used to be when the Great Spirit and the Great Mother got a little respect. I'm not going to hurt you."

"Can you call someone for me anonymously?"

"I don't care if you're in trouble or what your trip is. Really. I'm happy to help you. That's how simple it can be. Okay?"

"Okay." What could I have him tell Galen Nelson? If Toni hadn't come home, what message would Nelson take seriously, take straight to the police?

"Call Galen Nelson. If he's not in the phone book, ask around town; people seem to know each other. He runs Cyberdelics—he might still be there. You could check?"

"Okay."

"But even if he's there, even if Cyberdelics is still open, phone it, okay? Don't go in."

"I don't have to tell him the message is from you." He removed his hat, fanning his face. His stubbled scalp was much whiter than his cheeks. "Sometimes a message seems more important if it walks in. Versus phones."

"No, you don't want to talk to Galen Nelson in person," I insisted. "Call Cyberdelics if it's still open. Or get the number of his house. If Toni's not back, tell him Pan grabbed her in the woods. Tell him the spot. Tell him it was around ten-thirty this morning."

Hat still in hand, he executed an elaborate bow. Then, he took off through the scrub. He was right: He walked very damn fast.

I returned to the small lean-to, picking up Martin's paperback while there was still enough light to read. I checked it and every other paperback there, looking for an inscription or a name. One was stamped Rutgers University Library.

I looked through his clothes—yesterday's white shirt and blue vest, dark pants, two pairs of socks—looking for ID. I didn't find any.

He had a few cooking utensils and a small store of spices: salt, sugar, pepper, dried mushrooms. He also had water purifying tablets and, inexplicably, a handful of mothballs.

I found no notebook or walkie-talkie or laptop computer; nothing to suggest industrial spying.

I thought I remembered seeing the fire ring and drying rack on the other side of the lean-to yesterday, but other than that, nothing struck me as odd or amiss.

I lay down, keeping my hand between my cheek and the dirty rabbit fur. Maybe I could trust him, after all.

I hoped so. It was getting dark quickly. And I'd never felt so alone or insecure.

I lay still. The air smelled of dust and hot plants cooling in the night. I heard the scritching of birds or mice, the tap of a woodpecker.

The tapping was rhythmic, as quick as a racing pulse. It reminded me of Arthur's drumming last night. It reminded me of my strange waking dream.

I had seen a mountain lion, not unlike Tuesday

morning's. I had looked it in the eye, and it had communicated something to me.

It had told me to follow Arthur.

It had taken me over a surreally natural landscape, but that was the only statement it had made. To follow Arthur.

I wondered what it meant. I wondered if my subconscious mind had noticed something, heard something, worried about something. I wondered if it had been a warning, a clue, a guidepost.

And then I fell asleep.

I was shaken awake—moments later, I thought. But it was pitch black outside a circle of lantern light. A man squatted in front of the lantern, close by me. I could see his silhouette.

"Martin?" I could hear the quaver in my voice. I blinked, hoping it wasn't the spurious backpackers instead.

"Martin?" Edward's voice was impatient. "Who the hell's Martin, and what are you doing up here? Jesus, I've been looking for you everywhere. Everywhere. For hours. What did you come up here for?"

I threw my arms around him.

He stiffened. "What's wrong? What happened?"

"Toni," I said. "Have you seen her?"

"No."

"Pan grabbed her. I ran. I don't know what he did to her."

"Whoa, back up. When was this?" He pulled his lantern closer. It lighted his face eerily from the bottom up. "What happened to you? Did this Baker guy beat on you? You're not—" He checked my feet, I supposed to see if they were tied. "What happened?"

"Toni hit me. I ran, and she chased me into the woods. We fought—I hit her, too."

Edward looked astonished.

"Well, she tackled me, Edward. She started it."

"Just move along. What else happened?"

"Pan pulled her off me. I thought he was saving me, helping me." I could feel tears spring to my eyes. "I wasn't thinking. I took off, and then, when it occurred to me, I went back. Or I tried to. I was lost. I don't know if I've spent the day going in circles or what. But I didn't stop until I got here. And then Martin said—"

"Martin being?"

"The kid with the shaved head."

"Joel Baker? The guy Nelson says is Joel Baker? I gather he doesn't call himself that."

"He says the same thing today that he said yesterday." I decided not to mention having sprung the name Joel Baker on him. I didn't think Edward would approve.

"Well, he might say the same thing, but he ain't on the same hill."

"This isn't where we found him before?"

"Lewis and Clark, you're not. No. He's about a quarter-mile east."

I wondered what it meant. Had we spooked him? Had he moved to preserve his hermitage . . . or his secrets?

"So go on," Edward pressed. "You sent him out to look for Toni?"

"He had me describe the spot where it happened. He thought he could find it. That was right before nightfall."

"What did you expect him to find there? You think

Pan stayed there all day with Toni? Not likely." He rubbed the spot between his brows.

"I told him to phone the Nelsons. I told him to tell Galen. If Toni's not back, I mean."

He shook his head.

"Man," he said finally, "this is going to look terrible. If the cops come into this now, this is going to look really terrible."

I wanted to hit him. Martin Late Rain had at least tried to offer some consolation, some hope.

"I'm well aware of that, Edward, believe me. I've done nothing but worry about this all day. All day."

"Well, at least I found you. I was about five minutes away from getting hysterical." He rose, extending a hand to help me to my feet. "Let's get you out of here before this Martin-Joel comes back."

I cried out when I stood up. Everything ached, absolutely everything.

"Come on," he urged. "I don't want us anywhere around when he gets here. You sent him toward town, right?"

"He was going to go into town to phone."

"Yeah, sure," Edward said. "We'll try not to cross paths with him."

"I think he's who he says he is, Edward. One of his books even has a Rutgers Library stamp in it."

"So I guess you know where Joel Baker went to college?" Edward gave me his arm, started me walking.

I felt like a stiff seventy-year-old. "Rutgers?"

"How should I know? The point is, a book—probably a used book at that—doesn't prove zilchola. Come on, granny, I know it's hard. But try to hustle."

Such was the quality of my company for the next hour or so.

But it was worth it in the end. It was worth it to climb into Edward's Jeep, to be once again on a padded seat in a heated interior.

When we reached the rented cabin, I went straight into the bath. Edward was dialing the Nelsons, shushing Arthur so he wouldn't be heard in the background.

I had done all I could for now. For now, I would soak.

Edward tapped at the door with the news: Toni Nelson wasn't home. Galen had just walked in the door himself. He'd received no call alerting him she'd been snatched.

He expected us over immediately to tell him more.

I climbed reluctantly out of my bath. If I went to Galen Nelson's, he'd want me to talk to the police. And I couldn't do that: I couldn't take the chance they'd discover my identity. That would bring Don Surgelato back here; and he'd learn Edward had lied to him. He'd know I'd been hiding here—that I'd been an accomplice, not a hostage, in the Financial District getaway. Sooner or later, because of the local murder, because Seawuit was Arthur's assistant, Surgelato—or some other cop—would realize Arthur fit the gunman's description. As terrible as I felt about Toni, I couldn't risk leading the police to Arthur.

Didn't Edward see that?

I quickly dried off and dressed. I left the bathroom ready to explain, plead, argue with Edward.

He was nowhere in sight.

"He's gone," Arthur reassured me. "He didn't think it would be a very good idea for you to join him. He was going to tell them you went back to . . . did you ever say where you're supposed to have come from?"

"I'm not sure."

"Well, no doubt he'll think of a place," Arthur said. He bounced slightly, looking happy to be on an actual bed. "Do you know, it appears you have a black eye?"

"Part of my disguise. Like Abbie Hoffman's nose job."

I crawled into the other bunk, grateful Arthur didn't press for details.

It struck me that he wasn't a difficult companion, even under the worst of circumstances. He kept saying he'd been lucky to have Billy Seawuit. But Seawuit, I thought, had been equally lucky to have Arthur.

CHAPTER TWENTY-TWO

I hadn't slept in a real bed since leaving my own on Monday morning. But I didn't sleep well. Nightmares—the kind that leave you drenched and gasping—woke me several times. The last of these, at dawn, left me fully awake.

It had seemed so real. I'd been sitting behind a sewing machine stitching seams on blue curtains, while all around me women wept. It had seemed real because I'd once spent two months in the San Bruno jail. The matron had forced us to sew curtains all day, every day—I never learned why. I'd been shocked how much crying I'd heard there—heartbroken, constant weeping, some of it mine. On visiting day, mothers who'd seen their children were inconsolable.

I would do anything not to go back. I just wasn't sure I could think of any more to do.

I'd been lying there about half an hour when I heard voices. A woman seemed to be answering questions fairly close to our cabin. A man's deep rumble didn't resolve itself into words. But the woman's voice was sharper and higher. I heard her say, "No, nobody like that checked in," and, "No, I'd remember her."

I went to the window. Unlike Edward's place, this one had blinds. I parted the slats. A man in an olive uniform and a cop's utility belt stood with his back to me. I supposed he was a sheriff. He was speaking to a woman with a dog on a leash. He was showing her something.

My paranoia told me it was Toni Nelson's photograph. He was looking for someone who'd seen her.

I crept back to bed, heart pounding. The voices grew closer. Not half a minute later, I heard the woman say, "You aren't planning to go knocking on cabin doors, are you? Our guests expect their privacy."

I supposed the cop agreed; he didn't knock on mine.

But it seemed likely he was searching for Toni. And that meant she hadn't come home. All night.

What did Pan do to her?

I started shaking. How could I have been so stupid, so selfish, so shortsighted? I felt my fingers knot into my hair.

I lay there a long time, watching the room grow brighter, listening to Arthur's rhythmic wheezing.

When the door opened a while later, I screamed.

"It's just me." Edward shut it.

Arthur sat up in bed, looking alarmed. "Ah, the cat," he said.

"I thought you were in court this morning."

Edward, in gray slacks and a sport jacket, nodded. He set a paper bag down on our tiny Formica table. "Continuance. I came straight up from the courthouse."

"The sheriff was here earlier. I heard him ask the resort manager about a missing person."

Edward squatted in front of my bed. His face was grim. "Good. They must be searching for Toni."

"How did Galen Nelson react? What did you tell him?"

"I told him you saw this Pan guy drag her off." He scowled. "The way he took it was way odd. He basically dismissed it; let me know he didn't really believe us about Pan."

"But yesterday he apologized for not believing us."

"Bingo." Edward shook his head. "And last night he was saying, no, don't worry, Toni's out late all the time. I stressed that you'd seen her get dragged away. You know, naked man runs off with your wife, you're supposed to show a little concern." He shrugged. "He says she crashes on her ex-husband's couch once in a while. But he wouldn't give the guy a call. Obviously did *not* want to talk to him."

"Did you find out where Stu lives?"

"Yesterday afternoon. I went by there. The place isn't far from the Nelsons'—a hell of a lot more run-down, though. It didn't look like anyone had been there lately—garden parched, no trash in the can. I went by several times last night, finally took a look inside. Stopped there again this morning."

"You broke in?"

"Well, yeah." He ran his hand over his hair. "I had to make sure."

"But she wasn't there."

"And neither was Stu. The place was tidied up, no perishables in the frig, empty space where the computer should be."

"Did you tell Nelson?"

"I didn't want to let on I'd been snooping. I just tried to shame him into calling. But he kept saying you didn't seem reliable, that he didn't believe you. Giving me attitude. This kind of thing." Edward sucked in his cheeks, looking cold and guarded. I was shocked how much the expression changed his looks. "I reminded him I'd seen Pan, too."

"I don't get it, Edward. He said he believed us about Pan. He apologized for not taking it as a warning."

"I don't know what to tell you. That photo of the kid and his lean-to, it made a huge difference. When we went to the cops about the break-in, Nelson practically clapped his hand over my mouth when I brought up Pan. He gave the cops Joel Baker's picture and said—"

"I don't think he is Joel Baker. He probably just moved his camp for privacy. He says he's—"

"Whoever the hell he is. That's who Nelson wanted to talk about—and he pretty much wanted to do all the talking." Edward again ran a frustrated hand over his hair. "Last night, I started wondering if Nelson didn't have Toni stashed somewhere. It was almost like he knew she was okay." He raised his brows. "Or he absolutely didn't care."

"Maybe he thinks she ran off with Stu."

"Or wishes she did. Or wants people to think so."

"I'll bet Martin Late Rain did call him. I'll bet Nelson lied."

"Well, I guess Nelson finally got worried if the sheriff's looking for her. Unfortunately, they'll be looking for you, too, Alice."

Arthur asked, rather timidly. "Why would they be looking for Willa?"

"She witnessed a possible abduction. I assume they've got messages in to me by now, too. I phoned them last night."

"You called the sheriff?"

"It didn't look like Nelson was going to. So I went into town and did it. I told them they'd better call him right away about his wife because a friend of mine saw her get dragged off by a naked man. I didn't go in person, anything like that. I didn't tell them who I was or who my friend was. But I assume Nelson did. I thought they'd call me at home last night, but . . . Maybe Nelson didn't give them my name, I don't know. I don't understand the guy—what a cold fish."

"You're sure the police believed you—that they knew it was for real?"

Maybe I should have come out of hiding. Maybe I'd further endangered Toni Nelson by not going to the police in person.

"Well, the sheriff is looking for her," Edward pointed out. "Unless there are two missing women on this mountain. Speaking of which, I've got something for you."

"What?"

"A disguise, Watson."

Arthur seemed alarmed. "Another one? Why?"

"The BC cops might be looking for Alice, wanting to hear what she saw. Interesting to see your astrological chart this week, Willa: —You will be widely sought after.'" He rose from his squat and walked to the table. "It's time to lose that hair." He held up the bag. "Clippers and hair dye. And some makeup for the eye. We ain't leaving this cabin till you're cuter than Abbie Hoffman."

"I'm not cutting my own hair, Edward."

"Yeah," he said, "better let the prison matron do it for you." He tossed me the bag. "Hurry. Checkout time's eleven."

"We're not staying here?"

"Can't. You have a way of making a place too hot for you, baby." He seemed to think he was imitating James Cagney.

An hour later, I had blond hair again; luckily, the chemical-burn look was being popularized by techies and slackers. I'd hacked it so the sides angled into the bangs.

"From Prince Valiant to Friar Tuck," Edward commented. I noticed he'd changed into jeans and a T-shirt. "All right. So we're ready?"

"Where are we going?"

"Into town. Santa Cruz."

"No!" Arthur shook his head. "We mustn't leave the mountain."

"The hell we mustn't. We've got sheriffs running around here. They're going to be watching for Alice."

"Take Willa, then. But not me. I'm so close."

"Close to what?"

"To knowing."

"Arthur." Edward cast me a "you raised him wrong" look. "You can't talk to anyone up here, anyway. Right?"

"I can talk to the place," he insisted. "It's much less likely to lie than a person."

"So's your subconscious, wouldn't you say?"

Of all the times for Edward to get flaky on me. "Where do you want to take—"

"Right, Arthur?" Edward held up a hand to shush me. "If we could get into your brain and play a movie of everything you saw when that guy handed you a gun? All the stuff you consciously forgot. Wouldn't it tell you something about who killed Billy? You know the two events have to be related."

Arthur merely blinked. "But I'd planned to go to Bowl Rock . . ."

"What are you talking about, Edward?" I demanded. "What's this crap about Arthur's subconscious?"

"Yours, too. I know a guy who's a hypnotist. He's going to hypnotize you today. Tell us more about what happened in San Francisco."

I didn't know how to feel about it. "Do you trust him? He won't call the police?"

"No, he won't. I guarantee it."

Arthur looked uncomfortable. "I don't believe the brain is that type of structure, Edward. I don't believe consciousness is divided, you know, according to that Freudian paradigm. I don't believe it's like a suitcase, with a compartment for lingerie under the zipper. I see it as an access device, a way into an infinite number of realities."

"Well, but Arthur," Edward's patience seemed to be fraying. "None of that really matters. However it works, there are details you won't remember except under hypnosis. And they might be helpful. You guys can't be hiding out forever; we need a breakthrough. I'm just being practical."

Arthur continued to look troubled. "I've done a lot of journeying, Edward, shamanic journeying. I don't want to let anyone into those places with me."

Edward looked like he suddenly got it. "Oh, no; you have my word. He'll focus on what happened in San Francisco just before Wonder Woman here flew off with you."

"It's not just that."

"I'll make sure he backs away from anything personal. Honest."

"The minute you enter someone else's reality, even to retrieve a stray detail . . ." Arthur put his hand on Edward's shoulder. "I believe there's something in criminal law called the 'plain view doctrine.' " Arthur had spent time in prison because of it. He'd met my father there. "When the police come to your house for a legitimate purpose, and they see evidence of a crime in plain view—"

"I'm familiar with the doctrine," Edward assured him.

In Arthur's case, a policeman had seen a blowpipe containing a vision-quest snuff used in the Amazon. It led to a search that turned up LSD, which Arthur didn't know had been made illegal.

"I just don't want to have to worry about it for real," Edward continued.

"I'm afraid we've made Edward an accessory after the fact," I explained.

Arthur looked horrified. "But all he did was hide us."

I watched Edward grin.

"That's the main definition of the crime, Arthur. Edward's right. We have to do something."

"You don't understand the importance of what I *am* doing." Arthur's tone was gentle.

"It's just that we were both freaked out Monday morning. Who knows what we might have noticed but not registered?"

Having to back up Edward put me at a disadvantage. I wasn't sure I wanted anyone poking through my memories, either.

"When would we return here?"

"How long will it take the hypnotist to do his number?" Edward redrafted the question, perhaps unwilling to promise we'd return. "Maybe an hour and a half, two hours."

I felt panic rise. In a college town like Santa Cruz, someone might recognize Arthur.

"If they find Toni today, we can come back. Right, Edward?"

"Yes, we'll come back, won't we?"

Faced with my need for Toni to be all right and Arthur's need to commune with the mountain, Edward looked like a cornered parent.

And in fact, he said, "You kids will have to ask your mother about that."

CHAPTER TWENTY-THREE

I was nervous. We were in a tiny office with rattan furniture and a wall of windows overlooking a ravine. It had all the hallmarks of a therapist's office: a desk with a laptop computer and a big-numbered digital clock, a chair opposite a couch, and Kleenex on every end table.

I'd been in therapy a few months, stopping when it became unaffordable. I couldn't decide if it had helped or not. I preferred *not* discussing my problems on a regular basis. On the other hand, they weren't going away just because I was ignoring them.

Now, sitting on this couch, Kleenex at hand, I felt a Pavlovian need to whine. Or maybe it was because Edward sat beside me.

His therapist/hypnotist friend, an outdoorsy-looking man about our age, sat in the desk chair, which he'd rolled around to face the chair opposite the couch. He and Arthur sat almost knee to knee. He was holding up a device that flashed light, almost like a tiny strobe light. He also played an ocean-waves audiotape with, we were told, subliminal commands to relax.

He had warned us, after Edward's sotto-voce to pass the popcorn, not to say anything or make any noise, and to keep our movements to an absolute minimum. He usually preferred complete privacy, he told us pointedly.

Edward's response had been, "Yeah, yeah, Fred, let's get on with it."

We'd been sitting there several minutes already, watching Arthur watch the light. It seemed to me his facial muscles had grown flaccid. Though he'd doubted he could be hypnotized, he looked pretty well zombified to me.

But it was a little longer before Fred said, in that soothing therapist voice, "Can you hear me, Arthur?"

Arthur's face remained blank, his eyelids half-lowered. "Yes," he replied.

"Can you tell us your name and date of birth?"

I was surprised to learn the two of us had the same birthday.

"Can you tell us where you are now?"

"With you," he said dully.

"And where are we both?"

"In your office."

"Fine." He clicked off the audiotape. "Now we're going to go back into your recollections. Can you recall last Monday morning?"

A slight hesitation. "Yes."

"Tell us about waking up that morning, Arthur."

"Pain. Arthritis in my neck. I shouldn't fall asleep in a chair; it's painful when I rise."

"Where is this chair? Are you at your home?"

"No," Arthur replied. "I might have had a home

with Nina, but the regret has settled into my bones as arthritis. That was a long time ago."

Fred looked startled. I wondered if he was used to more direct answers from the subconscious mind. "Where is your home now, Arthur?"

"Ah, I wish I knew."

Fred showed a spark of ingenuity: "Where are your books and papers?"

"In storage. New Haven, Connecticut."

"And things you've acquired since leaving Yale?"

"Vancouver Island."

Fred kept the frustration on his face out of his voice. "And your daily necessities? Change of clothes, toiletries?"

"My hotel."

"What hotel is that?"

"In San Francisco. On Stockton Street."

Edward had gotten the address his first night with us. He'd made sure the hotel wasn't adding daily charges to Arthur's credit card. No one looking for Arthur would be led there based on this week's credit transactions.

"Did you awaken in your hotel room Monday morning?"

"Yes," he confirmed. "On a wing chair."

"Tell us what you did then."

"I bathed. I ordered eggs and toast. The coffee was very weak. I dressed."

"Where were you going Monday morning?"

It was difficult not to sit forward. Arthur had always been vague about this, saying only that he'd had no particular business, that he'd been strolling.

"To the place the dove specified."

Fred glanced at us, brows raised. His cheeks were

sun- or wind-burned, with goggle-shaped whiteness around the eyes. "And who is the dove?"

"My power animal."

"Can you explain?"

I looked at Edward. He had agreed to keep the hypnotist out of Arthur's shaman stuff. But Edward just sat there, chewing the inside of one cheek.

"I was advised while journeying. I was told I would meet someone on the street."

"When did this journey take place, Arthur?"

"Billy and I were in the rock."

"What day was this?"

"It was Saturday."

"Saturday, two days before that Monday morning?"

"Yes." Arthur's face remained slack, his speech relatively uninflected. It was almost as if a ventriloquist spoke for him.

"What time of day on Saturday were you inside the rock with Billy?"

I wondered how well Edward had prepped Fred. Obviously well enough for him to follow up on this.

"Sunrise."

"Why were you there together, Arthur?"

"We sensed a transition. A loss and a gain. Powerful forces at play. We had questions."

"Can you tell us more about this?"

I nudged Edward. We'd promised not to let Fred intrude. But Edward cast me a cranky glance, shaking his head.

"We had learned to journey together. We'd guessed the significance of the rock."

"And what is that, Arthur?"

"It's a boat."

"Can you explain what you mean by that?"

"The Makah and the Salish and the Kwakiutl, the Haida, the Nootka, the Tsimshian, all of them hollowed logs to make vast canoes fit for rough seas. This was a stone canoe, used not by the local Costanoans, but by shamans who predated them: This was our feeling. It was a vessel for a particular spiritual quest. It's at the edge of a clearing shaped like an inlet, the best place from which to launch. But a dugout canoe can't be managed by oneself, not through rough water. So we tried together at sunrise."

"This was last Saturday at dawn."

"Yes."

"And Monday—"

Edward waved to catch Fred's attention. Fred glanced over, scowling. He saw Edward shaking his head, and mouthing the word "Saturday."

Fred seemed irritated.

Nevertheless, he said, "Arthur, tell us what happened on Saturday."

"Our journey couldn't be completed." Desolation changed his voice. "The water was rough. It boiled with an emotion, a spell cast upon us, a terrible jealousy."

"Were you jealous of Billy, Arthur?"

"No."

"He of you?"

"No."

"Whose jealousy, then?"

"It was Hera."

"And who is Hera?"

I was afraid I knew the answer.

Sure enough, Arthur told him, "The wife of Zeus."

Fred cast Edward a glance that said, Satisfied?

"How long were you together in the rock, Arthur?"

"We got as far as we could. But we capsized. The dove and the raven came for us. The dove said someone waited for me in San Francisco. So I left Billy." His brow crimped. His eyes, open only slightly, glinted with tears. "How strange of the raven to say nothing, to offer no warning. Why?" Arthur moaned. "Where's Billy now? Why can't I find him?"

Fred's glance at Edward was furious.

"Let's go back to Monday, Arthur, this last Monday morning. You've eaten breakfast in your hotel room. Now what do you do?" He waited a moment for Arthur's response. Then he repeated, "It's last Monday, after breakfast."

"I check my clock, and I see it's time. So I leave my hotel."

"What is your destination, Arthur?"

"Montgomery Street. I've been told to follow the morning river to the Banker's Heart."

"Who told you this?"

"The dove."

"And what did you take it to mean, Arthur?"

"Montgomery Street."

I noticed Edward's smile. The Banker's Heart was a huge hunk of black marble set by some ironic sculptor in the Bank of America Plaza. On Montgomery Street.

"I had gone there Sunday morning," Arthur said softly. "And I'd found it deserted. The pedestrian river flows only on weekdays."

"So you went there again on Monday?"

"Yes," Arthur agreed. "To meet the person."

"Can you recall the moment that you reached Montgomery Street?"

"Yes." Arthur sounded surprised. "A blue car

honked at me when I crossed in front of it. A woman looked at me as if she knew my face. And there was a young man eating a brownie."

"That's excellent, Arthur. Can you describe what you see as you continue walking?"

Arthur's narrative rambled: an attractive woman, a man with an interesting umbrella, eyeglasses similar to ones he'd owned years ago, an unusual flower in a planter box. He listed things as if choosing them at random from a movie of his walk.

"That's fine, Arthur. That's excellent. Can you go now to the moments just before someone handed you a gun?"

Edward shook his head slightly. Did he consider this a leading question? Did he doubt Arthur's story?

"I had been walking quite a while, up and back. Not doubting—but I was slowing down. I was looking more particularly. People passed by me. A woman in a green raincoat, a man in pinstripes, they flowed past. Behind me, someone muttering; that's when . . ."

"Go on, Arthur."

"He handed me the gun."

"Why don't we slow down just a bit. Let's go back a few minutes before you feel the gun in your hand, Arthur. Can you go back to that approximate moment?"

Arthur didn't say anything. He frowned, a tic developing in the corner of his eye.

"Are you back in that moment, Arthur?"

"Yes."

"Can you freeze it in your mind as if you were pausing a film?"

A few seconds later, he said, "Yes."

"Then let's talk about what you see. What do you see closest to you?"

"A woman in a beige trenchcoat, a man raising his jacket collar, a young fellow with a hat over a shaved head, a canvas safari hat. There's an eagle feather in the hatband."

Edward nudged me.

"A girl trying to put up an umbrella," Arthur continued. "Such a lot of umbrellas up, and yet it isn't very wet. They look like corks bobbing in a river."

"Let's keep looking close by you for another moment," Fred suggested. "Who else is standing near?"

"A couple passing on my right, chatting. He says, 'We'll cream them in court,' and she says, 'That's naive.' A conversation behind me, too. I don't pay attention."

"Can you pay attention now, Arthur?"

"But it's not . . . it's only one person—" His voice picked up a whisper of bewilderment. "Talking to himself. Something about the police."

"Arthur, what can you tell me about his voice?" Fred looked much more excited than he sounded. I wondered if therapists took workshops from FM deejays.

"It's not an old enough voice."

"Old enough for what, Arthur?"

"For the man who made the fuss. It's a younger voice."

"Then what happens?" Fred was looking flushed in his unbuttoned shirt and earth-tone blazer.

"I feel something in my hand. I don't want it, I'm going to let it drop. But the voice is whispering, 'Take it take it take it.' Something hard with a sleek surface. I don't know why I let my fingers close around it. I suppose I don't want it to drop. Someone behind me values it, and so I don't want it to break. I try to see who's doing this, but we're too crowded, it's difficult. My neck won't turn easily this morning."

"What do you feel in your hand, Arthur?"

"The scarf. I raise my hand to look at it. It's a silk scarf."

"Can you describe it?"

"It's yellowish. It has a pattern of tiny brown dots."

"What style is the scarf?"

"I don't know. Masculine, perhaps an ascot. I can tell now that there's a gun in it. When I open my hand to look at the gun, the scarf slides away." He paused a moment. "Odd—it falls quickly, as if there's a weight attached. It slides away, and I hardly notice it." His frown looked painful. "I'm so surprised—I open my hand to look, and I almost drop it. I'm fumbling, perhaps that's why the scarf falls."

For a moment he said nothing. But his frown deepened. His eyes moved from side to side as if he were dreaming.

"What's happening around you now, Arthur? Can you freeze the movie at the next frame?"

"Two men pass me on my left. They rush past. One's bulky. He wears a fedora and a trenchcoat. One is smaller. He wears an anorak and jeans. He's hatless. He turns and glances at me. I've stopped walking, you see. He turns as if he's irritated. I'm a logjam in the river."

"Do you recognize him or his companion, Arthur?"

"No," he said. "A man in front of me raises his hands and begins shouting for help."

"Is this someone you've noticed on the street before?"

"No."

"Can you see where he came from?"

"No."

"Did he come from behind you, Arthur?"

"I was looking at the gun. Not at the street."

"But you noticed two men when they passed you."

"Yes," he confirmed.

"But you didn't notice this man approaching you?"

"No. I only stopped staring at the gun because I heard him shouting for help. I found him looking at me. It startled me."

"What did you do then, Arthur?"

"I tightened my grip on the gun. I was afraid it might discharge if I dropped it. And I looked around to see why the man was shouting."

"What did you see when you looked around?"

It took him a minute to respond. Edward was sitting forward, elbows on his knees. I held my breath, waiting for Arthur to say more.

"The young man with the eagle feather in his hat. He was behind me. I caught a glimpse of him over my shoulder, the back of his head. He was walking away from me."

"You'd seen him earlier."

"Yes. He'd walked past me some moments before. He was walking away from me again."

Fred looked at Edward, nodding. His voice remained phlegmatic. "What else did you notice, Arthur?"

"The man who was shouting. Before he put his hands up, he reached into his pocket. He fiddled with something there."

"Can you describe the motion, Arthur?"

"No. Just that he reached in and did something. Or checked something."

"Then what did he do?"

"He raised his arms and called for help."

"Can you see the people around him, Arthur?"

"Yes."

"How are they responding to his calls?"

"A woman is panicking. She backs into another woman. A man and a woman pass by quickly, hardly glancing at him. Another man looks irritated by the noise he's making. A woman on his left seems angry until she sees me, then she looks scared."

"And what is the man doing now?"

"He's telling me I can have his wallet."

"What happens then, Arthur?"

"Other people move over as they walk. A woman crouches. A man blocks foot traffic by throwing out his arms. He speaks over his shoulder to people coming up behind him. One of them doubles back, breaking into a run. A voice behind me says, 'Stay back, stay back, he's got a gun.' The man tells me not to shoot and that he'll reach into his pocket and give me his wallet." Arthur stopped. His breathing had quickened. " 'No, don't do that,' I tell him. And I see a policeman. I feel such relief. I can straighten it out now, you see. I say, 'Officer.' But I can't say more right now. Willa has suddenly put herself in front of me. I'm looking down at the top of Willa's head. She can't seem to part her hair properly; I've always meant to tell her."

My hand strayed to my part. It would have been straighter if I hadn't just run my hand through my hair.

"She says, 'If you back up, he won't hurt me.' And

so I try to back up, but there's someone behind me. I say, 'But Willa,' and she says, 'Will you what? Will you kill me?' I don't understand; I simply don't understand her. I look at the man in front of her and at the officer, and they seem very surprised. They're goggling as if Willa meant me, so I explain that I'd never hurt her. Then Willa says, 'Maybe if you let him go, he'll let me go.' I still don't comprehend who she means. The policeman is paying a great deal of attention to her, but I simply can't determine the context. There are so many people about. Some are backing away, and some are running. Everyone is staring at Willa. The policeman is very young and has a crewcut and has nicked himself shaving. There's minor pandemonium, and I'm hoping Willa will turn to me and tell me what she fears so that I can help her."

Edward looked at me, shaking his head.

"Go on, Arthur." Fred's tone was gentle. "What happens then?"

I listened to Arthur tell the rest of the story from his point of view. Having been there, I knew the facts. But he described a completely different reality from the one I'd experienced.

From Arthur's perspective, I had exploded onto the scene and demanded he come with me. I had pulled him into my gravitational field like a rogue comet, and he had followed and obeyed because my determination left him no alternative.

I slumped on the couch, arms wrapped around myself. Maybe if I hadn't intervened, Arthur could have explained about the gun, pointed out the scarf. Maybe the cop would have believed him. Maybe the whole thing would have been cleared up with only minor inconvenience.

I'd be at work right now, and Arthur would be dealing openly with the police about Billy Seawuit's murder.

I felt like I was staring at the corpse of my future happiness. I looked around Fred's office, hoping to distract myself before I cried. I glanced at the clock: We'd been here forty-seven minutes.

Fred was again guiding Arthur through the moment when I'd reached behind me, grabbing his arm and forcing him to follow me down an escalator.

Even in his trance state, Arthur looked bewildered.

I felt my hand wander toward the Kleenex. Any more of this and I was a goner.

Fred was prompting, "You followed Willa down the escalator, Arthur?"

"Yes, I followed her. Because I realized at that moment what it was really about. At that very moment, you see. I needn't have gone along with her. I knew Willa was running from the police and that running would not serve my interests. But I saw what it was truly about."

We waited. There wasn't a sound in the room except Arthur's breathing.

Finally, Fred said, "What did you realize, Arthur? What was it all about?"

"It was about Willa," he said firmly. "She was obviously the one I was supposed to meet. The dove had sent me there that morning to meet Willa." His face smoothed into relaxation. "And so I followed her and did as she wished. She was an emissary of a greater will, you see. Though I might not understand it in this context, she was clearly the vessel of grace."

Edward rolled his eyes.

I could only shrug modestly. It's not easy being a vessel of grace.

Moments later, Fred roused Arthur. He jumped, as if wakened from a dream.

"I was afraid I wouldn't be able to go under," he said apologetically.

"No, no," Fred assured him. "You were very clear in your remembrances. I'm sure it was very helpful."

Arthur's jaw dropped. "You mean we've been—?" He glanced at the clock. "Oh, my. We have been." He looked at me and Edward. "Was it useful?"

"Yes." Edward's tone was decisive. "Definitely. In fact, I think we can tell you who put the gun in your hand."

"Really?" Arthur sounded impressed.

"His name is either Joel Baker or Martin something, goes by Martin Late Rain, wears a safari hat. You spotted him—the hat, anyway—twice in the crowd on Monday. Me and Willa saw him up in the woods Wednesday; took his picture. Galen Nelson swears he's an industrial spy." Edward looked at me. "I shouldn't have let that photo out of my sight." Then, to Arthur: "Nelson talked me into letting the police have it. I haven't picked up the duplicate, and it's probably not the greatest idea for me to go into town today. Damn. Damn, I'd like to show it to you and get an ID."

I briefly described yesterday's encounter with him, feeling a little sheepish. "Martin Late Rain" had seemed so personable, so concerned about me. I'd much rather believe Galen Nelson was lying about him.

But the fact remained: "You told me Monday morning you'd had the 'feeling of an eagle,' " I reminded Arthur. "Just now, you said this person had an eagle feather in his hatband. I assume eagle feathers are pale gray?"

"Yes. With a black tip."

It sounded like Martin's—Joel's?—hat, all right.

"I'm impressed, quite amazed," Arthur said. "I didn't think this would come to anything."

Edward looked pleased with himself.

"May I remain when he questions you, Willa?"

"I guess so." But God, I hated the idea of Edward being there.

I reluctantly switched chairs with Arthur. It was no use asking Edward to leave. He was the private eye, after all. This was mostly for his benefit.

I sat there awhile, watching Fred's little strobe light and listening to his ocean-waves tape. My problems with Edward were insignificant compared to my problems with the police. If I could add anything to the knowledge pool . . .

A moment later, I seemed to wake up.

Fred nodded, smiling as if he knew me pretty well. I looked at the clock. Damn. A half hour had passed. What had I said?

I looked at Arthur. He wore a sentimental smile, and his eyes were damp.

I looked at Edward. He wore a huge grin.

"What?" I asked defensively.

Arthur answered, "I'm quite touched, my dear. Touched that you would risk so much for me. And impressed that you would act so decisively."

Edward laughed. "Mighty Mouse to the rescue!"

Fred wheeled himself back behind his desk. "You're being a jerk, Edward."

"You and your clinical jargon, Fred."

As soon as we left the office, Edward began humming the Mighty Mouse theme.

CHAPTER TWENTY-FOUR

We sat waiting for Edward in his Jeep. It was parked on what looked like a country road but was actually a rural pocket in the middle of Santa Cruz. Horses grazed in a wet meadow studded with huge oaks and ringed with Monterey cypress, their branches pointing inland. It was impressively bucolic, considering we were around the corner from a 7-Eleven. Edward was sitting atop a wooden fence, speaking into Fred's cellular phone. His booted feet were hooked between the rails. He faced the horses, giving us a view of his back.

Arthur seemed to be nodding out in the front seat. I could see his head bob.

Edward glanced over his shoulder, beckoning to me. I slid out the back, leaving the door open.

Edward had just clicked the phone off when I reached him. "Bad news," he said. "They still haven't found Toni Nelson. They've called for city cops to join the search."

He patted the spot next to him, offering me a hand

so I could climb up. "I need to talk to you about a couple of things."

"Okay." I tried to get comfortable on the rail, but I was still a mass of aches and strains.

Edward must have noticed my wince. "God, I almost forgot." He pulled something out of his pocket, handing it to me. It was a tiny container of pills. "Fred gets samples up the yin-yang. He noticed you were looking beat up and stiff. It's a painkiller. You're going to need it today."

"I thought Fred was a therapist." Only doctors got medicine samples. The label read: Tylenol with codeine.

"Psychiatrist. Which brings me to the first thing I want to talk to you about: Fred's not sure Arthur really went under."

I tried to unscrew the cap. "What do you mean? Of course Arthur went under. We were there, we saw him."

"His responses were pretty elaborate for a guy under hypnosis, that's what Fred thought. He just phoned to tell me. That's why I came out here to talk."

"I assumed you were just being rude."

"Thanks." He pulled the container out of my hand, opening it. "Take a couple—in case you need to 'rescue' someone later."

"Of course Arthur was under, Edward. You could see that, couldn't you?" I glanced behind me. Arthur was slumped in the front seat, sleeping. I hoped he wasn't hurting his neck. "His answers were elaborate because he's got that kind of brain. He's not your average man on the couch."

"That's true, too." Edward spilled two pills onto his palm, offering them to me.

I swallowed them without water. The way I felt this morning, anything would help.

"Fred did bring that up. And he admits there's a range in what you get from people under hypnosis." Edward shrugged, recapping the pain pills. "But he wanted me to know there was a significant possibility, as he put it, that Arthur was scamming us." He held up his hand to forestall my defense. "Just a possibility. Fred's no dummy—he's had a lot of experience. So I wanted to put it to you. It's no use me knowing something you don't."

"Well, I don't believe it." The pills had left a sour taste in my mouth.

"Okay. Subject change: We've got a choice to make, Willa. Either we go for it—go back up the mountain, cops and all, maybe bugger everything up so there's no talking our way out of it . . ."

"Or?"

"We get ourselves a lawyer right now and go that route."

A lawyer would pave the way for our surrender, negotiating limits to the charges against us. A man had been murdered, and a woman was missing; we might have information that would help the police investigate.

On the other hand, our futures would be at the mercy of San Francisco's district attorney, Mr. Law-and-Order himself, against whom my mother had organized rallies and about whom my father had written scathing cyberpamphlets.

Edward watched me. "I think it should be your decision, not Arthur's or mine."

I didn't disagree, but I wondered, "Why?"

"You're a vessel of grace, remember?"

"Ha ha."

"Because Arthur chose to trust you. In a weird way, you're his lawyer; he's put himself into your hands. And me, well, I came into this late."

I thought he was being uncharacteristically generous. "They'll throw charges at you, too, Edward. And your PI license will hang in the balance; you know that."

"Yeah, I do know that. I'm just telling you, I'll back you up either way."

I stared across the meadow at a cantering horse. Edward wasn't acting like himself. He was being overtly . . . well, loyal and kind. He might be those things at heart, but he usually kept them off the surface.

"Look, Willa, we've had a lot of hassles over the years. Especially over all that stuff . . ." He paused. We'd had a rough breakup, years ago. And he'd lied to me recently, using me to help an old girlfriend. "But, you know, I've always liked you a lot. I've always wished we could get past the bullshit and be friends."

This was a hell of an olive branch. He could end up in jail with no means of support when he got out.

"Okay," I said. "As far as I'm concerned, there's no choice. If we go to a lawyer, we're screwed. A little bad luck and Arthur's in prison forever."

He nodded. "That's what I thought you'd say. Well, today's going to be very interesting." He swung his legs over the fence and jumped off. "Arthur will be happy. We're going back up the mountain."

241

He walked toward the Jeep without offering me a hand down.

The engine was warming up when I climbed back in. Arthur was yawning behind his hand.

"Are we going to Bowl Rock now?" he nagged. "I know I can find out—"

"Yes," Edward said, backing the Jeep up. His head was turned as he looked through the rear windshield. I'd never seen him quite so somber. "But our first stop is Martin-Joel's. Assuming he's still in the same place."

I filled Arthur in: "He moved his lean-to after we saw him on Wednesday." Because we'd mentioned Billy Seawuit? "I guess that's the advantage of living like the local Indians—"

"No, no, Willa." Arthur turned to me, shaking his head. "The Costanoan tribes, including the Awaswas, lived in rucks, not lean-tos. They were much admired for their cleverness and mobility, as well as the durability of their ceremonial roundhouses."

"Oh. Galen Nelson thought he built the lean-to to impress Billy Seawuit. You know, with his knowledge of native culture."

"Nelson couldn't have understood Billy if he thought that. Billy used to lament that people expected him to be some kind of living monument," Arthur mused. "That historical interest in aboriginal cultures is just another way of rejecting today's natives." He sighed. "The problems they have now—no one knows how to deal with them. It's so much simpler to create exhibits and documentaries about who they used to be."

"Aren't you doing that, too, somewhat?" Edward

glanced over. "Keeping alive shamanic practices native people have walked away from?"

"Ah, but they haven't walked away from them, Edward. We persist in believing they perform rituals—rain dances, celebratory dances. But they really aren't 'dancing,' you know. They are journeying, just as they did thousands of years ago. Granted, many have converted to Western religions. And some just go through the motions, adopting the white man's misconception of a ritual reenactment. But shamanism is the one facet of the culture that fully survives. We simply have a blind spot about it. Perhaps I can show you a bit more of what I mean? When we go to Bowl Rock?" Arthur wasn't through lobbying for our return there.

"First things first. If Joel-or-Martin's around, you can ID him, and I can muscle him. We'll try to get the story on him. In the meantime, I've pulled in some favors. We'll get some information from Cyberdelics's bank, see how flush they are."

"Then we'll go to Bowl Rock?"

"Try to." With police combing the mountain for Toni Nelson, who knew how far we'd get.

Edward sped us up the mountain over dew-slick roads, occasionally hitting the windshield wipers. He took a different route this time, past a university that, from here, looked more like a ranch. We continued past smatterings of houses and fenced meadows onto a serpentine forest road.

As we wound through dark, wet redwoods, the pain pills began to silence my nagging body parts. I could spare the scenery the attention it deserved.

We began taking fire access roads, bumpy and muddy, so narrow in spots that limbs and vines scraped our doors. But we didn't see any other vehicles on the path less traveled.

Edward parked in a pocket of brush.

"Okay, brownie troop, we're here," he announced. "Time to win us a few more badges."

We hiked down a brambly ravine to a creek bed.

"Look familiar?" Edward asked me.

I murmured noncommittally.

"Well, it shouldn't. We're taking the back way in. Less visible from the chaparral; hopefully, Baker won't spot us."

Arthur, despite being twice our age and arthritic to boot, had no trouble keeping up. He seemed very much in the habit of covering rough ground.

Twenty minutes later, we climbed out of the ravine, through impossibly steep forest. We had to stop a time or two. I needed to catch my breath, though Arthur kindly pretended it was for his sake.

Eventually, the forest thinned to oak and pine and madrone. We started seeing stands of tough-leafed shrubs Arthur identified as coyote brush and ceanothus.

"It should be right over there." Edward picked up speed.

He pushed through the coyote brush, several yards ahead of us. I knew something was wrong when he said, "Oh, Jesus!"

I hurried. He'd already crossed to the lean-to by the time I saw it. He was squatting in front of it, waving his arm extravagantly.

He was waving away flies. I knew from the smell why he had to do it.

I stopped, staring at his back, at the cloud of black flies around him.

He turned. "Watch where you walk. We don't want to be messing up the scene."

Arthur had reached my side. "The scene?" he repeated.

"He's found a dead body."

"Who is it?" Arthur had good reason to sound alarmed.

"Martin Late Rain—Joel Baker. I assume." No other possibility had occurred to me. "Edward?" I could hear the fear in my voice. "Edward? It's not Toni, is it?"

"No." He appeared to be touching the body, looking beneath it. "No." He glanced back over his shoulder. "It's Pan," he said.

Arthur moaned.

"Pan?" It didn't make sense. I approached slowly, as if verification would lead to understanding.

"Watch where you walk. Don't step on anything, don't scuff any footprints."

He stood, stepping away from the fly-infested lean-to.

Pan lay there as if arranged in a glass coffin. His arms were folded across his chest, his eyes were closed, his feet were side by side. His pipes lay atop his chest.

He hardly looked real, he was so wide and powerfully built for his height. He looked like a blend of man and beast, with his ragged head and thick body hair.

And there were flies, more flies than I'd ever seen in one spot.

"He's cold as hell. He's been here awhile." Edward pointed to something strewn on the ground. "Smashed up mothballs. Camphor. Hikers carry it to keep animals out of their campsites. It kept the body from being snacked on. He looks like Sleeping Beauty, huh?"

There were withered manzanita blossoms at his feet and around his head.

"How did he die?"

Edward swatted away flies, covering his nose. "Let's back up a bit. But watch what you step on."

"Shouldn't we check how he died?"

"You're just not close enough to see. There's a huge wound under his hands. He was stabbed." Edward drew a line across his belly to indicate where. "Or rather, sliced open."

Arthur had walked slowly toward us, eyes glued to the sight. He seemed near tears.

"But he was magnificent," Arthur whispered. "Who would take such a person out of the world? Who would slaughter someone so unique?"

"I could hazard a guess," Edward said grimly.

The smell was nauseating me. "Who?"

"The tenant of this estate. You'll notice he's packed his bags and vacated."

"Why kill someone, then leave him in your own place? God, Edward, we're in a huge forest. He could have buried him someplace out of the way. Why beg the police to suspect you?"

"To suspect who? This guy doesn't realize we took his picture. He doesn't know Galen Nelson identified him." He wiped his hands on his jeans, looking disgusted. "He could count on it being a while before anyone stumbled across this body. Decomposed, it wouldn't show cause of death. The cops would assume this was the dead man's camp; that he died in bed, so to speak."

"Someone might find the body too soon." I shook my head. "Why take a risk you don't have to take?"

"Well, here's another possibility. Last night you sent Baker out to look for Toni—and Pan. Maybe he found Pan dead and carried him up here."

I must have looked shocked.

"Don't ask me why. Show him to you?" Edward sounded perplexed. "Perform some kind of native death ceremony?"

"Actually," Arthur offered, "the Awaswas and other Costanoans, like most Pacific Northwest tribes, cremated their dead."

"Maybe he was planning to do that. Maybe he laid Pan out, and then got spooked. Just picked up and ran."

I looked around. Martin's drying racks were dismantled, and his potatoes were scattered. The campfire ring stones were nowhere to be seen.

I stepped a little farther from the body. Perhaps the police would discover Pan's earlier identity now. Perhaps they'd be able to notify family members who'd long ago despaired of hearing news of him.

Would he turn out to be a scholar, a younger Arthur who'd crossed the line between reality and mythology?

"Or maybe the Pan thing was an act." Edward sounded more confident. "Maybe Baker knew him. They might have been working together. Or in competition. Hell, for all we know, 'Pan' was Toni's ex-husband."

"No, no," Arthur assured him. "This gentleman certainly believed himself to be Pan. Wouldn't you say so, Willa?"

"Yes." I'd almost believed him myself.

Arthur covered his eyes. "A brilliant musician." His voice was heavy.

"Why hasn't Toni gone home?" I fretted.

"Maybe Nelson's lying. Maybe she did go home." Edward brushed a fly from his cheek.

"Can you tell by looking at the body if Pan, you know, if he—"

"Raped Toni?" His brows climbed. "I did kind of look him over. I didn't see any fresh scratches. Not that she'd necessarily have struggled. I gather some women get paralyzed."

I touched my swollen eye. I couldn't imagine Toni freezing up under attack.

"What are you thinking, Willa? She went home and got a knife? Or told her husband—or maybe her ex— what Pan did to her? Nelson came up here and killed him?"

"Did you describe the lean-to when you talked to Nelson?"

"At the sheriff's office, yeah; it was in the photograph. But hell, it's not like I gave Nelson coordinates. Not to mention the camp got moved a quarter-mile. He would have had to look pretty hard for it."

"Why didn't the sheriff find it? Wasn't he supposed to be searching?" My pique sounded childish; exactly how I felt. "Why didn't the sheriff find this body?"

"Nelson said his stuff got sabotaged, not taken—no stolen goods to recover. Sheriff probably just shined it on."

"But he should be searching for Toni."

"They just started this morning."

I tried to master the pouts and sneers that threatened, like loud Trotskyites, to take over my personality. I summed it up: "I don't trust Galen Nelson."

"Now you sound like his wife."

Toni had been right about me lying to her; maybe she'd been right about Nelson lying, too.

"But I hear you—I don't trust him, either," Edward agreed. "I'd like to try to sneak a look at that basement of his. See for myself if things got trashed."

"Edward?"

"Yeah?"

"She'd have fought Pan. Toni Nelson would have fought back. There should be scratches and bruises on him."

"Well, who knows . . . maybe you were right at the time." Edward sounded almost apologetic. "We don't know Pan confused Toni with Syrinx. He might have just been protecting you when he grabbed her. He might have let her go after you ran away."

I felt tears spring to my eyes. If so, I owed him.

No matter what, Arthur was right. The world had lost someone unique.

CHAPTER TWENTY-FIVE

I screamed when Edward's borrowed cellular telephone rang.

We'd left the chaparral and were back in the ravine. It was a wild and tangled place, nowhere you'd expect a modern intrusion.

Edward grinned as he flipped the phone open. Then he said, "The connection's lousy. Can you speak up?" He moved toward the creek bed. "No. Let's just do the best we can. I appreciate your call."

For a few minutes, Edward stood there, hand clapped over his other ear, shoulders hunched in concentration.

He said, "Give me those dates again?" Then, "Okay, now the stock?"

I was putting all my energy into eavesdropping, so I wasn't pleased when Arthur spoke to me.

"Willa, something happened to you night before last, didn't it?"

I gawked at him. Unfortunately, something had happened to me every day this week.

"You began a journey, didn't you?" Arthur persisted.

I shrugged. "I kind of bopped around in, well, just in my imagination."

" 'Just' your imagination? Is your imagination a poor relation, then?" A wan smile crinkled his face. "Your body has a kind of magnetic pull for your spirit, you know. You won't stop being aware of your body until it's comfortable being ignored. But that doesn't change the nature of your experience. You did have one, didn't you?"

"I'm not sure." I stared at Edward. He was frowning as he listened to the person on the phone.

"Come with me to Bowl Rock," Arthur urged. "I can't journey in that canoe alone. You can help me."

"I wouldn't be able to do anything like that." Daydreaming to the pounding of a drum was one thing. But a voyage in a stone canoe? If it did happen, it would freak me out. "And I wouldn't want to."

"Ah, you see? You see, Willa?" Arthur was getting more, not less, excited about the idea. "You know in your heart it will work. Your future self is speaking to you in your present reaction."

"My future self?" My tone was dismissive.

He didn't seem to take offense. "How many times have you continued with something because you knew, simply knew, it would happen for you? Or conversely, how many times have you worked against an inner conviction that nothing would come of your endeavor?"

Edward was speaking, and I was being kept from eavesdropping. I was brusque. "So?"

"We're in the habit of accessing time in a linear manner," Arthur explained. "We know the past shapes the present. And we know our plans and expectations do, too. But there are other ways the future affects the present. Where do our gut feelings come from?"

Edward was profusely thanking the person on the other end of the line.

"Where?" I asked absently.

"Your future self has conversations with you, my dear. Think how often you mull over your past, deciding such and such was a mistake or that you were right to persevere in something. Your mind is a vast structure, only partially bound by linear time. Sometimes your past self is able to hear those whispers of perspective. It interprets them as hunches or fears or, as we often put it, 'feelings.' " He must have noticed my impatience. He concluded, "What you feel now is a dread of the mystery accessible to you. It's your future self telling you you will be able to journey with me."

"If my future self is saying anything, it's saying, avoid scary situations." Maybe I could send my past self a message to call in sick last Monday.

Arthur grinned. "No, that's a misinterpretation. You aren't being warned not to do this.You're being warned of its success. And of the changes it will make in you and your life."

Edward walked up. "I've got very interesting news, children."

He stuffed the phone into his pocket. Saved by Ma Bell.

"Without getting into the details:" Edward looked happy as a boy. He'd certainly gone into the right line of work. "The last two times Nelson deposited a big chunk of cash, his stock went down within the month."

"How much money? From where?" It was a relief to discuss something concrete, something usual people might talk about in the course of ordinary reality.

"Fifty thousand. Deposited twice. And about a month after each deposit, a competitor beat him to a patent."

"What would the products have been worth?" Fifty thousand wasn't much for a moderately successful product.

"I couldn't even guess," Edward admitted.

"Because a product would have to earn way more than that to justify development costs. God, Nelson pays his attorneys—" I shut up. Curtis & Huston deserved my reticence, at least. "Even a patent search gobbles up money. A product's got to generate a lot of profit to be worth the work."

"So fifty grand's chicken feed?" He looked a little crestfallen. "But he's got partners, right—Louis Drake, even that surfer-nerd kid gets a percentage. Maybe by the time he pays his lawyers, his partners, the manufacturers . . . maybe fifty thousand in the bank puts him ahead."

"You've ruled out other sources of cash?"

"Some of the obvious ones: court settlements, accounts receivable, inheritances." Edward rubbed his forehead. "Maybe Nelson wasn't selling information about the products per se. Maybe he was selling tips about the direction his company was taking. Thinking other companies would back off if they saw how far ahead he was?"

"But he lost two patents. That's money right out of his pocket." It was hard to believe Nelson would sabotage his own company, undercut his own stock. "Besides, Cyberdelics walks on the wild side. Most computer firms are making better trackballs and motherboards. Cyberdelics is making computers that can smell."

"Still, a bird in the hand, and all that." Edward seemed determined to bolster his theory.

"Was it the same company both times?"

"That beat them to patents? No. But Nelson might have worked with the same middleman. The guy who broke into my Jeep, for instance. Or even Joel Baker." Edward shot me a look. "Given that Arthur saw him in San Francisco. We think."

We think: Meaning we couldn't be sure it was the same man with a shaved head? Or that we couldn't be sure Arthur had really been hypnotized, had really been telling the truth?

After we'd hiked a while longer, Arthur excused himself for a moment, going behind some bushes.

Edward grabbed my arm. "I need Arthur to talk me into leaving him at Bowl Rock. Only I'm not going to leave."

"He won't do anything sinister there, Edward. You don't have to spy on him."

"Just go along with it if it happens."

Later, when Arthur asked if we were on our way to Bowl Rock, I felt uncomfortable hearing Edward lie.

"I'm going to the Nelsons. With any luck, Galen's at work, and I can get a peek at this famous basement."

Predictably, Arthur insisted. "If we could take the time to go to Bowl Rock first?"

"To do what?" Edward asked innocently.

Arthur glanced at me. "Willa?"

Edward looked at me, brows raised.

"He wants me to . . ." I didn't have the vocabulary,

much less the inclination. "He wants me there with him."

Edward couldn't leave it at that. "To do what?" he repeated.

"I can't handle the boat alone," Arthur explained.

"The—? Oh." Edward got it. "The rock canoe. You need help rowing it." He couldn't disguise a smile. "Okay. I'll drop you guys off and go to—"

"Edward." Arthur put his hand on Edward's arm. "Billy and I were able to chant. But Willa can't. So I need someone to provide the rhythm. I can improvise something for you to use, and I can teach you the beat. But please, this may be my last chance."

Edward glanced at the wrinkled hand on his sleeve. "Sure. No need to break my arm." He conceded, "It's probably better. I don't want you trancing out, letting the cops creep up on you."

Maybe that was Edward's future self talking.

Three-quarters of an hour later, Arthur and I faced each other inside Bowl Rock as if we were bathing together. The rock interior was cold and slimy with moss. Behind Arthur, traces of Billy Seawuit's blood remained.

My present self felt damp and cramped and downright silly. Edward's smile told me he'd remind me of this moment some day.

"I thought drum vibrations did something to brain waves," I said nervously.

Edward was holding two pieces of tree branch. Arthur had rehearsed him so he clapped them at a precise pace, a few beats per second.

"Your mind knows how to do it now," Arthur explained. "You can trust it to hear the rhythm and find the place again. Just look for me, Willa. Instead of looking for your animal, look for me."

I tilted my head up. Part of the rock "eggshell" curved up around us. It didn't look much grayer than the sky. I hoped we didn't get rained on. It was chilly enough in here.

Edward, with a skeptical shake of the head, began banging the sticks. I closed my eyes and tried to get comfortable—not an easy project with rock torturing my back and a half inch of water and slime soaking through my pants.

I tried to relax, which only invited the rock to grow harder and itches to take hold. The stone seemed to suck warmth from my body.

I was humoring Arthur, I reminded myself. I didn't have to do anything but sit here. Edward had some kind of agenda, and so did Arthur. But I was just being Miss Congeniality. I was just along for the canoe ride.

I allowed my mind to wander for a while. I listened to innumerable stick beats, time passing slowly. The sound was lulling, like the ticking of a clock.

I felt myself begin to drift into a nap. I'd slept poorly, despite last night's real bed; I'd been too worried about Toni Nelson, about Arthur, about myself. I could still hear the sticks, but faintly. I dozily recalled my previous attempts to visualize a tunnel. The memory carried me into sleep.

Suddenly, Arthur was there waiting, standing at the tunnel exit, beckoning desperately.

"Willa," he called, "we have very little time. Edward will grow impatient. Come. Hurry."

It was a funny kind of sleep, I decided. I could still

feel the rock against my back and hear Edward bang the sticks. Or maybe that was part of the dream.

"Call it what you will, my dear." Arthur continued beckoning. "But please hurry."

I stepped out of the tunnel.

He took my arm. "It will be less confusing for you if you close your eyes."

"Okay," my dream self told him.

Suddenly, something grabbed me from behind, bunching up my clothing. I forgot to close my eyes. I could see the feathered belly of a huge bird, feel its claw pull my sweatshirt tight. Wind rushed past my ears as the landscape shrank beneath me: I was being carried high into the air, Arthur beside me. Vast wings made a sound I'd heard in aviaries, but never so loud.

"Close your eyes," Arthur shouted over it.

Below me, the scene was so surreal I thought my heart would fail. I closed my eyes.

I could feel the lift of wind and the powerful beating of wings.

Dreams can be very strange; I reminded myself several times.

I felt myself being deposited into something unstable, something bobbing. I opened my eyes to find Arthur opposite me in a boat. Around us, rain hit the sea in loud sheets, drubbing our wooden craft.

Arthur had prepared me to expect a canoe, but this one was thirty feet long, with sides as thick as walls. It bore the marks of the tool that had hollowed it.

Arthur handed me an ornately carved oar. "Do your best, Willa," he shouted over the storm.

We skirted swells as green as jade. In every direction, there were islands covered to the shore with pines and cedars. Their evergreen faded behind the rain.

"Where are we going, Arthur?" I shouted back.

He pointed over his shoulder. "Watch for whirlpools. Watch for rocks. Don't be frightened by anything that rises out of the water." His hair was plastered to his face. Rain dripped off the tendrils.

I tried to row, but the water seemed too thick. "We're not getting anywhere. Where are we?"

"We are inside the myth. We are in the place it came from. The Greeks transplanted it and added their own scenery, but the story is inside us. It's right here. You know it already. You know what to expect."

The rain battered him, but he looked younger and desperately determined. Over his shoulder, the island seemed no different from the others.

"Why that one, Arthur?"

"We tried the others. That's the one we couldn't get to. Something always capsized us."

"What's on it?" I could taste the rain, feel it chill my skin.

"We thought it would be the people who made this boat, who moved Bowl Rock."

"Do you still think so?" I was cold and scared; the dream was too real.

"Billy Seawuit," he shouted over the torrent. "Billy's on that island. That's why we couldn't reach it. He was already there."

The dream suddenly faded. It faded literally, as if someone had thrown a veil over a television.

And then it was completely gone. I saw only the insides of my eyelids.

I opened my eyes to find Edward hovering over us, saying, "Come on come on, come out of it!"

"I was having the weirdest dream," I told him.

"Hurry. Get out. Cops."

I hurried, taking Edward's hand.

It took both of us to get Arthur out. He looked absolutely bereft. We had to haul him out by the armpits and drag him into the brush.

"Jesus," Edward muttered, "you guys are soaked."

I told myself water had collected at the bottom of the rock bowl. My clothes had wicked it, that made sense. I touched my hair; why was it wet?

We got Arthur on his feet, pushing him along. The three of us crashed through the brush till we'd gone far enough to take cover.

"Keep hidden. Stay still," Edward commanded.

I tried to quiet my breathing. Close by, Arthur curled over his bent knees, head bowed.

I could hear voices now. A man shouted someone's name, then told him to wait up.

He and two other men milled around the rock for a while, then moved on. They passed us, but not near enough for it to matter.

We sat in the shrubs a little longer. Edward was probably being cautious. I was being frightened. Arthur remained draped over his knees.

Edward stood first. He spoke to Arthur. "Are you okay? I didn't know it was so wet inside there."

Arthur looked up. His skin was ashen. "Those were sheriffs?" he asked.

"I think so; one of them, anyway. I caught their movement through the trees. Incredible they didn't hear me banging those sticks."

I got up, brushing myself off. "They must have heard you. Why else would they come straight to the rock?"

"Woodpecker," Arthur said, rising. "I've had the experience before, of sticks being mistaken for a woodpecker."

"Could be why they didn't search harder," Edward agreed. "They could have talked themselves into believing it was a woodpecker."

He was eyeing us strangely. "Did I stop at a bad time or something?"

"No," I reassured him, "stopping before the police arrest you is a good time."

I glanced at Arthur. I wished we could go forever without talking about it. I was afraid he'd describe the same "vision" I'd had. And I'd much rather continue thinking I'd dozed.

"So what happened?" Edward persisted.

To my relief, Arthur said, "It's better not to dilute the experience by discussing it. It sometimes tells you something later if you don't disturb it."

I nodded, trying not to smile.

We walked back the way we'd come, avoiding Bowl Rock and keeping to the woods.

When Arthur lagged behind, Edward leaned close. "So . . . did you go boating?"

"What did it look like?"

"It looked like you were asleep."

"Mm," I hedged. "What about Arthur?"

"Looked like he was sleeping, too. Which might have made my little experiment useless."

"What experiment?"

"Did you hear me say something while you were sitting in there?" he asked me.

"Hurry up, the cops," I paraphrased.

"You didn't hear me maybe five minutes earlier?"

"No. What did you say?"

"Something like, You must go to Montgomery Street. I wanted to know if you'd hear it, or if you'd incorporate it into whatever else was happening."

"Incorporate it?"

Edward looked a little uncomfortable. "Remember Arthur talked about a dove telling him to go there? I thought if he was fantasizing about a dove and someone came along—"

"And whispered it in his ear?"

"People around here know he's into this 'journeying' stuff. Call it a figment, daydream, self-induced acid flashback—whatever. But if Joel Baker saw him in the rock, and realized he was tripping . . . Maybe he walked up behind him and told him to go to Montgomery Street."

"And Arthur attributed it to his dove." It wasn't a bad theory.

"But you didn't hear me?" Edward confirmed.

"And nothing in my dream told me to go to Montgomery Street."

"Ask Arthur for me. As his fellow traveler."

"No way."

He looked a little surprised by my vehemence.

"Edward, I almost totally believe I was dreaming. Even if I'm wetter than I should be."

"You're wet because the rock—"

"Fine. But I'm not going to compare notes with Arthur. I don't want to know what he thinks happened."

To that end, I staked out the middle ground between Arthur, who trailed dispiritedly, and Edward, who couldn't seem to go fast enough. We hiked single file back to the creek bed.

I caught up to Edward. "Where are we heading?"

"Right now, to the Jeep. Arthur's not going to make it much farther. Then we're off to the Nelsons'."

"The Nelsons'? That's exactly where we'll find the police."

"We'll find them any damn place we go from now on. And we should, too, with Toni Nelson missing, and Pan up there . . . And look at us," he added, matter-of-factly. "Never mind you two, now I can't go home because someone made off with my keys. I'm paranoid about using my credit card. I'm reduced to borrowing money and a telephone from my brother."

"Fred is your brother?"

"I never told you about Fred?"

"No."

"Well, he used to steal all my girlfriends. That's probably why."

I nodded. "He is kind of cute."

"Naw. That's a post-hypnotic suggestion."

I glanced over my shoulder. I was glad we were on our way back to the Jeep. Arthur walked slowly, shoulders drooping.

"See." Edward followed my glance. "We need to get all this settled as soon as we can. We need a plan."

"I don't suppose you have one?"

"I thought I'd keep it to myself so they can't torture it out of you."

"You always could keep a secret." Like the girlfriend he acquired while we were together.

He shot me a paranoid glance. "I was going to tell you about her. But you got yourself thrown in jail before I had a chance."

"I can be so inconsiderate that way."

When we reached the Jeep, we were a bedraggled threesome with damp hair, muddy clothes, and no spring in our steps.

Before we climbed in, I begged Edward, "Tell me you really do have a plan."

"Would I kid you?" he asked.

CHAPTER TWENTY-SIX

Edward stashed the Jeep in another off-road pocket, commanding us to wait there. I knew we were somewhere near the Nelsons'; I recognized the road.

Arthur sat in the front as motionless as a rag doll, staring at nothing in particular. He didn't seem inclined to talk, but I was taking no chances. I got out and moseyed through the woods within sight of the Jeep.

The sky glowed with twilight colors behind a low overcast. A thin wind rustled duff and branches. If I closed my eyes, I could almost resolve the sounds into speech, I could almost believe the trees were conversing. I wished I could listen hard enough to hear Pan's pipes. I wished I could hear that perfect music, perfectly suited to the woods, again.

I took the opportunity to mourn the strange man who'd rediscovered himself as a demigod. I put my forehead against the rough, spongy bark of a redwood and closed my eyes.

When Edward returned an hour later, my skin felt

refrigerated, and I was as goosebumped as a raw chicken. It was dark out.

I climbed back into the Jeep. It was beginning to feel like my home.

Edward sighed, long and loud. "It wasn't easy—obviously, I wanted to be careful, not be seen. Plus, a high-tech guy like Nelson, I wanted to be sure he hadn't put up security cameras."

"Cut to the chase, Edward. Did you get a look at the basement?"

"Through a window, yeah. It looked tidy as a pin to me. I checked the garbage, too. Nothing weird, just food." He let his head loll against the seat back. "Plus I broke into the mother-in-law unit; poked around, went through Seawuit's duffel bag. Nothing interesting there, not that I noticed."

"You think Nelson's lying about the break-in?"

"I have no idea," he admitted. "I don't know what he meant by 'damaged.' It could be pretty subtle, damaging computer parts. I don't know." He slumped over the steering wheel, looking discouraged. "I guess I was hoping for a smoking knife."

He started the engine.

"Where are we going?"

"Beats me," he admitted. "Off the mountain. I am truly out of steam. I think Nelson's full of shit, but I don't have a handle on why I think so, and I can't think of any way to prove it."

"If we could get him to say something, admit something," I vented.

With Toni missing and Martin-or-Joel gone, we'd run out of options. All we could do was keep hiding, keep hoping for news.

Arthur surprised us by saying, "May I make a suggestion?"

"Sure." Edward pulled the Jeep back on-road.

"About Billy." Grief deepened his voice. "If I could give you a better sense of him, perhaps it would help you understand his relationship to the Nelsons."

"It couldn't hurt," Edward agreed.

"The other thing," Arthur said slowly, "is nightmares."

We were barreling down the fire road now.

"Nightmares?" Edward repeated.

"Willa's need to believe she was in a dream rather than a journey, that's what made me think of it," he explained.

"Think of what?"

"Nelson, you say, hoped to create a shamanic computer program. This reflects certain beliefs about the nature of reality, beliefs that are more . . . receptive, shall we say? Perhaps we could use those beliefs against him?"

"In what way?"

"From what I understand, Nelson is most intimate with, and most attuned to his computer. It would seem to be the only thing getting his full attention," Arthur mused. "Perhaps a custom nightmare, something we could load onto his system?"

"No way we're going to hack into a pro's hard drive." Edward sounded a little wistful. "Jesus, with Nelson's paranoia about spying, his computer's probably the equivalent of a medieval fortress."

"I doubt he's even on-line, not with his sexiest machines," I agreed. "That's the most foolproof way to keep hackers out. No modem connection, no way in."

"Perhaps we could load something manually?" Arthur persisted. "Unless his computers are somehow locked?"

I'd watched Toni Nelson fire up one of them and start a program. She'd hit a switch and selected a menu item, just like us lower-tech folk.

"Rather than break in through a network," Arthur continued, "couldn't we simply break into their house? Turn their computer on the usual way?"

"Say we did get inside," Edward didn't sound optimistic. "What kind of program would you put on there? What are we talking about?"

"We'd need several things before we could even . . . We'd need a good graphics application."

"I could get that," I intruded. "If Edward has a modem, we could download one from my dad's computer."

"Of course I've got a modem." Edward sounded insulted. "And I know how to do two whole things with it."

"My father's got every artsy application you can imagine—bootlegged, of course." Cyberpunks believe "information wants to be free"—which was about all my father could afford. "But the programs are huge; it would take hours." Still, I'd rather do anything than nothing. The illusion of forward movement would be a big improvement over the reality of hiking around avoiding sheriffs. "It'd be much quicker if you knew someone here who had them."

"Piece of cake." I couldn't tell if Edward was being sarcastic.

Arthur took him at his word: "We'd also need an instamatic camera, or better yet, a video recorder. And a way to feed the images into a computer."

"Yeah," Edward said. "I could swing it."

"You'd have to have a video-ready computer," I pointed out. "A fancy one."

He surprised me by saying, "Done." He turned to Arthur. "Anything else?"

"I would need to get into Billy's possessions."

"Jesus—you couldn't mention this before I went through his duffel?"

"Not Billy's clothing, no. I was thinking of his rattle, his drums. But they're in San Francisco, in the trunk of my rental car."

"Do we have to use Billy's? Can't we get something similar?"

"These aren't items you'd find at a supermarket," Arthur pointed out.

"Oh, but you don't know Santa Cruz." Edward nodded. "If we can get there before it closes." He stepped on the gas, careening wildly down the mountain.

A half hour later, we walked along a downtown alleyway. We entered the oddest specialty shop I'd ever seen: a boutique of tribal instruments from around the world.

Arthur looked like a boy in a candy store. "Look," he cried, "South African talking drums. And Kenyan rattles!"

Edward shushed him. "Don't talk to the clerk, don't invite anyone to notice you," he begged.

Two walls and much of the floor were devoted to drums, drums with metal kettles, skins stretched over hoops, ceramic drums.

A group of men in tie-dye and Jerry Garcia T-shirts tapped on them, earnestly discussing their tones.

Behind them were shelves of rattles made from gourds, skin, wood, even tin cans. There were also strange xylophones and instruments I couldn't begin to place. One wall was hung with African masks and figures. The back was lined with books, compact disks, and tapes, apparently of tribal music.

"Can a place like this do enough business to stay open?" I wondered to Edward.

"It's been here for years," he whispered back. "You can't buy a set of sheets downtown, but you can pick up a hookah, curly-toed slippers, a real scarab, or an African drum, no problem. I'd better go baby-sit. We've got to get him out of here before some college student recognizes him."

Edward squatted beside Arthur, who was pawing through a bottom shelf full of rattles. He whispered some sort of entreaty.

Twenty minutes later, we walked back into the alley carrying a bagful of rattles, two skin-on-hoop drums and a leather striker. We'd spent most of the cash in Edward's wallet.

So he looked a little disconcerted to hear Arthur say, "Now we need paint and some sewing supplies."

"Looks like we'll be hitting Fred up for dinner," Edward said. "Unless you feel like panhandling."

Edward's brother, we soon learned, lived in a condo full of photographs of his children from three previous marriages.

"He keeps marrying my girlfriends." Edward told me again. He didn't sound like he was joking. "These guys," he pointed to the rogue's gallery of kids with front teeth missing, "could be mine genetically. How about that? I get to throw around the football with them, but I don't have to pay their college tuition."

The condo was conventional and sparse, with wood floors, white walls, and white couches. It might have belonged to Everybachelor.

Except for one thing: a living room table was taken up with a computer and its peripherals. I stroked the scanner and digitizing pad: They were at the top of my "to buy" list. I guessed psychiatrists did pretty well for themselves.

As if in response, Edward said, "You should see the place he moved out of—mansion city. But wife number three got it. He's paid for more houses than I've lived in."

Arthur was already busy on the floor, pulling shells off one rattle, beads off another.

He kept shaking his head. He was muttering, "Raven, wolf, bear." He looked up at us. "I've seen them so often, but I'm not an artist."

"You've seen what?"

"Depictions by the Kwakiutl and Haida. They are absolutely distinctive, and I certainly recall the elements, the shapes within shapes. But painting them . . ." Again, he shook his head. "Of course, Billy was a carver. But I couldn't begin to achieve anything like that. We'll just have to hope . . ." He reapplied himself to the task of stripping rattles.

What Fred would think of the mess was of little concern to Edward. "Place looks worse," he nodded at the littered floor, "when the kids visit."

Edward had already foraged though Fred's cupboards, bringing forth crackers, cereals, and paté samplers from a gift basket. We'd eaten them without complaint. I hoped Fred was feeling generous. Bad enough we'd made him an accessory. Now we'd eaten all his food. I hoped I didn't screw up his computer as well.

I turned it on, relieved to see he had some hot-rod

programs: Morph, Photoshop, Adobe Premiere. He had more CD-ROMs than a rich teenager.

"And the video camera?" Arthur asked suddenly. He was unscrewing the tops from hobby shop paint jars. "Help me, friend," I heard him murmur.

Edward stood. "Fred's going to love me rummaging through his porn collection looking for a camera." He left the room.

I had no real work until Arthur was done, but I thought I'd better load the programs and see how well I remembered them. I fussed for a while, getting more and more frustrated, as I usually did at a computer. I could see no evidence the programs had even been opened before. I could understand that; they were more fun to own than to use.

After a while, I lay on a throw rug, not wanting to inflict my dirty clothes on Fred's furniture. I watched Arthur paint precise patterns on a rattle. Either he was more of an artist than he thought, or friend Billy was indeed helping him.

I'd been napping awhile when Edward prodded me with his foot. "Okay, cyberlawyer: Show time."

Fred also stood over me, arms folded across his chest.

"Don't get any ideas about her," Edward told him. "She's not our type."

CHAPTER TWENTY-SEVEN

I'd fed a video of the newly altered rattles and drums into Fred's computer, which was indeed "video ready" (code for "very expensive"). This had entailed connecting it to a VCR with a special cable and following Abode Premiere's directions. I'd changed the video background by substituting clip-art forest for everything white—that is, for Fred's wall. I'd blurred the images—Arthur's artwork was barely passable, according to him—and made them more dramatic with lighting tricks. Now, I was experimenting with Morph, blending one object into another for smooth transitions.

It wasn't much of a feat, but it pushed the envelope of my capabilities. And it certainly wasn't the custom nightmare Arthur had envisioned; at best, it was a half-baked crochet. I'd taken computer tutorials, I'd messed around with these programs. But my agenda had been to get a job, not to truly "learn" the skills. I was shaking as I worked.

As I struggled with the video, Arthur told us a story.

He described the night he met Billy Seawuit.

"I'd heard tell of a shaman," he began sadly, "who lived in a remote area on the northern tip of Vancouver Island. I found him living in a longhouse he'd built himself from the cedars there. Have you ever been inside a longhouse? They're magnificent structures, thirty or forty feet long, perhaps twenty feet wide, with roofs of overlapping shingles that can be moved to make skylights. And the smell—it's literally the inside of a cedar box. Billy had erected four totem poles, topped by the eagle or the raven, with the wolf and bear below. He had another pole inside the longhouse, partially carved. And of course, he had two carved beams facing the fire.

"He wore his hair long. He was a very handsome man with a stoic face and an intense brightness in his eyes. He told me he'd set out to become a carver, an artist, not a healer. But the trances were powerful for him. He knew Raven and Bear and Wolf intimately, you see, from carving them. And in his trances, they would give him gifts of spirit and energy for the sick. But he was best at finding souls that had fled from their bodies."

"When people died?" Edward stood behind me, watching the computer screen, making me nervous.

"Shamans believe that trauma causes a person's spirit to flee. It's not unlike the recent views of psychiatrists." He cast a glance at Fred, who sat on the couch sipping wine. "When a person is traumatized, psychiatrists say they dissociate; they retreat, if you will, into insanity. Well, shamans believe the same thing. Except they don't view the mind as a structure with a subconscious or unconscious. Because they have journeyed to the lower and upper worlds, you see. And when you do that, you do quite literally see those pilgrim souls. You see where the sane part of a traumatized person has fled.

"Shamans have had phenomenal success in the treatment of mental illness," Arthur asserted.

"I've heard something like that." Fred looked interested, if easy in his European ways.

"Shamans ask the spirit to return. A depressed or traumatized person is literally seen as 'dispirited.' And when the errant part of the spirit is returned, well, I've never seen transformations so dramatic."

"Similar to faith healing, I'd think," Fred said comfortably.

"No," Arthur disagreed. "The person is not healed by a belief in the grace of God, or a god. The person can be quite mad, you see; scarcely cognizant of the shaman beside him. But when the shaman blows the spirit back into that person, he'll sit up like his old self. The sick don't begin with the same depth of belief and sense of petition as someone visiting a faith healer.

"But my point is that Billy set out to be an artist, not a shaman. And yet he acquired a reputation as one of the foremost shamans in the world." Tears sprang to his eyes. "In the treatment of mental illness, he'd never failed.

"I was traveling in British Columbia. I had visited a family there whose child had been brutalized. She had retreated into clinical autism, which I understand is highly resistant to psychiatric treatment."

Fred nodded.

"The family had tried for three years to bring her back. They begged me to take her to Billy Seawuit. And I did. Her nurse went with me—she was in a wheelchair, poor child; she'd retreated even from movement.

"And so the first time I met Billy, a group of us were in his longhouse with this child. He asked us to journey with him. He said he needed many eyes to search for her spirit because it had obviously run very far away."

Fred was sitting forward, apparently taken with the metaphor.

"It was one of the most arduous journeys I've ever undertaken," Arthur said, paintbrush poised over a drum he felt he'd botched. "And one of the longest. We traveled for hours, searching, at one point through fire, through a sea of it. But we did finally find the poor child's spirit, running as fast and as far as it could, running and running and running, using up all the child's energy and mobility. It took several of us to catch her and soothe her. But only Billy could persuade her to return."

He stared ahead, not seeing us. He was back on the journey, back in Billy Seawuit's longhouse.

"When he breathed the spirit back into the child, she reappeared behind the child's eyes just as surely as a face appearing at an empty window. She looked around, asking for her mother, as naturally as if she hadn't been silent for three years. She was alive again. She was with her spirit again."

Fred continued to look interested, if not convinced.

"Her legs were too weak after the hiatus to carry her, but she wanted to stand, to move and stretch. And though it took time, she is quite normal today, I believe. But what interested me most as a scholar, as a documentor of these experiences, was that, beneath the metal wheels of the girl's chair, deep scars had been burned into the wood floor. She had come through the fire with us."

He stared at each of us in turn. "I photographed the burn scars, and the photos have appeared now in several journals along with my commentary."

"I'd be interested in seeing them," Fred commented.

"I'll be happy to send you copies. I'll jot down the citations for you tonight. I believe very passionately that psychiatry should open its mind to so-called primitive medical practices."

He bowed his head, taking a few deep breaths.

"But the true miracle," he continued, "was Billy Seawuit himself. He was free from our modern pettinesses and envies. And he understood what he knew, which is even rarer. He was a blessing. The embodiment of a blessing."

Arthur went back to painting the drum: A stylized raven—looking somewhat improved—stood atop a clam shell.

Edward, still hovering behind me, said, "Okay, so what was he doing here? What was Seawuit doing for Galen Nelson?"

Arthur looked up from his work. "I can't believe Billy was contacted to help develop a computer program. Nor would he have been interested in coming to do that." He looked confused. "Once he was here, of course, the rock held his attention; Bowl Rock, I mean. And the Pan legend."

"They contacted Billy?" I looked up from my work. "Galen Nelson told me they brought you here as a consultant, to help them create mythological background images. He made it sound like Seawuit came along for the ride and got interested in the project."

I racked my brain. "I can't remember exactly how he put it, but that was my impression."

Arthur looked astonished. "But no. Nelson himself asked Billy to come here. I came later, when Billy told me about Bowl Rock."

"What reason did he give Seawuit?" Behind me, Edward sounded frustrated. Because it was time to cut to the chase?

"I don't know. Billy didn't tell me."

"I thought you guys were close." Edward was sounding suspicious.

"But this was a mundane matter," Arthur explained. "Simply a travel arrangement, something Billy planned to do for a matter of some days. Days in which we had no plans together."

"So because you had no plans, you didn't ask him what Nelson wanted?"

"I have only this feeling to offer: that Billy can't have been there in regard to a computer program."

"Why?" Edward demanded.

"Because no program can substitute for the spirit. It's truly that simple. It may be that Billy was told this was a pretext and was asked not to contradict it. But it's important to remember who he was: a powerful healer of mental illness."

None of us bothered to say it: Toni Nelson did not act like a sane woman.

CHAPTER TWENTY-EIGHT

We weren't burglars, more's the pity. We had no choice but to knock on Galen Nelson's door.

Nelson answered immediately, looking crestfallen to see us. He glanced curiously at the cap that hid my newly blond hair. He looked pale, surprisingly more gaunt. His hair was tousled. He was fully dressed and shod in hiking boots despite the late hour.

He said, "The police have been wanting to talk to you." He moved backward to let us enter.

I walked in first, as we'd arranged. Edward would linger to make sure the door was unlocked. Arthur would watch through the window for Edward's penlight to flash. Then he would creep inside, go downstairs, turn on Nelson's computer, and load in three diskettes worth of data—we hoped.

Such was our "plan." If it didn't work or didn't generate a reaction, this would be a long, wasted night.

But if things went optimally, Galen Nelson would mention seeing Toni today, or speak of Pan in the past tense, or contradict something he'd said about

Joel Baker. Perhaps, shocked and goaded, he'd admit he'd summoned Billy Seawuit on a pretext, that TechnoShaman was a facade. Any tidbit from this taciturn man would be a coup, a stepping-stone, a reason to delay despair.

We'd do our best to trick him or, at least, surprise him. The plan was long on desperation, short on logic. Arthur felt that was a plus. Edward said he'd write to me in prison.

I apologized to Galen Nelson: "I'm sorry. I was out of town. Edward says you've been looking for me."

He shook his head cynically. "I'm supposed to believe you saw a naked man drag my wife off, and then you left town?"

"I had to leave. I have a life, you know. It's not like I didn't have Edward tell you about it."

"Yeah?" Nelson said. "And what is this life of yours, Alice Young? Why is it none of the Alice Youngs on SelectPhone are you?"

"What's 'select phone'?" Edward asked, stepping up beside me.

"A CD-ROM telephone directory of the whole country," Nelson explained.

I'd hate to see his next phone bill. "I have an unlisted number."

"And what would that be?"

"That would be none of your business." The get-huffy routine; any lawyer can do it. "Are you accusing me of lying about Toni?"

"Yes."

"I wish I were! She's not back yet, is she?"

"No." He looked more annoyed than concerned.

"You're not worried about her." Edward was as subtle as ever.

Not surprisingly, Nelson looked offended.

"She attacked me," I told him. "Out in the woods. I've got makeup over my eye, but I'll wash it off if you want proof. I think Pan was defending me when he pulled her away."

"But you didn't stay to make sure? I doubt it. I doubt your whole story." His tone certainly matched his words.

"I was afraid of her. She scared the hell out of me, so I took off."

"Well, thanks for the details—a day later." He ran an exasperated hand over his hair. "Maybe Toni did fight with you, I don't know. She's got a temper, and she's been upset—you saw how she jumped on me the other day. But—"

"But you're married to her."

"Meaning I had it coming?" He sounded martyred.

"Meaning men will put up with a lot from someone who looks like Toni," I was sorry to say.

"And you think I'm proof of that?"

"I hear Seawuit thought she was a knockout," Edward continued prodding. Arthur hadn't convinced him Seawuit's intentions were shamanic.

"Seawuit?" Nelson's tone was dismissive. "If he did notice her looks—so what?"

"So you moved him onto your land. Your own back-door man."

"What makes you think Seawuit had any interest in Toni? Why should he be?" His hands were shaking. He tucked them beneath his armpits. "What's Seawuit got to do with—?"

"Were you jealous?"

"There's not much point in getting jealous," he said

carefully, "if your wife thinks anyone who cares about her is a liar."

He had us there.

Behind him, the front door opened slowly. I could smell the night air, feel the cool draft.

I watched Arthur enter, looking as frightened as a mouse. Toni Nelson had complained her husband ignored outdoor perfumes; I hoped she was right, I hoped he didn't notice the sudden scent of forest.

Luckily, Nelson's attention was diverted by Edward's cell phone ringing. I wondered if Edward had planned it somehow, timed it with Fred.

"Do you mind if I take this?" Edward looked as surprised—and far more annoyed—than I was.

I tried not to follow Arthur with my eyes as he crept along behind Nelson, heading for the basement stairs.

Edward fumbled with the phone, perhaps to keep Nelson focused on it.

"Yeah?" he answered curtly. Then he listened, his face expressionless.

Whatever was being said to him, it must be important. Edward was not naturally nonchalant.

"Thanks," he said, before hanging up. To Galen Nelson, he explained, "Family. Sorry."

He barely glanced at me. But he was telling me something. Family, he'd said: meaning Fred had called?

"I have a niece who's autistic." He still didn't look at me.

Arthur had made it to the stairs and was on his way down to the basement.

"There's been some kind of mix-up with her treatment. Her records are lost—they can't find them where they're supposed to be." Though Edward looked calm, he'd grown pale. "Private eye in the family, you know how it is. Anything fishy, you get a phone call."

Nelson didn't seem to care about Edward's family woes.

But Arthur was downstairs now. It shouldn't take him but a moment to turn on the computer, open the video-player program, and insert a compression software disk. These would expand and play my tromp l'oeuil masterpiece, two diskettes worth of QuickTime movie—a brief loop of a shaking rattle and a drum being pounded.

A niece who's autistic, Edward had said. He must be referring to the story Arthur had recounted. *They can't find her records where they're supposed to be.*

When I used Fred's computer, I'd seen a list of his programs. One of them was MedLine, a National Library of Medicine on-line service. It provided modem access to medical and psychiatric journals and data bases.

Had he looked up Arthur's citations? Had he searched for the articles Arthur claimed to have written?

Had he phoned to tell Edward they didn't exist? To warn him—as he had after the hypnotism—that Arthur might be lying?

Why else would he call at so awkward a time?

I could feel Edward withdraw from the situation before us. I could feel him retreat into a corner of his mind to think.

If Arthur had lied about Billy's reason for being here—lied late and long—then maybe Nelson was telling the truth. Maybe Billy had come to help with a computer program, after all. Maybe Nelson had had good business reasons to want Seawuit alive. Maybe it was Arthur—determined to exalt "spirit" over technology—who hadn't.

And maybe it was Arthur who'd needed Billy's shamanic healing. Maybe years of travel and drug-induced journeying had taken their toll.

I'd been told in a sleepy fantasy—I hoped it was "just" my imagination; I hoped reality was roughly as I perceived it—to follow Arthur.

Maybe that had been the voice of my suspicions, roiling beneath the surface. Maybe my subconscious—never mind the spirits of the upper and lower worlds, never mind my future self—had been speaking to me, telling me to keep an eye on him. Maybe my fond feelings for Arthur were actually transferred protectiveness toward my parents. Maybe my daydreams were telling me I felt something else, underneath.

I glanced at Edward. He'd been polite to Arthur, but he'd never bought in, not like I had. He'd remained detached enough to voice some skepticism.

I looked at Galen Nelson and felt like a fish out of water. I didn't understand him or his wife or their relationship or what was going on now. And yet somehow, I'd become committed to entrapping him.

"Well, shall we call the police?" Nelson suggested. "Is there anything about Toni you haven't already told them through me?"

That's when we heard the rattle and drum downstairs.

"What in the—" Nelson looked at least as shocked as we'd hoped. He bolted toward the stairs.

We followed, less surprised but in just as much of a hurry.

Nelson charged down to the basement, with us not far behind. He stopped at the foot of the stairs, stopped as if suddenly turned to stone, one arm forward, one leg back.

He stopped, staring at his computer.

I knew what was on its screen: an altered rattle shaken by a computer-darkened hand.

I looked for Arthur. We'd told him to hide quickly; but we'd had no suggestion where.

He'd certainly done well: I couldn't see him.

In a moment, however, I heard him. I heard the plaintive *waaa oo aa waaa aaa neeee* I'd heard our first day here, when Arthur lay alone inside Bowl Rock.

Behind me, Edward whispered, "No trace of Arthur's journal articles. Fred checked."

I nodded.

I watched Nelson move cautiously forward, apparently mesmerized by the display on his computer monitor.

He bent closer to the image. I'd morphed it; it was changing from a rattle to a drum now. The sound changed, too, from shaking to banging. Soon, this drum would morph—jerkily, to my embarrassment—from one with a raven to one with a bear, both blurred to disguise maladroit brush strokes.

For a moment, Nelson stared as a chimpanzee might stare at his first television. He tilted his head.

Then he got savvy. He grabbed the computer mouse. But I'd made the image full screen with no menu bar. There was no place a mouse might click to stop the program.

Nelson turned to stare at us. He was flushed with excitement. He asked, "Did you put this on here?"

"We just walked in," Edward pointed out. "What is it?"

"You really didn't put it on?" Nelson repeated. He looked near tears.

Edward stepped closer, hand in his pocket. He was pointing a tape recorder microphone at Nelson. With all this extraneous noise—Arthur continued his *waaa oo waaa aaa neee*—I hoped the tape picked up Nelson's voice.

This was our only chance to record Nelson saying something unscripted, spontaneous—and, we hoped, illuminating, if not incriminating. I wished Arthur would stop, I wished he'd shut up.

I became a little obsessed: with trying to hear what Nelson would say, with needing the moment to provide resolution, with wanting to get on with my life.

I saw that Nelson looked happy, hopeful, excited to the point of stuttering. "Tech-TechnoShaman." He pointed at the screen. "Look."

For a man we'd decided didn't believe in this project, who'd hired Seawuit as a healer and not a consultant, he looked thrilled. Not cynical, not scared, not any of the things we'd expected.

I looked for Arthur again, wishing he'd stop the *waa uh waa nee*. He was standing in a corner now, solemn and pale. His mouth was closed. He wasn't chanting at all.

"Do you see this?" Nelson said excitedly. "I didn't put this on here. I just reconfigured this hard drive yesterday; it wasn't on here then. It's been imported. You didn't put it on? You really didn't?"

I stared at Arthur. But the moment I saw his lips weren't moving, I stopped hearing the chant.

Arthur looked as shocked as I was.

Edward was assuring Nelson we had nothing to do with it. Responding to his nudge, I motioned for Arthur to drop back behind the couch.

But Arthur seemed frozen, his expression not unlike Nelson's. Had the computer drumming sent him off on a journey? Was he in a trance?

If Nelson turned his head slightly, he'd discover Arthur. Our chance was slender to begin with. And Arthur was about to blow it.

Not caring what Nelson might think, I gestured broadly. When Arthur sank, I wasn't sure if he'd cooperated or fainted.

Nelson knelt, fingers poised over his keyboard. A simple force-quit command would reveal this was a program, not magic. Further inquiry would reveal its time of installation. It wouldn't take Nelson long to realize he'd been duped.

But for the moment, he looked ecstatic. "We've been trying to import pheromone-based images. We've indexed images to scents. It looks like the computer went into the image banks. Maybe. It's picked up . . . I don't know what scent, whose scent; I don't know what it reacted to." He knelt in front of the machine. "And I don't recognize this loop. But we have thousands, some I haven't seen."

So much for our assumption he'd recognize Billy's drums and rattle.

To Edward, I whispered, "Did you hear the chanting?"

He seemed annoyed by the distraction.

"Did you, Edward?"

Tersely, "No."

Maybe the drumming had affected me. Maybe I'd

drifted into mental vagary, conflating my current stress with memories from Bowl Rock.

"Where's my— Nelson patted the littered table top. "Stay with it. Tell me what it does. I'll be back with the handicam."

He dashed up the stairs. He didn't want to force-quit the program. He wanted to memorialize its appearance on his screen.

Edward turned as if to strangle me. "What the hell is Arthur—"

Arthur bolted from his hiding place then. He ran up the stairs, taking them two by two like a young man.

"Wait!" Edward cried.

But Arthur was gone.

"Jesus, what's he doing?" Edward fretted.

He ran up the stairs, too.

I watched the computer program loop back to the rattle in "Billy's" hand. Soon the first drum would appear, morphing into the second.

Arthur had lied about his articles, perhaps lied about the autistic girl. And judging from Nelson's reaction to this program, he was indeed sincere about TechnoShaman: It hadn't been a mere excuse to bring Seawuit to his mentally ill wife.

I wasn't sure what that meant.

Nelson returned with Edward, talking excitedly to him, holding a video camera in his hand.

"Arthur?" I mouthed to Edward.

He shrugged, nodding toward the window.

Arthur, I deduced, had run outside. He'd heard the chanting, too.

The voice in my daydream—on my "journey"?— had commanded me to follow Arthur.

I ran upstairs. I ran out the door. I could hear Edward shout my name.

Whatever the command meant, wherever it had come from—a subconscious observation, my future self—I had to do it. Whether it warned me he was guilty or directed me to protect him, I had to do it.

I had to follow Arthur.

CHAPTER TWENTY-NINE

I stood outside the Nelsons' house, looking from side to side wishing I could see more. The night was overcast, windless, damp. Where the light from the open door faded, everything melted into deep gray and black.

If Arthur heard the chanting, I could guess where he was heading. He'd go to Bowl Rock. But I wasn't sure I could find it in the dark.

I shivered with cold and fear. I didn't want to be out in the woods again. I wanted to stay close to Edward, close to the Jeep. Close to safety.

But safety wasn't worth much in and of itself. If I couldn't clear Arthur—or, I was afraid, prove him guilty—I'd be nice and safe in a jail cell.

I set out. I took the first steps out of the light and toward the forest. Follow Arthur, try to find Bowl Rock; that's all I could do.

I called his name. I didn't care if Nelson heard. I didn't care if he realized someone else was with us tonight, that the computer images weren't triggered by scents or beta waves or shamanic magic.

I just didn't want to lose Arthur. I started down Toni Nelson's landscaped path, thinking it led in the right general direction.

I screamed Arthur's name, over and over.

I ran along the trail until it became narrow and wooded.

I ran until I stumbled over him.

Sprawled on the mud and duff, I scrabbled and turned, kneeling close.

"Arthur?" I looked down at him. Even in the dark, I could make out his face a little.

I could tell his eyes were open. He whispered something to me. I leaned close to hear it.

He said, "Behind you."

I wheeled in time to see her, huge and pale against the night: Toni Nelson, wearing a white shirt, her long hair wild, her arms raised high, hands together. She was brandishing a knife. I couldn't actually see it, but nothing else would account for her posture—or Arthur's.

I had only an instant to act. Still low to the ground, I dived for her ankles.

I hit her legs hard, sending her sprawling backward. She started trying to kick loose. From the feel of it, she wore jeans and boots.

I'd never felt more vulnerable. Every sense screamed to me she had a knife. Waves of dread warned me it could hit at any second. I lost courage, knowing I couldn't fight a knife I couldn't see.

Faintly, I heard Arthur: *"Waaa ooo waaaa aaa neee."* Over and over, the merest whisper.

"Stop!" Toni screamed. "Stop it, stop it!" as if the nonsense syllables flayed her. "Stooooop!" She shrieked hysterically.

I scrambled away from her. I had to protect Arthur. I couldn't let us both down.

I watched her get back on her feet. The chanting had distressed her and delayed her, but she wasn't stupid. She knew what she had to lose.

She'd killed Billy Seawuit; everyone would realize that now. She'd killed Pan. Soon, the police would know that, too.

She stood out against the night like the ghost of Syrinx. She looked wild and voluptuous, her white shirt cinched at the waist by her fanny pack. She stood like a marble goddess, knife raised as if to avenge herself.

The woods were full of crazy people. And some of them lived in fancy houses.

"Don't hurt him," I pleaded. "He never did you any harm. We never meant to do you any harm!"

But she took a purposeful step forward. What we'd done didn't matter. Toni Nelson lived in her own world just as surely as Pan had. Just as surely as any of us do.

Toni lived in a world where everyone was a liar. Her husband, even a mere acquaintance like me, might be chastised and derided for it. She lived in a world where no one would admit the alleged perfidy, further fueling her anger.

Her fury—indiscriminate and unconcealed—might have made her a suspect in the murder of her houseguest . . . if his employer hadn't suddenly dropped out of sight.

I spread myself over Arthur. Looking up at Toni, I knew it would be useless to continue telling her we meant her no harm. Anything I said, she would dismiss as a lie; in her reality, as firmly entrenched as mine, everything seemed a lie. And it would be useless to brawl with her. I'd already learned the hard way that she'd pin me and pummel me. And I was painfully conscious that she was armed and I wasn't.

Arthur was barely whispering his chant. The same chant I'd somehow heard—imagined I heard?—in the house.

Toni took another step forward. She seemed surreally visible because of her shirt, frighteningly white. Both arms were raised to poise the knife. I did a panicked inventory: I couldn't use logic or brawn against her, and I had no weapon.

But I had something, a feeling I couldn't put a name to. I'd carried it away from Bowl Rock today. It was a glimpse into an impossible potential.

So I warbled with Arthur, as faithfully as I could, *"Waaa ooo aa waaa oo neee, waaa . . ."*

A shape leaped over us. I was certain for an instant that it was a mountain lion: The mountain lion from my dream, from my journey; my power animal.

But it turned out to be Galen Nelson.

He and Edward had chased out after me.

Nelson brought his wife down. Edward jumped over us, too, pulling the knife from her hand.

When Toni saw her husband, she said, "Hi, Galen," as if they'd just met at the supermarket.

I heard sobbing, but I knew it came from Galen, not Toni.

"I think Arthur's hurt!" I tugged at Edward's pant leg.

My eyes were growing used to the dark. I could see Arthur's sweater was torn, spread with blood.

Edward tossed the knife away as if it were hot. He looked over his shoulder.

Toni seemed docile now, nestled in Galen's arms as he bent his head over hers and wept. But I heard her mutter, "You think you're fooling me, but you're not. I know what you've been doing. I know what you did to our company."

Edward looked down at Arthur.

Arthur said, "Only a scratch."

"Are you sure? It's important I know." Edward's tone was urgent. "You've got to tell me the truth."

"It's not deep. Truly."

"Then we need to get you out of here. Now." He scrambled over to Nelson, speaking to him in a low voice.

A moment later, he was back, handing me the phone. "Call 911." He picked up Arthur and staggered toward the house with him. "Don't say anything about anything. Just tell them to come here. Talk in a deep voice."

I trotted behind them. I did as I was told, though the emergency operator nagged me to be more specific.

To my surprise, Edward deposited Arthur in the back of the Jeep, checking his wound briefly, then slamming the door.

To me he said, "Hurry up." He took the phone from me and tossed me the Jeep keys. "Get out of here. Go to Fred's right now. He'll take care of you. Then get the hell out of there before they trace the cell phone to him."

I was dazed. "But, Edward—"

He gave me a push. "Do it. Go."

I climbed into the driver's seat, hoping I could handle a vehicle this large.

As we zoomed down Highway 9, I saw an ambulance and a police car pass me going the other way.

I didn't understand how leaving would help. Galen and Toni had seen us, they knew us. I nearly signaled to the ambulance to stop, to tend to Arthur.

I tried to speak to him, to reassure myself he was all right. But my throat was too tight. I couldn't say anything.

I drove as fast as I dared back to Fred's condominium.

CHAPTER THIRTY

Fred waited for me on the street, carrying a medical bag.

He flung wide the backdoor of the Jeep, looking at Arthur, feeling his pulse.

I craned my neck, watching him pull open Arthur's sweater and shirt. He exposed a long wound on the torso. It wasn't bleeding much.

For a moment, I was hopeful. Then I checked Arthur's face: What if he'd died? What if I'd let Arthur die?

I'd tried to keep him out of prison. I'd tried to help him. What if it had led to—

"God damn that brother of mine!" Fred sounded more annoyed than scared. "He's no doctor—telling me it's a scratch. How the hell would he know?"

He climbed into the back and slammed the door, hovering over Arthur as he opened the medical kit. "I could lose my license for this." He began ministering. "What are you waiting for? Drive."

I was shaking with anxiety, soaked with perspiration. "Drive?" I repeated incredulously.

"End of the block, go right. Take it easy. We do not want to get pulled over."

I drove slowly, smelling Fred's antiseptics, listening to his nonstop litany about how irresponsible Edward had always been, what a cocksure, irritating pain in the butt he still was.

"Take a right," he said suddenly. "Not so sharp! You want to get us killed?"

His bedside manner left a lot to be desired.

"Okay, here. Turn into this driveway."

I pulled close to a huge stucco house, painted and landscaped to look like silent-era Hollywood, with flowering vines and huge palms.

Fred jumped out of the car, striding to the front door. To my surprise, he inserted a key.

He came back and carried Arthur inside.

I closed the Jeep doors, timidly following Fred into the mansion.

He'd lain Arthur down in the middle of a marble foyer. He lifted away the gauze he'd applied to Arthur's sunken, gray-haired chest.

A six-or seven-inch cut was exposed to view.

Fred rummaged through his medical bag, shooting me a furious look.

"You two should be taken out and shot." For a moment, I thought he meant me and Arthur. "Edward knows better than to mess around with a wound like this! What if it had been serious? What if it had nicked an organ? He could be dead by now!"

Arthur opened his eyes. "Ah, Fred," he said. "I forgot to tell you my pen name."

"Pen name?" Fred looked bewildered.

"For my articles. While I was at Yale, the department asked me to take a pen name; protect its reputa-

tion for dull academe. But everyone knew it was me."
He smiled weakly. Then he looked around at all the
marble. "My lord," he said. "Are we in a library?"

"We're at my ex-wife's house. She's in Cancún with
the kids. How are you feeling?"

Arthur tucked his chin down, looking at the wound.
"I was pulled back out of the way. Just as she struck,
I was pulled clear. Almost clear."

"What?" I hadn't seen anyone there with him. Was
he going to tell us he'd seen Billy Seawuit's ghost?

"A young man wearing a hat," Arthur explained.

"The one you saw in San Francisco?"

"I don't recall the young man in San Francisco.
Though you tell me I saw him."

"You saw him twice," I reminded him. "He almost
certainly handed you the gun."

"Well, that would explain why he ran away." Arthur sighed, closing his eyes. "It's not deep, is it? But
it stings. Like a paper cut."

"Which way did he run? Did he say anything?"

"Can't this wait?" Fred fretted. He poured disinfec-
tant over the wound.

"The man with the hat, Arthur?" I needed to know.

"Nelson identified him as an industrial spy; didn't
Edward tell us? That's very likely who he is. Only I'd
think he worked with Toni. Money deposited in Nelson's account would be hers to spend, as well. Perhaps
she was jealous of Nelson's achievements. She had so
few of her own." Arthur reached for my hand. "We
felt that, Billy and I, on our journey. A terrible boiling
envy beneath our boat. We—"

"I need to stitch this," Fred interrupted. "You'll
have to shut up."

"Don't bother; I don't mind a scar," Arthur objected. "No one will see it at my age, you know."

Fred snorted. "When you get proclaimed doctor, I'll let you make the decisions. In the meantime, don't talk."

Arthur flinched while Fred stitched the wound. I looked away, not wanting to watch.

An hour ago, I'd seen Toni Nelson in a white shirt, not the sweater of our previous encounter. The first time I'd met the young man in the lean-to, he'd been wearing a white shirt under a blue vest. Had Toni gone home and changed—or had she borrowed his clothes? Had she asked him to get rid of Pan's body?

If so, they might be in league. They might have been doing business.

Perhaps ten minutes later, Fred put his needle and thread away. "It's been a long time since I did one of these. You will have a scar," he promised. "But at least the cut won't reopen."

I heard Arthur's sigh of relief as Fred covered it with gauze.

"I've been thinking, Willa," Arthur continued. "From what you've said, Toni accuses everyone of lying. And yet, it appears that she's the liar. Isn't there a psychiatric term for that, Fred?"

"You mean projection? Projecting some aspect of yourself onto others."

"Yes, that's right. Think what a dose of it poor Billy must have endured as her houseguest. I wonder if he didn't suggest a healing journey." Tears filled his eyes. "I'm afraid to think how she'd have reacted."

Billy Seawuit had returned the sane spirit to many people as crazy as Toni, I would guess. Maybe he had described his beliefs and methods to her. Maybe he had offered to help.

But few people part willingly with their worldview, mad or not.

I pictured Billy sitting in Bowl Rock with her, commencing a healing journey. Maybe the flash of Toni's knife had pulled him out of his trance. I pictured him leaping to his feet inside the rock.

Or maybe he'd been there alone, his mind's eye focused on jade seas and evergreen islands. Maybe Toni had crept up on him.

Either way, the only witness had been Pan, standing in feral majesty in a field overlooking the rock. He'd seen Toni there, knife in hand.

"Her spy." Arthur's eyelids fluttered. He looked pale and exhausted. "Needed more information from her, perhaps—couldn't let her be the only suspect, could he? Didn't know about the new three-strikes law; or didn't know I'd been arrested before. It's not in character otherwise: He's chivalrous. Kind to you when you needed it. Properly laid out poor Pan's body. We should have known then. Understood from the gentlemanliness of the gesture."

The gentlemanliness of framing an innocent man to cover up your industrial informant's murder? There might be no honor among thieves, but there was arguably gallantry among spies.

It certainly looked like Galen Nelson was right. The man I'd known as Martin Late Rain must be Joel Baker. He'd paid Toni Nelson for her husband's computer secrets. Toni had been jealous of Nelson's success—of his "children," whom she wanted to kill.

But Toni couldn't visit a competitor's office without being conspicuous. She was too striking—and too ungoverned. It was safer to meet her in the woods. Maybe Joel Baker enjoyed camping in a lean-to. Maybe he'd hoped to attract Billy Seawuit and talk to him. Maybe it was just convenient in the short run.

"Chivalrous?" I tried to think the concept through.

Arthur's eyes glinted as he winced. "The gun must have a significance, Willa. He'd heard that's how Billy was killed. But there must have been some reason he thought handing it to me would take the brunt of the investigation off *her,* poor woman."

"It must have been Toni Nelson's gun. Nelson mentioned something of hers being missing from the basement; he thought it might be somewhere else. But I'll bet it was a gun. Joel Baker must have seen it when he was looking at TechnoShaman. He probably took it last weekend, after hearing Billy was shot. Either he assumed Toni killed him or she admitted something."

"Something but not everything. Not her use of a knife. The proverbial 'a little information.'"

"Then he must have gone to your hotel—I suppose Billy told Toni you were there; he wouldn't know not to. Baker followed you out Monday morning. He thought Toni shot Billy, so he gave her gun to you, Arthur."

"To protect her." There was a hint of admiration in his tone.

"Can we please discuss this tomorrow, people?" Fred sounded highly exasperated. He was taping the thick pad of gauze over Arthur's cut.

"If I hadn't thrown the gun away—"

Fred and Arthur interrupted simultaneously.

"No more!" Fred insisted.

"Ironic," Arthur agreed.

Had Arthur been arrested with the gun, it might

have linked Toni Nelson to a crime for which she wouldn't otherwise have been a suspect. And perhaps the man who'd called himself Pan would be alive now.

Arthur reached out and squeezed my hand.

An hour later, assured that Arthur was all right and sleeping peacefully, Fred left.

He didn't know whether Edward had stayed with the Nelsons or fled. He didn't know what, if anything, Edward planned to do about the fact that 911 had recorded the cell phone's number. But Fred wanted to be home, and ostensibly in bed, if the police came by.

"If I end up in jail for that mutt—" He shot me a look. "I should have drowned him at birth."

He sped off in Edward's Jeep, leaving me in a house that recalled my solvent days as a corporate lawyer.

But I might as well have been on Mars. The week had carried me light-years from my past.

I sat up half the night watching Arthur, wondering what would happen next.

CHAPTER THIRTY-ONE

"It's so embarrassing," I said again to Cary Curtis. "I felt like a fool when I phoned my father and he told me what had happened."

"Well, I admit, Willa, we thought you'd jumped ship."

I smiled at my new boss as if the very notion were preposterous. It was one week to the hour since I'd encountered Arthur around the corner from this office.

"I was so surprised!" I lied. "I phoned to check in, and my dad told me you expected me in last week. I couldn't believe it. I had him check my datebook, my computer calendar. I don't know how it could have happened. I don't know how I could have written down the thirteenth when you wrote down the sixth."

"You can imagine our relief when he phoned on Friday and told us he'd spoken with you. Explained the mix-up."

My father had taken it upon himself to make excuses for me, though he'd heard nothing from me since Monday. Insurance, he called it, in case things worked out.

"I wish I could have called you myself. But it's not easy to get a good connection from there."

"As long as you don't do this with your court dates!" He laughed, but we both knew it wasn't a joke.

"No." I sounded sure. "This definitely won't happen again."

"By the way," Curtis said, "I like your hair like that."

"I got it cut on vacation." It had taken a very short style to disguise the botch job I'd performed.

"Well, let's go ahead and get you settled into your office." He stood, preparing to walk me down the hall. "We certainly got to know Lieutenant Surgelato well," he said archly.

I tried to smile. When I couldn't quite manage it, I preceded him into the hall.

"We hear he even hired detectives to look for you," Curtis continued.

"No, that's just someone's embellishment."

The two phony backpackers had indeed been off-duty cops. Surgelato hired them to search the woods near Edward's cabin. Edward was livid when he heard. He was especially angry about his camera, which they took to check for snapshots of me. He was even more displeased that they'd fired into the air to keep him at a distance.

Cary Curtis ushered me into a tastefully furnished office with some phenomenal computer equipment in it.

A newspaper was folded beside a carafe of coffee. I'd already read the story that interested me: that Arthur Kenna had come forward after a brief retreat to learn of the tragic death of his assistant.

The version tucked into the business section had been of greater interest to Curtis & Huston.

"It's awful about Mrs. Nelson," I said. "I realized when I read the article that it was the Cyberdelics people."

Curtis nodded. "She's been selling secrets to its competitors. They still haven't found her middleman, though I believe they know who it is. The rumor is he bought himself a mansion somewhere up in Canada. But they don't know what name he's using, and Canada's a hell of a big place."

It was hard to visualize Joel Baker in a mansion.

"Nelson tried to keep the whole thing quiet," he continued. "He's like a lot of us geeks, I suppose— lets the wife handle the money." He leaned closer. "Confidentially? It turns out she sabotaged the hardware and software he keeps at home. He thought they'd had a break-in. So sad: He'll be way out of pocket by the time he reimburses his partners."

"Not to mention pays for her defense lawyers."

"Oh, I don't know about that. I imagine they'll plea bargain. She's admitted the killings."

She'd used the same knife—tucked in her fanny pack the day she and I grappled—on Billy Seawuit and John Doe, as the police blandly renamed Pan.

"I assume they'll go for an insanity defense?" I tried to sound merely curious.

"Well," Curtis sighed. "Good thing we don't have to worry about it. We're not down in the trenches like criminal lawyers. We're nice and insulated from the muck. We've got our own kind of muck, but at least it's bloodless; no one loses anything but property or money. Or worse, creative effort." He glanced at the stack of file folders on my desk. "You know we're defending Cyberdelics in a suit brought by Mrs. Nelson's ex-husband? He was in town last week meeting with his lawyers. He claims Cyberdelics used his beta-wave research. It's tricky: It involves work he and Mrs. Nelson did together."

No wonder Galen Nelson didn't want to talk to—or even about—him. I just prayed I hadn't been assigned the case.

"I'll be taking care of it personally," Curtis concluded.

We exchanged a few more pleasantries. Then, with great relief, I shut my office door behind him.

I sat in my swivel chair, absolutely exhausted. I'd only had a day to get everything together.

Edward had persuaded Galen Nelson not to involve "Alice Young" in all this. He'd called it his quid pro quo for disappearing Toni's last victim, Arthur.

Edward had arrived at his ex-sister-in-law's house in the wee hours of Saturday morning, and we'd made our arrangements. Others in Boulder Creek had met Alice, but Edward would pretend she'd been a pickup, just a one-week stand.

The police had Toni Nelson; they didn't care about much else.

Only Don Surgelato had required extra persuasion. But I'd shortened the time we needed to talk by phoning him at home when his wife was there.

As far as I was concerned, there was only one loose end. I phoned the Biltmore Hotel.

"Hi, Arthur," I said.

"Willa." His voice was fond, tired, familiar. "I miss you, my dear. I was just about to phone you."

I swiveled my chair so that I looked out my window, down at the Financial District's morning foot traffic.

I had nothing in particular to say. "I'm calling from my office. Last Monday seems like a long time ago."

"Willa?" He sounded apologetic. "Do you really want to be a lawyer?"

"I'm sitting here, aren't I?"

"So they made no fuss?"

"No. They chalked it up to miscommunication."

"But do you *want* to be there?"

"I went to law school. This is what people do if they've been to law school. It's somewhat expected of them." That was the sad truth of the matter. If you worked hard enough, you got what you worked for.

I put my hand on my stack of file folders. I couldn't talk long. I'd have to be a real hot dog for a while to make up for the lousy first impression.

"The reason I bring it up, the reason I was going to call . . ." Arthur paused. I could visualize his face clearly after our week together: I could see the tentative inclination of his head, the brightness of his eyes. "I can't quite cope without Billy, you know. I need an assistant."

"They'll jump at the chance, anyone you interview." I imagined Arthur's assistant traveling to visit shamans, living in longhouses, gliding in dugout canoes. What an experience for some lucky young anthropologist or ethnobotanist.

"Will you do it, Willa? Will you be my assistant?"

"Me?" Save me from major life choices at my age.

"Edward didn't feel you had the . . . how shall I put it?" Arthur struggled to edit him. "A Spanish word not used in polite company."

"Cojones?" But one thing I was sure of: "Edward

knew you'd tell me that. He thinks I'll do it now just to show him." To show I had (to sink to guyspeak) the "balls."

Arthur chuckled. "He suggested I ask you if your new employer considers you a vessel of grace?"

I flipped open a folder: the fine print of a patent application.

The last time I'd made peace with work I didn't like, it backfired. I hadn't been able to hang in long enough to boost my career. I'd run through the money I'd saved, winding up worse off than before.

This job was supposed to be my way out of that predicament.

"Is another law firm really the answer, Willa? Or are you repeating the same mistake?"

I tried to think of a rejoinder: my career, right or wrong. I tried to think of a facet of law, an aspect of practice, I loved. I opened more file folders: unfair competition, software copyright, breach of contract. The cases involved sexy new gadgets and Hollywood special effects, but it was still business law, the same old common law rules and obtuse new regulations. It was back to carping briefs and bad-tempered phone messages, back to twelve-hour days and big-city egos.

Oh God, maybe Edward was right.

I gripped the receiver tightly. I didn't want to hang up, I didn't want to let go.

Perhaps that was my future self, casting its vote.

I closed my eyes, begging my present self to be sensible.

"Arthur, I can't."

"Oh?" He sounded disappointed. "But I feel certain you'll change your mind. I was sent to Montgomery Street to find you; this has to be the reason."

There was a knock at my door. "Come in," I called.

My secretary, a plain young woman with intelligent eyes, walked in. She was carrying a foot-tall live pine tree in a pot trimmed with colored cellophane and ribbon. She smiled as she set it on my desk. She handed me the florist's enclosure card, then left.

"Willa?" Arthur sounded sad. "Will you call me if you change your mind?"

I wondered if I was limited to a certain number of calls per day.

I pulled the card from its envelope. It read, *Go for it*. I knew it was from Edward.

My former boyfriend apparently agreed with my future self.

If only the present Willa weren't so stubbornly practical. "I will call you. Soon. Either way," I promised.

The scent of evergreen filled my office. It wasn't easy to hang up and get to work.